"What happened to my father?"

A worried frown creased Tina's forehead. "He's pouting like a little boy."

Russell relayed the conversation he'd had with the old man. "Ty accused me of planning to leave him. He heard the mechanic ask me when I was going to California."

"What happened next?" Tina asked softly.

"He begged me to take him with me."

Tina was silent. It gave her a jolt to think that her father would want to leave her and the family ranch he'd always loved. But then, of course, this wasn't the real Ty. This was a man who didn't even recognize his own daughter half the time.

"God, I feel just terrible about it," Russell told her.

"Well, take heart. Chances are good Dad will have forgotten all about it in about an hour."

But, she added silently, it's going to take *me* much longer to get used to your leaving.

ABOUT THE AUTHOR

Barbara Kaye's fourteenth Superromance
novel comes on the heels of her very
successful Hamilton House trilogy. Once
again, this Oklahoma author has given her
readers an insightful look at human nature. In
Love Me Tender, she treats a sensitive topic
with a great deal of empathy.

Books by Barbara Kaye

HARLEQUIN SUPERROMANCE

HARLEQUIN AMERICAN ROMANCE

Don't miss any of our special offers. Write to us at the
following address for information on our newest releases.

Harlequin Reader Service
P.O. Box 1397, Buffalo, NY 14240
Canadian address: P.O. Box 603,
Fort Erie, Ont. L2A 5X3

Love Me Tender

BARBARA KAYE

Harlequin Books

TORONTO • NEW YORK • LONDON
AMSTERDAM • PARIS • SYDNEY • HAMBURG
STOCKHOLM • ATHENS • TOKYO • MILAN
MADRID • WARSAW • BUDAPEST • AUCKLAND

Published April 1992

ISBN 0-373-70495-X

LOVE ME TENDER

CHAPTER ONE

RUSSELL CADE DROVE the eighteen-wheeler into Red Star Trucking's main terminal and eased it into a slot between two identical trucks. After making some final entries in his logbook, he retrieved his belongings from the sleeper in back and swung down from the cab. Closing the door, he patted the distinctive Red Star logo painted on it.

"So long, sweetheart. Don't think it hasn't been fun."

His codriver, a burly, good-natured man named Junior MacRae, rounded the front of the truck and fell into step beside him. "You know somethin', Russ, I'm bettin' you don't really quit. I'm bettin' you're jus' gonna take some time off. You'll be back."

"You're wrong, Junior. I'm quitting. I've been planning this a long time."

"California?"

"You bet. The North Coast. I'm going to do nothing but fish and commune with some redwoods for a year. After that, who knows?"

"Once you make your mind up, it stays made, don't it?"

Ten years had passed since Russell had first seen California's North Coast. He and Junior had been making a run from San Francisco to Oregon. He'd taken one look at the rugged coastline, ancient trees, quaint Victorian towns, solitary beaches and had been hooked. "This is where I'm going to settle down someday," he'd announced. Junior had scoffed, but since that day, every dollar Russell had made that hadn't been needed for subsistence had been put in Red Star's credit union, all of it earmarked for settling in California.

"I never found a place I liked better, and I guess you and I have seen just about every navigable inch of North America in the past thirteen years," he now told Junior. "But I think I'd quit even if I'd never seen California. I'm tired of the life, and I'm getting a paunch from driving for ten hours at a stretch, then eating truck-stop food and crawling into the sleeper. I need a more active life."

"Hell, that ain't no paunch," Junior declared, rubbing his own ample belly.

"It's the beginning of one."

"I jus' hate this, damned if I don't. I ain't never gonna find me a partner as easy to get along with as you."

Russell grinned. "Sure you will. Find some young buck and train him the way you want him, like you did with me. You weren't so all-fired crazy about me in the beginning. If I remember right, you said I'd never make it, that I was a sorry-ass pip-squeak."

"Hell, that was years ago. I jus' wanted to keep you humble, son."

They crossed to the parking lot; each man tossed his belongings into his own car and went inside the office building. The front lounge was almost deserted. In a glass-enclosed cubicle just off the main room two men in Red Star caps sat drinking coffee. Seeing Russell and Junior, they nodded a greeting, then resumed their conversation. Since it was after five o'clock the office help had gone home. The partners headed down a long hall to the dispatcher's office, where Russell turned in his log and signed out for the last time.

"When you leavin'?" Junior asked.

"Right away."

"You mean like tonight?"

"Maybe."

"I got three days off," Junior said, "so 'spect I'll go down to Muskogee and see that wild woman I'm married to. Wanna come along?"

"Junior, we've been on the road three straight weeks. You and Sara need some time alone."

"Hell, we ain't newlyweds, ya know. It ain't like I walk in the door and we hit the sack. Our twenty-fifth anniversary is comin' up."

Russell shook his head in wonder. "Twenty-five years with you. Somebody ought to strike a medal in Sara's honor."

"We hardly ever see each other. Remember that, Russ—it's the secret to a long, happy marriage. Sara would love seein' you. Sure you won't come along?"

"No, thanks, pal. I'll say goodbye here." Russell stuck out his hand.

Junior clutched it in a bone-crunching grasp. "Won't forget me, will ya?"

"I won't forget you. So long, Junior."

"So long, pal. Remember, ya gotta go down the hill in the same gear ya went up it."

"Yeah, I'll remember."

Russell was filled with a surprising sense of loss as he stared after Junior's retreating figure. He hadn't expected saying goodbye to the old buzzard to be so hard. He waited until he was sure Junior had had time to get in his car and pull away, before he, too, left the building.

While driving the fifteen miles from Red Star's terminal to the pretty college town where he kept a room, he searched his mind for second thoughts, regrets or doubts and found there were none. He was thirty-seven years old, and about half his life was behind him. He didn't have a home, only a rented room that he slept in maybe three or four nights a month. His parents were retired and living in Florida, and his sister and her husband lived in Atlanta. He had no family of his own. There had been a wife once, but that hadn't lasted long enough to produce anything but a lot of bills and a determination not to try marriage again until he gave up trucking.

He really didn't have much of anything but a comfortable nest egg in the company credit union, a lot of dandy memories and a burning desire to settle in California. Life, as most people lived it, was as foreign to him as driving ten-hour stretches every day would be to them. So the previous month, during a midnight run down a lonely interstate, he'd simply made up his mind. It was time. He'd been planning it and thinking about it for ten years. It was time to just do it.

Although saying goodbye to Junior had been hard, the rest was easy. He didn't have any attachment to the solitary furnished room, or to the Ozarks town where it was located, and there was nobody to say goodbye to. He had no real friends, just a lot of acquaintances scattered all over the continent. If ever there was a man who was footloose and fancy free, it was Russell Cade. Now the time had come to put down some roots.

In his room Russell looked around. He had packed up everything before he and Junior had left on the last run. All there was left to do was gather it up and turn his key in to the manager, who wished him well with a discernible lack of genuine interest. They probably hadn't exchanged two dozen words in the three years Russell had been paying rent there. He left the building, threw his things in the trunk of his car and slammed the lid.

The car, a 1988 Thunderbird, was his proudest possession, the only extravagance he had allowed himself in ten long years. When he was on the road, the vehicle waited under a protective custom-made cover. He was happy to say it still was in showroom condition without a scratch in sight. Now all he had to do was point it west.

He stopped in Fort Smith that night, got a room in a too-expensive motel, had a couple of drinks and an excellent dinner, also too expensive. Then he watched television until midnight and slept like a well-fed baby. But the following morning he awoke with a nagging sense of duty. It had been a long time since he had visited his sister and her brood. He called her frequently, and several times when he'd been able to stop in Atlanta she had met him at the truck stop for lunch. But he couldn't remember the last time he'd seen her husband and kids. California had waited for him all this time. He supposed a week or two either way wouldn't matter. Atlanta would be his first destination.

Helen was almost pathetically glad to see him. It had been longer than he'd thought. His twin nephews, whom he remembered as little kids, were in high school, and his brother-in-law, Ed, was losing his hair. Russell intended staying two days, three tops, but ended up staying four. Every time he turned around, Helen plied him with food, as though she feared he'd been existing on a starvation diet. In truth, truckers as a group were probably the most overfed people on earth. The boredom of the road made food the one thing they looked forward to.

Leaving Atlanta, he again was seized by a call to duty. He had come this far, so he knew he should go on down to Pensacola and visit his parents. His mother cried copiously the first hour he was there, while his dad kept slapping his shoulder and swallowing thickly. Again he was bombarded with home cooking. He spent a week lazing at their pool and saying, "Really, Mom, thanks, but I can't eat another bite." He left Florida just before he lapsed into a food-induced stupor.

Now he really was heading west. But first there was a two-day stop in New Orleans, a city he had driven through countless times but had never really seen. Then on to Galveston, Houston, San Antonio. He spent three nights there, devouring mariachi music, margaritas and Mexican food and giving serious thought to heading south to spend some time in Mexico. Then he took stock.

He was growing horribly soft and having far too much fun. His comfortable nest egg wouldn't stay comfortable for long at this rate. For three weeks he had been enjoying himself, eating and drinking anything he wanted and tossing money around with reckless abandon. And he'd seen the same things he had seen from a rig—miles of smooth interstates and endless fast-food places. So when he left San Antonio he opted for back roads, driving through the scenic hill country, rolling farmland, then flat ranching country. The farther he traveled in a northwesterly direction the sparser the towns became and the fewer the people. Cows outnumbered humans; gas wells dotted the landscape. One could look a long way and not see much of anything. At about noon, Russell's stomach, which was accustomed to being filled at regular intervals, started complaining noisily. Earlier he had promised himself he would skip lunch altogether, but he had about changed his mind. A sandwich or a burger would taste awfully good, and he could have something light for dinner. The trouble was, he seemed to be in the middle of nowhere, with not a single café or restaurant in sight. He switched on the car radio to take his mind off his hunger.

"It's a minute past high noon," a masculine voice announced. "Good afternoon, everybody. High today should reach ninety-two. Moderate to severe thunderstorms are forecast for late afternoon. Folks from Dalhart to Dumas might want to look out for some hail. The storms should cool things off, and we'll have a low in the mid-sixties tonight. There's a system building in the Pacific Northwest that will—"

Russell turned the radio off. Ninety-two in June? What was the place like in mid-August? Not that he'd want to stick around and find out. It was lonely, unlovely country. He drummed his fingers on the steering wheel and wondered how long he would have to drive before he found a real town. Finally he stopped for gas at a tiny village whose sole reason for existence seemed to be to supply liquor to the surrounding counties. The hamlet consisted of five liquor stores, a gas station and a small mercantile establishment. A sign near the gas station read Leatrice, 35 miles.

"Is Leatrice any bigger than this place?" he asked the gnarled man pumping the gas.

"Almost any place is bigger'n this one."

"Does it have a café or restaurant?"

"Oh, sure. There's a brand-new Dairy Queen on the right after you get in town."

"Is there anything between here and Leatrice?"

"Yep. Five or six windmills."

TINA WEBSTER PULLED into a parking space in front of the Dairy Queen in Leatrice. Already the day was very warm, too warm for June, portending another scorcher of a summer. She could stand the heat—she had lived in it most of her life, but, dear God, she hoped the weatherman was right about that rain. Early April showers had pleased everyone for miles around, but they had been a short-lived blessing. There had been only an occasional drizzle since. Leaving the pickup's windows open an inch or two, she got out and went inside.

A blast of refrigerated air greeted her. When the bell over the door heralded her arrival, a young woman behind the counter looked up and smiled. "Hi, Tina."

"Hi, Marge." Tina walked up to the counter. "A couple of tacos, I guess, and a large iced tea."

Marge turned and yelled through the kitchen's serving window, then plucked an enormous paper cup out of the tall column of them on the counter and crammed it full of crushed ice. "How've you been?"

"Not too bad."

"How's your dad?"

"Oh . . . there's no change, not really."

"I'm so sorry. That's bad stuff."

"Yes, it is." Tina carried her tea to a small table for two near the counter and waited for her food. "You don't happen to know of anyone around here who's looking for work, do you?"

Marge frowned. "Can't say I do. Seems like everyone who's looking for work heads for Amarillo."

"Tell me about it. I've hired and lost two men already this year. No one wants to farm or ranch anymore, and Jake has so much to do. Sure would be nice to find an extra pair of hands. I do what I can, but Dad takes the lion's share of my time now."

"Yeah, that's rough. If I hear of anyone, I'll sure tell him about you." Marge set the paper basket containing the tacos on the counter. "Want *picante* sauce?"

"Yes, please." Tina got her food, then carried it back to the table to eat in solitude. She had been gone from home since early morning, and she felt guilty about taking the time for a peaceful bite to eat, but sometimes she thought that if she didn't get out of that house she would go mad. The constant demands on her time and patience had her feeling far more exhausted than a woman of thirty-three ought to feel.

Could it have been only eighteen months since Ty Webster, her once-strong bull of a father, had been diagnosed as having Alzheimer's disease? It seemed a lifetime ago. Now she knew there had been symptoms for at least a year before that, symptoms she had dismissed as stemming from other causes. Her father had never been the most placid of men, so the outbursts of temper had simply been "one of Dad's moods." And the forgetfulness had been attributed to age. But then he began forgetting people he had known all his life. Suddenly she realized that not only did he forget where he'd put things, he forgot what to do with them when he found them. His reactions to common events became totally inappropriate. But it wasn't until he forgot who she was that Tina finally had sought medical advice and had heard the term *senile dementia* for the first time.

Since then she had been through the predictable stages—disbelief, denial, rage, then resignation. And resentment that her father's illness had placed her own life in limbo. She didn't want to run the family ranch. She was young and needed to be working in a city, where she could go places and meet people. Yet just thinking such thoughts brought on guilt. And during their last visit to the doctor in Amarillo, one more blow had been heaped upon too many others. "You have to prepare yourself, Tina," he'd said. "The day will come when you simply won't be able to care for Ty any longer. He'll have to be placed in a home where there are people trained to look after such cases."

Lord, Tina thought, *where will I find the courage to put Dad in one of those places?* More guilt.

She was vaguely aware of the tinkling of the bell announcing the arrival of another customer. A man strolled up to the counter, placed an order, then sat down at the table next to hers to wait for his food. Idly Tina studied him, mainly because he was a stranger. He was probably in his mid-thirties, though it was hard to tell. A sun-streaked mop of brown hair covered his head, and he had a ruggedly attractive profile. His arms were muscular; he didn't look like a man who made his living behind a desk. He had seemed tall while standing at the counter, maybe six feet. He was just passing through, she guessed, and she wondered where he was from and where he was going. She often wondered that about strangers because she knew she couldn't go anywhere for a very long time.

"You feel trapped, don't you?" the support-group counselor had asked at the last meeting, and Tina had admitted she did. The counselor had smiled sympathetically. "Such feelings are normal. Don't be ashamed of them. And don't be afraid to ask for help from family, from friends, from anyone who'll give it. No mere mortal can be on-duty twenty-four hours a day."

Tina's gaze was drawn back to the stranger. In the grand space of a minute he had come to symbolize the kind of freedom that was lost to her. Then she chided herself. For all she knew, he had a wife, five kids, a mortgage and a job he hated.

Then Marge called his number, and he stood up. Yes, he was about six feet, and well-built if one could ignore the slight overhang at his belt buckle. Still, he looked strong. The short-sleeved cotton shirt he wore with his jeans stretched across an admirable pair of shoulders.

The man reached back to lift his wallet out of his hip pocket, paid Marge, then carried his food to the table. Apparently noticing Tina for the first time, he nodded and smiled.

"Hello."

"Hello," she said. She took a bite of a taco, holding it over its paper dish.

He chomped down on a burger and chewed thoughtfully. Swallowing, he turned to her. "Is it always this warm here in June?" he asked.

"No, not this warm. We need rain."

"Driving in, I heard a fellow on the radio say some's on its way."

"We'll see. There'll be a *chance* of thunderstorms every afternoon from now until October."

"It was raining like crazy down in Houston a few days ago."

"Funny how those who don't need it get most of it."

Doubtless there were places in the world where strangers striking up a conversation in a place like the Dairy Queen was unheard of, even dangerous, but rural West Texas wasn't one of them. It was one place where outsiders could overdose on friendliness. "Where are you from?" Tina asked.

Russell smiled. "Nowhere. Lots of places. A long time ago I was from Kansas. More recently, from Arkansas."

"Where are you headed?"

"Northern California."

"That must be beautiful country."

"It's that, all right. At least, it was the last time I saw it. I hope it hasn't changed much."

"What line of work are you in?"

"I was a trucker for more years than I care to remember. I finally got tired of it, so I quit." He bit off another chunk of the burger.

Tina waited for him to finish chewing before saying, "So you're unemployed."

"Currently, yes."

"Do you have a job waiting for you in California?"

"No. In fact, I don't know a soul in the whole state. I'm going because it's something I've wanted to do for a long time."

A little tingle raced through Tina. It was probably ridiculous to ask, but . . . "Would you be interested in a job? It could be a temporary thing if that's what you want."

"Doing what?"

"I have a ranch about fifteen miles from here."

Russell shook his head. "I'm afraid ranching's something I've never done. Worked the wheat fields some, but I never ranched."

"We also grow wheat, cotton and corn. You wouldn't have to ranch. Most of the time the cattle look after themselves, especially this time of year. When they don't, Jake takes over. But there's more to running the place than tending cows. Equipment needs repairing, fences need mending, the cornfield has to be tended. I'm desperately in need of another hand—two if I could find them. Fifty dollars a day, a nice clean room and the best food for miles around."

Russell hadn't paid close attention to her before, but now he did. She wasn't a kid, but he guessed she was younger than he was. And she was pretty in that unsophisticated, homespun way that screamed of fresh air and sunshine. Her hair was a marvel—a chin-length, wavy, russet cap—and her eyes were a startling green, not even slightly flecked with gold or gray. Looking at them was like staring into a clear mountain brook. Her left hand rested on the table, and he noticed she wasn't wearing a ring.

Fifty dollars a day, three hundred a week—he supposed ranchers took Sundays off. He had routinely pulled down three times that when he'd kept the wheels rolling. Of course, when room and board were thrown in they sweetened the pot considerably. He wasn't interested, but he was enjoying the conversation. In the interest of keeping it going he asked, "Who else besides that Jake fellow do you have for help?"

"Nobody. Well, there's Ruby, Jake's wife. She helps in the house. Outside, too, when she's needed."

"How big a place are you talking about?"

"About eleven hundred acres," Tina said.

Russell started to laugh, thinking she was having a little fun with him, but he saw that she was completely serious. "You and one guy work eleven hundred acres?"

"Oh, we hire day help occasionally, when we can find it, and we contract out the wheat harvest every summer. Mostly, though, it's Jake. Like I said, cattle look after themselves most of the time, but we do need some help."

"I probably wouldn't be much help, ma'am."

"You look able-bodied to me. Look, mister, you wouldn't have to sign on for a specific period of time. Even a week's worth of help would be a godsend. If you don't like it, just move on. All the others did. There are no guarantees in this business, on either side."

That didn't sound promising, Russell thought. Maybe the working conditions were intolerable. Maybe this lady rancher was impossible to work for. That, however, was hard to believe. If he had to use one word to describe her, the word might be *sweet*. She had a sweet-sounding voice, a sweet expression, as though she'd never harbored an unkind thought. That, of course, was impossible, but that was the impression she gave.

Meanwhile Tina was sending up silent prayers all over the place. This man was the first unemployed male she had come across in months, and she couldn't let him get away. Besides, he was a cut above average— neat, clean and mannerly. He would have to be more reliable than the drifters she'd hired in the past. If he'd just give them a chance...

But her prayers were destined to go unanswered. Though for a minute he appeared to be seriously considering her offer, he finally shook his head.

"Sorry, ma'am. Thanks, but ranching just isn't what I have in mind. And this country isn't what I have in mind, either. I've been looking forward to California a long time."

Tina sighed in resignation. "Well, it was worth a try."

"I hope you find someone soon."

"Yeah, so do I." She gathered up the remains of her meal and carried them to the trash bin by the door. The stranger was right behind her. He opened the door and stood aside to let her precede him. The heat was an assault on the senses.

"It was nice talking to you," Russell said.

"Thanks. Happy trails . . . or whatever."

Tina watched him cross the parking lot and get into a snazzy Thunderbird with Arkansas plates. She smiled ruefully. No man who owned a car like that would be interested in the kind of work she had to offer. The Thunderbird backed out, then straightened, and the stranger threw her a jaunty wave as he drove off.

Tina might not have planned to be a rancher, but she possessed a rancher's instincts. From force of habit she scanned the northwest horizon, hoping to see gathering storm clouds. There was nothing. What she really needed to hire, she thought with a sigh, was someone who could do a real good rain dance.

CHAPTER TWO

TINA MADE one more stop—Foster's Drug to have her father's prescription refilled—then she headed for home. Though most of the highway was a straight-as-an-arrow ribbon of blacktop, there were a few bends. One was about a mile south of the entrance gate to her ranch. There the road curved and climbed slightly. As Tina reached the top of the rise she saw the accident. A pickup and an automobile had been involved in a collision.

She shook her head in disgust. It had happened at the entrance to the Higgins farm, so that meant old Willard had, literally, struck again. The crusty eighty-five-year-old farmer had had his license revoked two years before because of poor eyesight, but that hadn't stopped him. Whenever he could sneak away from his family, he took off in the pickup, and Willard behind a steering wheel was a lethal weapon. His accident record was legendary in the county.

Tina braked and eased off the road to offer her assistance. Then she noticed the Arkansas plates on the car involved. Oh, Lord, the man in the Dairy Queen. She walked over to assess the damage. Willard's truck seemed to have escaped without a scratch, but it had done a masterful job of demolishing the Thunderbird's right front. The stranger was probably fit to be tied.

That was an understatement. Russell was livid! He hadn't believed it when it had happened, and he still didn't believe it. Naturally he had seen the pickup, and naturally he had assumed the driver would yield. But the old goat had just kept driving, hadn't even slowed down coming out of the gate. As he surveyed the damage to his car, his anger tasted like bile in his throat. If the guy hadn't been so goddamn old, Russell was sure he would have decked him.

He also was heartsick. Squatting, he stared numbly at the crumpled metal. His car, his beautiful car! Even with expert bodywork it would never be the same again. He stood in the blazing heat, fuming and feeling helpless, until he heard a soft feminine voice say, "Oh, that beautiful car! How awful."

Russell looked up. It was the woman he'd spoken to in the Dairy Queen. He straightened.

"What happened?" she asked.

"This idiot drove right into me, that's what happened!"

Tina looked at the farmer. "Willard, you know you're not supposed to drive."

"I jus' wanted to go into town for a spell. I didn't see this fella."

"How could you not have seen me?" Russell yelled. "You can see twenty miles in all directions in this godforsaken place!"

"Willard can't see twenty feet," Tina said. "Are either of you hurt?"

The men assured her they both were fine.

"We'll have to notify the police," she reminded them.

"I'll do it," Willard said, and started to climb back in his truck.

But Tina detained him. "Oh, no you don't, Willard. You'd be leaving the scene of an accident. I'll go back into town and get someone. Don't either of you leave."

Russell sighed his frustration as he stared at his car. Fat chance he'd be going anywhere. Why, oh, why hadn't he stayed with the interstates?

Tina's trip back into Leatrice and return to the scene of the accident took half an hour. She was followed by Bob Louvin of the police department and Leon Shaw of Shaw's Garage and Body Shop. While Bob took down all the pertinent information and checked Russell's driver's license, Leon studied the damage to the Thunderbird, shaking his head and making *tsk-tsking* noises.

Bob handed back the license. "Sorry this had to happen, Mr. Cade. Mr. Higgins here will get the citation." The policeman shifted his attention to the farmer. "I'll swear, Willard, the next time I catch you driving a car, I'm going to let you cool your heels in the clinker overnight. Do you have your liability insurance information with you?"

"No," the farmer said.

"Well, let's go up to the house and get it. I'll follow you. And once you park that truck, don't you ever get behind the wheel again, you hear?"

Leon Shaw was still shaking his head and Russell didn't like the look on the mechanic's face. "This baby's gonna have to be towed into town," Leon said. "The wrecker's out on another call right now, but as soon as it's free, I'll have it out here."

"And just what am I supposed to do until then?" Russell wanted to know.

"Wish I could help you, sir. I'd like to give you a ride into town, but our insurance doesn't allow us to carry passengers in the company truck. Sorry. But I'll get your car into the shop just as soon as I can and let you know what damage has been done."

Russell had serious doubts about the quality of workmanship available in a town like Leatrice. "Perhaps the car should be taken somewhere else," he suggested. "How far is the nearest city?"

Leon looked downright offended. "Well, sure, sir, I guess it could be towed into Amarillo, but—" he rubbed the Thunderbird lovingly "—she won't get the personal attention there that I'm gonna give her."

"Leon really does do excellent work," Tina interjected. "We've used him many times. I'm so sorry it happened, but since it did, you couldn't do better than Shaw's Garage."

Russell wanted to hit something. Everyone was sorry about everything, but that didn't put him back on the road. He took out a handkerchief and mopped his perspiring brow.

That prompted Tina to step forward. "My house is two minutes away. Why don't you wait there? It'll be cool, and Leon can call you there. I'd take you back to town right now, but I really need to check in at home. Jake or I will drive you into town later."

Russell glared at her, then remembered that the lady wasn't part of his problem. She was only being kind, and he obviously could use her help. The afternoon heat was murderous. "All right. Thanks."

"You'd better get your stuff out of your car."

"Yeah, I guess you're right."

Russell cleared out his trunk and glove box, surrendered the keys to Leon and stowed his belongings in the bed of Tina's truck. Then he climbed into the cab with her.

She smiled at him. "By the way, I'm Tina Webster."

"I'm Russell Cade, Tina. I wish I could say it's a pleasure meeting you. I'm sure it would be under different circumstances."

"I know. It's a shame. Somebody's got to keep old Willard off the road." She turned the key in the ignition and eased the pickup onto the highway.

The terrain wasn't as flat as it looked, Russell noticed without much interest. Once Tina turned off the highway and drove under the arch that proclaimed the spread to be the Webster Hereford Ranch, he spotted numerous arroyos, all of them bone-dry. And the road that had looked so smooth was like a washboard. But it didn't seem to faze Tina. She drove the truck like a bat out of hell, stirring up a cloud of dry earth that looked like a miniature tornado.

The ranch house they approached was typical of most of those built on the high plains in the 1920s and thirties—two storied with a covered porch that spanned the width and swept around one side. The building was pristine white except for the red brick foundation, and it was surrounded by magnificent old cottonwoods. There were several buildings behind the house, along with a windmill and water tank. The cluster of structures sat alone on a sea of grass, like a fleet of small boats on an ocean. Tina parked the pickup behind a Jeep and a blue compact sedan, and she and Russell got out.

They entered the house through the back door, which led directly into a big, pleasant kitchen. In the center stood a round oak table with six chairs encircling it. The room reminded Russell of the Kansas kitchen of his youth. At least, it did until he noticed something very odd. All the drawers and cabinet doors were labeled in large letters: Cups, Silverware, Towels, and so forth. And he saw that some of the cabinets had heavy locks on them. Maybe there were children around.

A gray-haired woman with an ample bosom was at the sink. When the door opened, she turned. "You're back," she said, eyeing Russell curiously.

"Ruby, this is Russell Cade," Tina said, and gave the woman a succinct account of Russell's misfortune.

"That's too bad," Ruby said. "Somebody ought to do something about Willard before he kills half the county. Can I get you something to drink, Russell?"

"Thanks, no, Ruby."

"How are things?" Tina asked, addressing Ruby.

"Not too good. No, I wouldn't say we had a good morning at all."

"Where is he?"

"In the living room. Grumpy, grumpy." Ruby affected an exaggerated shudder.

Tina sighed. "Then I'm sorry I left you."

"You can't stay here every minute," Ruby said.

Russell was left slightly puzzled by the exchange between the two women, but he said nothing.

"Where's Jake?" Tina went on.

"He was right out back a few minutes ago, tinkering with the tractor."

The words were no sooner out than the back door opened and Jake Yearwood entered the kitchen. Jake was a wiry man in his late fifties, lean and hard with salt-and-pepper hair. There were permanent lines around his eyes from working in the sun most of his life, and his face had the texture of a pecan shell.

"Pleased to meetcha," he said as he shook hands with Russell. "Where ya from?"

"I've been working out of Arkansas for a lot of years."

Tina then told Jake about Russell's accident, prompting Jake to frown. "Why don't them grandkids of Willard's hide the goddanged keys?"

"I've heard they do, but sooner or later someone leaves them out, and Willard finds them."

"How can a body find keys when he can't see?" Jake went to the sink, got a drink of water, affectionately patted Ruby's hip, then headed for the door again. Halfway there he stopped and looked at Russell. "I'm fixin' to make my rounds, young fella. Wanna come along, or do you wanna stay here and jaw with the women?"

"I'm waiting for a phone call, Jake. Thanks just the same."

"If you think you'd enjoy seeing our operation," Tina said, "I can take Leon's call for you, and you can get back to him later."

Russell thought about it. The call might not come for an hour or more. Making the rounds with Jake actually held little appeal, but neither did sitting around a kitchen listening to the chatter of two unknown women. "All right, I think I'd like to go along for the ride."

When the two men had left, Tina went in search of her father. She found him slumped in his easy chair in the living room, sound asleep. Ty slept so much, maybe too much, but at least when he was sleeping none of them had to watch him. Tina knew that one reason they would be able to let him remain at home so long was the ranch's remoteness. Most dementia patients roamed, and he was no exception. But even if he wandered off and forgot where he was, as he often did, he couldn't actually get lost. She couldn't imagine trying to take care of him in the city, where he could wander so far afield that he could come to real harm. He would have to be kept under lock and key. As it was, the hardest part was just keeping an eye on him and trying to find simple things for him to do, things that required a minimum amount of concentration. Tina quietly turned and went back to the kitchen.

Ruby was seated at the table, shelling butter beans. Tina sat down across from her. "Give me some and I'll help. Tell me about Dad."

"Ty gave Jake a hard time about getting dressed this morning. He said he wanted to leave his pajamas on. I remember you said you didn't want him doing that, so I told Ty he had to take a shower, shave and put on real clothes. My God, he exploded! Called me a bossy old bitch and said he'd get dressed when he blankety-blank pleased . . . or words to that effect."

Tina sighed and shook her head sadly. "I shouldn't have left the house without getting him dressed. Ruby, I'm so sorry you have to put up with that kind of thing, but try to remember . . . that's not Dad talking."

"I know. I'll admit it's hard hearing Ty say things like that to me after all these years, but I understand."

"Sometimes I think that's the worst part of the disease—the alteration in his personality."

Ruby looked up from her work. "I think the worst part is the alteration in *your* personality. You used to be so bright and lively."

"Come on, Ruby. I haven't been bright and lively since the day I found my darling husband in the throes of passion with Mazie Stephens. Let's be honest."

The two women worked in silence for a few minutes, their fingers flying. Finally Ruby spoke. "The real shame of it is that you have to do for Ty alone. Your sister ought to share some of the responsibility."

"One person usually winds up being the primary caregiver," Tina said. "They told us that in support group. And we have to remember that Becca has a family."

"She has money. She could hire someone to watch the kids for a few days. Or she could leave them with your mother. I don't know why Joan can't help out now and then. Ty was her husband for fifteen years, and a darned good one, too. It wasn't his fault that she hated ranch life. She knew what he did for a living when she married him." Ruby sniffed her disdain. "Becca and Joan could give you a hand if they had a mind to."

Tina said nothing. For once she wasn't inclined to rush to the defense of her sister and her mother. She loved them both, of course, but she wasn't blind. They were two very self-centered women.

"I still say," Ruby persisted stubbornly, "you ought to tell Becca she's just going to have to stay here a few days and let you get away."

Tina smiled. "I'm afraid if she actually agreed, dear Ruby, you would find yourself with two invalids on your hands."

She scooped more beans out of the sack. "Have you talked to Connie today?" she asked, referring to the Yearwoods' daughter who lived near Clarendon.

"Uh-hmm. She called this morning."

"How's she doing?"

"Coping," Ruby said.

"It must take a lot of coping." Connie and her husband, John, after fifteen childless years of marriage, had recently adopted an entire Bolivian family of orphans—a brother and two sisters. Tina was sure it must be akin to finding oneself with triplets when only one baby has been expected. Both Connie and John were teachers, but Connie had quit to devote all her time to the children. She was even studying Spanish so that she would be better able to communicate with them. "Connie's a remarkable lady."

"She's just doing what we all do—whatever we have to."

Again the two women worked silently. Tina knew that both Jake and Ruby had tried to talk Connie out of the adoption, feeling that three children was two too many. But Connie had been adamant, feeling perhaps that they might never get another chance. But from a word here and there, Tina had ascertained that things weren't going as nicely as everyone had hoped. "She must feel enormously tied down after being childless so long."

"She's not as tied down as you are, Tina," Ruby said.

"But I have you. That makes a world of difference."

Ruby, Tina thought, gave her the most curious look.

"GIT OVER THERE!" Jake hollered in a tough voice. "Git!"

Russell sat paralyzed in the Jeep, unable to believe his eyes. The creature on the receiving end of Jake's wrath was a slobbering black bull that weighed two thousand pounds if he weighed an ounce.

It was late afternoon. Russell and Jake had been heading back to the house, when they'd encountered a small part of the herd in a back field. Jake, using the Jeep as expertly as cowboys used horses, had begun steering them closer in, when the bull had balked, just put on the brakes and refused to go a step farther. To Russell's utter astonishment, Jake had stopped the Jeep, gotten out, picked up a switch and headed for the animal.

"I told you to git!" Jake hollered. "When I say git, I mean move!" He snapped his wrist, and the switch popped across the bull's rear.

The animal snorted and fumed and raised his head. Russell's heart was in his throat. He was certain he would soon be witnessing a tragedy.

The enormous animal swished his tail defiantly, snorted again and set his legs apart. Then he lowered his head as though going to charge.

"Git!" Jake hollered again, and cracked the switch across the bull's rump once more.

The ensuing sound was as loud as a pop of thunder. And right before Russell's stunned eyes, the old bull backed up and rejoined the herd.

Jake returned to the Jeep, shifted, and the machine lurched forward. "Gotta show 'em who's boss," he said laconically.

"Weren't you afraid of that bull?"

"Nah. He's just stubborn. Likes to test me every once in a while."

Jake, Russell noted, was not a man one should cross.

It had been an interesting afternoon, far more interesting than Russell would have imagined. And the ranch was a far more complex operation than he had thought. Now Jake was telling him that the Webster ranch had once been three times as large as it was now, a vast cow-calf operation, but now wheat, cotton and corn were as vital as cattle.

"We contract out the harvestin', though. Don't pay for an outfit this size to tie up a hun'erd-thousand dollars in a combine," Jake explained. "Ty sure hated seein' them first crops go in the ground. Ty's Tina's daddy, an old-style cattleman. He said he'd 'bout as soon run bare-ass nekkid through Leatrice at high noon as put a plow to his place, but you can't live off cows alone, not anymore."

"I really expected to see a lot more cattle," Russell said.

"There's more, but they're in feedlots, where a bunch of nutrition experts decide what they oughta eat. That's who we sell our corn to. Ain't as romantic as grazin' on the open range, but it's better bi'ness."

The Jeep bounced along. "How long you been here, Jake?"

"All my life. Fifty-eight years."

"Guess you know people for miles around."

"'Bout eighty-seven percent of 'em."

Russell wondered how he had arrived at such a precise figure. "Anybody famous ever come from around here?"

"Oh, sure. An army general, a Dallas banker, a Midland oilman and a Texas U quarterback. Oh, and a guy who played fiddle for Merle Haggard for a while."

"Impressive."

" 'Course, we also had some guys who ended up in jail. And some who didn't but shoulda, more'n likely. Shee-ut! Looka that!''

"What?" Russell's gaze followed Jake's gesturing finger. To the north the sky was boiling black. It was a strange landscape. Behind them and to the south were blue sky and puffy white clouds. Up ahead, the lowering sun was putting on a spectacular show. But that rolling mass to the north looked downright menacing, and it was heading for them at an alarming rate of speed.

"We might have us a little blow 'fore long," Jake said.

Russell glanced at him nervously. "What's a 'little' blow?"

"Can't never tell, not this time of year. Might be a twister or two in that baby."

It was said offhandedly, but Russell noticed that Jake pressed his foot down on the accelerator a little harder.

BY THE TIME they got back to the house, Leon Shaw had phoned, so Russell returned his call. His news was not good. The Thunderbird had suffered extensive frame damage, and there were parts that had to be ordered from the factory. Leon couldn't get them in Amarillo. Once the parts arrived, they were looking at a minimum of eight to ten working days. Then, if everything went right, they would need a week to prime, sand and paint the vehicle. Russell couldn't believe his lousy luck. What in hell was he going to do in Leatrice for more than two weeks?

Hanging up, he noticed Tina staring out the kitchen window and frowning.

"Russell, you'd best get your things out of the truck. Looks like that promised storm is finally on its way."

"Listen, folks, I can't impose on your hospitality any longer. Looks like I'm stranded for two weeks or more, so I really should get back to town and do something about finding a room."

"Well, you certainly can't go anywhere until after the storm," Tina said. "Besides, Ruby is planning on you for supper. Let's get your things. And if the storm sticks around all night, we have extra room."

"Please, that's awfully nice, but..."

Ruby silenced him with a glance over her shoulder. "Guess you're not familiar with the way we do things around here. We look after folks, especially strangers in trouble."

Russell saw no sense in protesting further. He really was in a bind, and these people were literally offering him a port in a storm. He got his belongings out of the pickup and stowed them in a corner of the dining room, out of the way. Then he joined Tina, Jake and Ruby in the kitchen.

Supper was on the table when the storm hit. First came wild wind gusts, then cracks of lightning so loud they sounded as if they had hit right next to the house. Outside it was as black as midnight. Russell found himself wondering if the ranch had a storm cellar and how quickly they could get to it. He nervously glanced around the table, but no one even looked concerned, much less scared. With some difficulty, he concentrated on the food, which was excellent. If corn bread cook-offs were held, Ruby surely would win any she entered. And while he ate, he listened to Jake's reminiscing about other storms the Yearwoods had lived through. If one could believe his accounts, many a town for miles around was remembered for the last time a tornado had "'bout blowed it plumb away."

A curious, peaceful glow suffused Russell's insides. He had no idea what caused it, since he couldn't think of anything he had to be happy about. Perhaps it was the sense of family that prevailed. While a certain camaraderie existed when a bunch of truckers gathered at a favorite truck stop to eat, drink coffee, swap tall tales and outright lies, it was nothing compared with this. Outside, all hell was breaking loose, but in the kitchen it was cozy and serene.

Ty Webster, Tina's father, had joined them, and he was a surprise. For some reason, Russell had expected a modern version of the quintessential Texas cattleman—strong, tough and energetic. Ty, however, was quiet to the point of being mute, and he looked rather frail, as though he'd been sick. He also looked too old to be Tina's father.

Upon being introduced to Russell, he'd looked at him blankly and asked, "How's the family?"

"Well...ah, fine, sir." Russell assumed Ty had mistaken him for someone he knew. The man had nodded, grunted, then sat down at the table and waited to be served. There hadn't been a word out of him since.

Russell became aware that Tina was asking him something.

"How was your afternoon?"

"Interesting. Jake is a fountain of information." There was a clap of thunder so loud Russell would have sworn he felt the house shake. Through the window over the sink he could see the rain coming down in silvery sheets.

Tina made a soft, contented sound. "Oh, listen to that! Music to my ears. The gullies will be full tomorrow."

"Maybe," Jake said. "The ground might be so dry it'll jus' suck it all up. Now if it'd do this all night..."

Ruby passed the big bowl of ham and butter beans around the table so they could have seconds. Russell knew he shouldn't eat more, but he did. After helping himself, he handed the bowl to Tina

She turned to her father. "More beans?"

Ty gave her the same blank look he had given Russell earlier. "How are you related to me?"

Russell turned, startled and puzzled. Everyone else kept on eating.

"I'm your daughter."

"I have a daughter named Becca."

"You have two daughters. I'm Tina. More beans, Dad?"

Ty stared at the bowl. "No, they taste like hell."

"You always liked Ruby's butter beans," Tina said calmly, setting the bowl in the center of the table.

"I want Becca to cook my beans from now on."

"Becca would be hard-pressed to boil water," Tina snapped, then immediately regretted it. Rule number one was, don't argue and don't try to explain. It did no good and often further confused a dementia sufferer.

"What did you say your name is?" Ty asked.

"Tina."

A few seconds ticked by; then Ty stood and kicked back his chair. "I think we're going to have to go home soon. I don't like the food here one damned bit. I don't like anything about this place. I just don't know...why everyone went away." With that he stomped out of the room.

"You better see where he's going," Ruby said to Jake.

"Right," Jake said, getting to his feet.

An awkward silence fell over the room. Tina had so hoped that supper would pass uneventfully, particularly since there was a stranger in their midst. Sometimes meals did. She tried never to be embarrassed over anything her father did; he was ill and could no more help his actions than she could help drawing her next breath. She pushed the rest of her food around on her plate and finally gave up on it altogether.

"What's wrong with him?" Russell asked softly when he could bear the strained silence no longer.

"Alzheimer's," Tina answered.

"Aw...what a lousy, rotten break."

That was a nice response, and he sounded genuinely sorry. Tina smiled at him sadly but gratefully. "Yes, it is. You would especially think so if you'd known him five or six years ago."

"Then he's the reason for the labeled drawers and locked cabinets."

"Yes, but I don't think the labels help anymore. The locks have to stay, of course. There are locks in some awfully strange places in this house."

"Would you like more of anything, Russell?" Ruby asked.

"No, thanks, not another bite. Everything was delicious. I think that's the best corn bread I ever ate."

Jake came back into the kitchen. "He's okay. He's noddin' off in his chair again. I turned the TV on."

Tina didn't think her father could follow story lines because his attention span was so short, but he seemed to enjoy the movement and noise. She stood up. "The rest of you go watch if you like. I'll clean up, Ruby. You did the cooking.''

Ruby didn't protest. When Ty acted up, Tina liked to find something that needed cleaning. Physical activity that didn't require much thought helped take her mind off her father.

"I've got some mending that needs doing," Ruby said. "I'll go sit with Ty and get it done."

"Don't look like the storm's gonna end anytime soon," Jake told Russell. "Looks like you might have to bunk with us tonight, young fella. The road to the highway's gonna be a loblolly."

"You folks have been awfully nice to me. I sure hate to intrude."

"It's no intrusion," Tina assured him. "There's no way you can get into town tonight."

"I'll check out the spare room," Jake said, turning on his heels. "It ain't been used in a spell."

Tina bustled about, clearing the table and carrying the dishes to the sink. Russell watched her. She had just about the cutest tush he'd ever seen, high and firm, and it sure filled out her jeans. For a pleasurable minute he simply sat and looked at her. Then, remembering his manners, he pushed back his chair and got to his feet. "Let me help," he said, gathering up some glasses and silverware."

"Oh, please, no."

"I'm pretty good at this sort of thing. I've lived alone a long time." He deposited the dinnerware on the counter near the sink and returned to the table.

Tina glanced over her shoulder at him. "Ever been married?"

"Once."

"Divorced?"

Russell deposited more dishes on the counter. "Yeah. Truckers' marriages aren't known for their longevity."

"Why didn't you give up trucking?"

"I tried for a while, but she didn't like that, either. She missed the money. It was a no-win situation. I tried, but nothing I did worked. I finally decided that what she really didn't like was me."

Tina looked at him. His small smile was appealing. The self-deprecation was charming, too. "What made you take up trucking in the first place?"

"I was restless, I guess. I went to college for a couple of years, but school and I didn't take to each other too well. I figured driving would be a good way to see the country, and it was. I saw just about all of it."

"I guess it's hard to meet people when you stay on the go all the time."

"You meet lots of people. You just don't get to know any of them."

"Is that why you finally quit?"

"Maybe. I'm thirty-seven, and I don't want to still be alone when I'm fifty. It's time to settle down."

"What made you decide on California?"

He told her about the North Coast, how spectacular the scenery was, a surprise around every bend in the road.

"Not much in the way of spectacular scenery around here," Tina said. "Not many bends in the road, either."

It occurred to her that this was the first time in ages that she'd had a conversation with someone near her own age. There was Becca, of course, but she and her sister were poles apart. Mainly she talked to Ruby and Jake, less frequently to her mother and the people in the support group. Even there, everyone was much older than she was. "Would you like coffee?" she asked hopefully. She hated to have the conversation end.

"Are you having some?"

"Yes, I think so."

"Then I'll be glad to join you."

Somehow while they had been talking, the table had been cleared and the dishes rinsed and put in the dishwasher. Tina quickly made two cups of instant coffee in the microwave oven. "Ruby or I always make a big pot of brewed in the morning," she said as she and Russell sat down at the table again. "Dad hates instant. Or at least he used to. He isn't much interested in food anymore. You saw how much he left on his plate tonight."

"Is that part of the disease?"

"Yes. It's a daily battle to get him to eat something."

"How long has he been sick?"

"Who knows? Probably longer than any of us are aware of."

"I've heard of Alzheimer's, of course, but I can't say I know anything about it. For sure I've never known anyone who had to live with it day to day. What made you suspect it in the first place?"

Tina looked at him with a wan smile. "Russell, it's so complicated. I'm still learning something new every day. Once I start talking about that hideous stuff I can't seem to stop."

"I'd like to hear it if you don't mind talking about it."

"Oh, I don't mind." She took a swallow of coffee, closed her eyes and let her mind wander back to the time when she'd first known there was something very, very wrong with her father....

CHAPTER THREE

"IT'S SUCH an insidious thing," she began. "Looking back, it seems to have hit suddenly, but it actually sneaked up on me little by little. About two and a half years ago, I came back home after living in Forth Worth for years. I was in the process of getting a divorce, so I had problems of my own and wasn't as aware as I should have been. The only thing I noticed right off was that Dad had lost weight, that he didn't look as robust as he always had. But everyone's so weight conscious these days, I just assumed he was watching the pounds. I had planned to stay home only a month or so, but after I'd moped around, licking my wounds for a few weeks, I began to notice a lot of things."

Russell sipped his coffee and watched her intently. He was surprised to hear she had been married, since she had introduced herself as Tina Webster, but he supposed a lot of women reverted to their maiden names when a marriage went sour, particularly if no children were involved. He guessed no children had been involved. There sure weren't any around here. He listened to her with interest and looked deeply into her sad, tired eyes.

"The first occurrence that I remember clearly," Tina continued, "was the afternoon when Dad and I had gone into town to do some shopping. We came out of the hardware store and were going home. Dad suddenly stopped, looked around as though he was confused. The car keys were in his hand. He glanced down at them, frowned, then handed them to me, just like that, with no explanation or anything. So I drove home. That doesn't sound earthshaking, not unless you knew Dad. He never wanted anyone else to do the driving, especially not a woman. At the time I thought it was strange, but I didn't think about it long. Now I suspect that he'd forgotten which car was ours. He might have forgotten the way home. He might even have forgotten what the keys were for or how to use them.''

"That's rough," Russell said.

"Then, not long after that, I began to notice how he asked the same questions over and over again—what time it was, what day it was. But I chalked that up to preoccupation or not paying attention. And he would tell me the same story over and over again, but I remembered my grandfather doing that very same thing as he got older. You see, Dad married late in life. He was forty when I was born, so he was getting along in years. I denied there was anything really wrong with him because so much of the time he acted perfectly normal. That's what you regret most when you discover there's a disease involved. It pains me now to think how many times I've said, 'Dad, for heaven's sake, look at the clock,' or 'Why do you ask me questions if you're not going to listen to the answers?' ''

"What made you finally go to a doctor?"

"So many things. One, he was unusually cranky. Two, his attention span was about thirty seconds, and the simplest chores just threw him. Three, he'd come downstairs in the morning and his shirt would be buttoned wrong or not buttoned at all and his fly wouldn't be zipped. This from a man who had always been so fastidious. Then I began receiving past-due notices from the drugstore, the feed store, the dentist, you name it. We Websters have always paid our bills, so I snooped around in the office. It was in chaos. Bills had gone unpaid for months, correspondence hadn't been opened and the checkbook hadn't been balanced in ages. It took me forever to straighten everything out. When I tried talking to him about it, asking him why on earth he'd let things get in such a mess, he stormed and snorted and said he couldn't trust anyone anymore. When I asked him who 'anyone' was, he said it was the person who was supposed to do the bookkeeping. Well, I knew something was wrong. Dad was the only one who'd ever kept the ranch's books. He wouldn't even hire an accountant to do our taxes because he didn't want anybody else to know how much he was worth.''

She paused to sigh and run her fingers through her hair. ''Then he began wandering, just roaming from room to room as though he were looking for something. The psychologists will tell you that he *was* looking for something—himself. You see, in the early stages the patient knows he's confused, so he looks for something familiar and comforting to hold on to. I could cry when I realize that Dad knew there was something wrong with him long before I did.''

Russell winced. ''Is that when you went to a doctor?''

''Would you believe it wasn't? I honestly thought Dad was just displaying classic symptoms of old age. But one morning...'' Tina paused and her chin trembled slightly. ''One morning he came down to break-

fast, and when he saw me, he . . . asked me who I was
and what was I doing in his house. Then I finally knew
something was dreadfully wrong. I made him go see a
doctor on the pretense of being worried about his losing weight. The doctor sent us to a gerontologist. His
diagnosis was senile dementia . . . or Alzheimer's, just
one of a whole family of dementias. You know, I was
almost glad when somebody gave it a name. I thought
Dad and I both were losing our minds."

"And nothing can be done?"

"Oh, research goes on. Maybe someday. Right now
I think it's the only disease I've ever heard of where
help is aimed primarily at the person who cares for the
patient. The monster really has two victims. And one
thing's for sure—the brain damage that Dad's already
suffered is irreversible. How I wish it would just stop
dead in its tracks right now while I can still handle him.
He can't ever be left alone for long, and he needs help
with his showers and getting dressed. That pretty well
ties me to him, but at least I can handle him."

Russell pursed his lips thoughtfully. She had come
home for a short visit and now was stuck. She'd probably never say such a thing, but she wouldn't be human if she didn't occasionally feel it. "Tina, I'm
probably asking too many questions, so if I come up
with one you don't want to answer, just tell me so."

"I don't mind talking about it. In fact, the support
group counselor says that talking is the best therapy."

"Why do you have to be the only one to take care of
your dad? You have a sister, or was that a figment of
the imagination?"

"No, I have a sister."

"And your dad is obviously taken with her."

Tina uttered a bitter little laugh. "Now there's a fig-ment of the imagination. Our folks split up when Becca and I were in high school. I stayed here, and Becca went to Amarillo with our mom. She's hardly been back since. She hates this ranch."

"But she could help you."

"If you knew Becca, you'd know she'd be little help. Besides, I'm more fortunate than some caregivers."

"How on earth do you figure that?"

"I have Jake and Ruby, but it's what I don't have that's a plus. I don't have a husband and two kids who are resentful of the time I have to spend with Dad. More coffee?"

"No, thanks." Russell admired her positive think-ing. "Can't you hire help?"

"To come all the way out here? I doubt it. And caregiving is expensive. The day will eventually come when I'll be glad for every dollar I didn't spend."

At first Russell didn't catch the meaning of that. But then he understood. "He'll have to be put in a home?"

Tina nodded. "It's inevitable."

No wonder she looked beat, Russell thought. What a hell of a thing to have hanging over your head—the knowledge that some day she was going to have to commit her parent. "Your dad said something else at supper, something about going home..."

"Yes, that's the latest phase. He seems to think we live somewhere else, that we're just visiting here."

"And when we were introduced, he asked me how my family was. Did he think I was someone he'd met before?"

Tina shook her head. "No, that's his standard greeting to everyone. That's what makes me think that part of his brain is clicking along nicely. Think about it. Almost everyone has some family—parents, siblings, aunts, cousins, someone. Dad doesn't remember who people are or if he's ever met them before, so he asks them how the family is. Pretty smart if you ask me. I clutch at all straws, no matter how thin.''

"Tell me something, Tina—do you have friends close by? Do you ever get out to go to dinner or the movies or things like that?''

"No, not really. Most of the friends I had when I was growing up are long gone from here. And I don't like to leave Jake and Ruby with Dad too often. Since I have to go into Amarillo occasionally, that pretty well does it.''

"So how do you spend your time?''

"Dad takes most of it. When he's napping, I do the ranch's paperwork. And I'm in charge of totin' and fetchin' for Jake.'' She smiled wanly.

Russell expelled his breath in a long sigh. It sounded like a hell of a life for a beautiful woman her age. And Tina was beautiful. The longer he looked at her, the more beautiful she became. She belonged almost anywhere else, doing almost anything else. He wished she didn't have such problems. He didn't know why he cared; he just did.

"Russell?'' Tina had her chin propped in her hands, and her eyes were closed.

"Yes.''

"Since you're stranded, you're welcome to stay with us until your car's fixed.''

"Well, Tina, I . . .''

"I'll be honest with you. It's been nice having someone new to talk to. Sometimes I think my mind's going to atrophy. Not many family friends come to call anymore.'' She paused, then added, ''As a matter of fact, no one does.''

Her honesty was disconcerting. He didn't know what to say. The situation was pretty ridiculous when he thought about it—to move in with strangers for two weeks . . . or more. It was odd that he'd even consider it.

But he liked these people. They reminded him of the folks he had known when he was growing up in Kansas—honest, hardworking, unpretentious, friendly. That afternoon he had felt an instant rapport with Jake, much like the one he'd shared with Junior. And he liked Tina. She had problems that he wouldn't have wished on anyone, but if she felt sorry for herself, she didn't let it show.

Tina misinterpreted his hesitation. ''Sorry. Guess I have my nerve, huh? If old friends won't visit because Dad's condition makes them uncomfortable, why would a stranger want to be around him every day?''

''Oh, it's not that,'' Russell said quickly. ''I just wondered—wouldn't I be in the way?''

''I doubt it. You can talk to me, tell me all about that big, wonderful world out there.''

''Some of it isn't so wonderful.''

''Then you can tell me more about Northern California. At least it sounds wonderful.''

Again Russell hesitated, then made up his mind. Wouldn't this friendly house beat a motel room? ''All right, Tina. You put it so charmingly that I can't refuse. Now, may I ask another question that's none of my business?''

''Sure.''

''How come you went back to your maiden name after your divorce?''

"I didn't want anything to do with him, so that included his name."

"No kids?"

"No kids, thank God."

"Sounds like it wasn't an amicable parting."

Tina was sure she'd never talked so freely to a stranger, certainly not about her divorce. The hurt and bitterness were still fresh after more than two years, as was the feeling of rejection. But she was starved for conversation, and Russell just seemed to pull the words out of her. "Amicable? Hardly. You see, my husband couldn't stay away from other women."

Russell accepted the explanation without comment. He pushed back his chair, got to his feet and carried his cup to the sink.

"The guest room is the first on the right at the top of the stairs," Tina said.

"Thanks. I'll put my stuff away so the rest of you won't have to step over it."

"The offer of a job still holds if you want. But I'd like to have you stay with us whether you work or not."

"Maybe I'll take you up on that, Tina. I can't imagine just doing nothing for two weeks or more." Russell turned to leave the kitchen, but at the threshold he paused. "Do you know what I think?"

She cocked her head and quizzed him with her eyes.

"I think your husband was an idiot." With that he left the room.

Tina stared after him. Her cheeks felt unusually warm, and a prickling began at her nape. It was a sensation she always experienced when something pleased her. If she wasn't mistaken, she had just received a compliment from a nice-looking man. That hadn't happened in so long she was almost in shock.

LATER THAT NIGHT, in the privacy of their own room, Ruby told Jake that Tìna had asked how Connie was.

"What'd you tell her?" Jake asked.

"The same, that Connie is fine. I hate lying to Tina."

"You ain't lyin' to her, jus' not tellin' her every little thing."

"I don't dare. If she suspected that Connie needed me, she'd insist I go, and I don't think she could cope with Ty without my help." Ruby sighed. "Connie says Alejandro's mouth is a mess, and the dentist is going to cost two thousand dollars. Maria needs eyeglasses, and poor Connie sounds plumb worn out."

"I knew she was bitin' off more'n she could chew when she signed up for them three kids."

"I thought so, too, but the adoption agency never would have accepted Connie and John if they hadn't agreed to take all three. The kids were considered ... unplaceable ... or some such. But at Connie's age I figured she'd have a hard time adjusting to one young'un, much less three. And Lord, that agency's picky. Everything has to be just so. I can't imagine why. I mean, those kids came out of a village that didn't even have running water." Ruby sighed. "I just wish I could help Connie more."

"By livin' here with Tina, we can help her the way she needs it most—with money," Jake said firmly. "Sure she's tired. Bein' tired goes with bein' a momma. She'll do fine." Seeing his wife's worried expression, he went to give her a reassuring pat. "We can't leave, babe. Connie's young and strong, and she has a husband. If we left, Tina wouldn't have anybody."

"I know," Ruby said, "but you can't blame me for worrying about my own baby."

"Yep. That goes with bein' a momma, too."

CHAPTER FOUR

AFTER BREAKFAST the following morning everyone went about their own chores. Tina's morning, as was almost always the case, was devoted to Ty, while Ruby did the housework.

Jake was more than happy to have Russell's company and help. "But you need a big hat. Them little baseball caps ain't worth screw-all for keepin' the sun off." And he produced a straw Stetson from his own closet.

The two men stepped out onto the back porch. Last night's storm had left the air fresh and clean. "Don't think it's gonna be so hot today," Jake observed.

It was hot enough. Russell had thought unloading thirty-five thousand pounds of cargo was work, but it was a song-and-dance routine compared with what Jake did. First the corn had to be weeded and sprayed, which took most of the morning. At noon Tina drove out with their lunch—four of the fattest sandwiches Russell had ever seen and a gallon of sugary iced tea. They ate the food in the only shade they could find, the shadow of a tin shed.

"Now me personally, I think we should ditch the corn," Jake informed Russell.

"I'd certainly second that."

"Oughta jus' plant cotton, maybe some wheat, but cotton's the crop. Takes a mite more machinery than

corn, but not near as much fertilizer and water. Water's jus' sumpthin' we don't have enough of. Once
upon a time ever'body thought that ol' underground
aquifer would last till the end of time, but it ain't
gonna. It's droppin' all the time. When that happens,
guess all this'll jus' go back to what it used ta be—pasture.''

That suited Russell just fine—his interest in the ter-
ritory's future was nil. By midafternoon he knew with
certainty that he was not cut out for ranch work. He
was closer to physical collapse than he'd ever been in
his life. His arms ached; his back hurt so much he was
sure his spine would snap in two when he straightened. In spite of the hat, his skin burned from the sun.
He was on top of a swaying windmill, oiling the
damned thing and experiencing his first bout of acro-
phobia, when it dawned on him that he was a moron
for getting suckered into this kind of work. He could
be back at the house, or in a cool motel room in Leatrice, sipping cold beer and watching TV. At supper
tonight he would tell Tina he sincerely appreciated the
hospitality, but he didn't think ranch work was up his
alley. It wouldn't be easy to admit that a fifty-eight-
year-old man could work circles around him, but what
the hell? He'd never see any of these people again.

The day did finally end, but Russell didn't feel much
better even after a shower and another of Ruby's delicious meals—roast beef this time, with three vegeta-
bles, homemade biscuits and cherry pie. He couldn't
believe food could taste so good or that the human
body could hurt so much. All he could think about was
getting into bed. When the meal ended, Jake wandered out the back door, Ruby went to get Ty settled in

front of the TV and Tina began clearing the table. Russell couldn't even move.

"Tired?" Tina asked kindly as she whisked away his plate.

"You could say that, yes." He took a deep breath. Even that hurt. "Tina?"

"Yes."

This was the time to tell her he was quitting. If he could catch a ride into Leatrice in the morning, he'd get out of their way. He'd vanish from their lives as abruptly as he had entered, and this would become one of those incidents guys relate over an after-work beer: Did I ever tell you about the time I worked on a ranch in West Texas for one entire day?

Hell, who would he tell? He had walked away from anyone resembling a friend when he'd quit Red Star. He'd have to go back to Georgia or Florida to find anyone who really cared about him. These people had taken him in, invited him to sit at their table, treated him like one of the family. It was only two weeks out of the rest of his life, for God's sake, and California wasn't going anywhere.

"Russell, was there something you wanted to say?"

"I . . . I think I'll turn in early, if that's all right."

She smiled. "It's all right. I understand." Opening a drawer, she took out a jar and handed it to him. "Put some of that on your face and neck before you go to bed. You got a lot of sun today."

Russell nodded numbly and pushed himself away from the table, wondering if his legs would support him. Miraculously they did. With as much dignity as he could muster, he left the kitchen and went to the stairs. The distance to the second floor looked like a mile. It was only seven-thirty, but when he reached his room, he whipped off his belt, took off his shoes and fell across the bed fully clothed. Within seconds he was sound asleep.

RUSSELL DIDN'T CHANGE his mind the next morning or the next. Things got better. Not immediately, but by the fourth day he actually could get out of bed without groaning. And he actually could stay up past seven-thirty at night. As the days passed, his skin darkened, but he was careful to wear sunscreen whenever he was outdoors, which was damned near all the time. He wouldn't have wished this life on his worst enemy, but it had its compensations. He could feel his body getting harder, and he'd shed a few pounds, despite Ruby's cooking. And he was receiving an education—albeit unwanted—in all manner of things: drainage systems and water wells and circuit breakers and septic tanks, things he fervently hoped would be of absolutely no use to him in the future. He would never understand why not calling a plumber or an electrician when things went wrong was such a matter of pride to rural people.

If someone had asked, he wouldn't have been able to say why he'd stayed. He hadn't fallen in love with the work by any means. He hated having his skin covered with a mixture of sweat and dirt. He hated the calluses on his hands. But at night, with the day's work and a shower behind him, he thought there was nothing on earth quite as wonderful as one of those grand meals in that cozy kitchen, listening to Jake's tall tales and the banter between him and Ruby. He liked the Year-woods—he really did. They were what people meant when they referred to "the salt of the earth."

Then there was Tina. He liked watching her—maybe too much. She looked awfully good to him. He loved sitting with her at the kitchen table after supper. She wanted to know all about his life on the road. He told her about various characters he'd met, about how pretty Virginia was in spring and how breathtaking New Hampshire was in fall. Maybe he romanticized his anecdotes a little, but those sessions at the table seemed to put life into her. She didn't laugh much, or even smile a lot, but when he talked to her, her face became more animated. Sometimes she looked almost happy.

And, unwittingly, she had told him more about herself than she'd probably intended. Her divorce had just about done her in. If Ty's illness hadn't forced her to push aside her own problems who knows how long she might have taken to recover?

Russell couldn't begin to imagine the kind of man who would cheat on a woman like Tina. His own marriage hadn't been close to idyllic, but he'd been as faithful as a cocker spaniel while he'd been locked into it.

Tina, it seemed to him, would be a perfect wife. Apart from her looks, he could tick off all sorts of other attributes—intelligence, resourcefulness, sweetness. The man must have been nuts to risk losing her. She was the most agreeable companion Russell had ever known.

Not even a status report from Leon Shaw saying a certain vital part had to be back-ordered could upset Russell. So the car wouldn't be ready for three or four weeks. It would be ready one of these days. And when that day came, it was going to be very hard to say goodbye to these people.

ON THE LAST WEDNESDAY of the month, Tina left the ranch at nine-thirty and planned to be gone until mid-afternoon. There had been a time when she'd managed four or five trips into Amarillo every month, but as Ty's illness had progressed, she had reduced the number to three. One was with her dad for his monthly visit with his doctor; another was for shopping that couldn't be done in Leatrice; still another was to attend her support-group meeting. On meeting days she drove in early enough to visit her mother and her sister. Those visits were the biggest chores of all. She always came away from them feeling that she was a dismal disappointment to both women.

Her first stop was at Becca's two-storied brick house, with its beautifully manicured lawn and sweeping drive. Rebecca Webster Jennings was married to the scion of the third or fourth richest man in Amarillo; Tina could never remember the exact rating. The clan had its fingers in many pies, construction among them. Her sister liked to boast that the Jenningses had built a third of Amarillo. Becca had met Derek Jennings at a friend's wedding. Three months later they had one of their own, followed by a honeymoon in Spain. They went to the Bahamas every year. Their children attended a posh private camp every summer. Becca, as Joan Webster pointed out to her younger daughter on every possible occasion, had done very well.

"Teee-na!" Becca screeched gaily, appearing to float across an Oriental rug. "You look adorable." She grabbed her sister and hugged her ferociously.

"Thanks. You look pretty spiffy yourself." Tina had on a sensible rose-colored shirtwaist that didn't wrinkle. Becca wore billowing crimson hostess pajamas.

Long, sparkling earrings dangled from her lobes. At thirty-five, she was a full-blown beauty, a vision.

"Coffee, tea, something?" Becca asked.

"No, thanks. I really don't have a lot of time. I'm having lunch with Mom, then I go to the support-group meeting."

"Oh, you always just pop in and out. I wish I could join you and Mom, but there's a luncheon to kick off the museum fund drive. Come on in and sit down."

As young girls, the Webster sisters had often been told they looked alike, and in those days Tina had seen something of a resemblance. She no longer did. Her own looks, as far as she could see, were of the homespun variety. Becca's were sophisticated and lush, from her highlighted hair down to her sculpted nails. Tina had never heard of anyone who didn't like Becca. Some possibly were overwhelmed by her, but everyone always liked her. She was open, warm, sexy and energetic. The only thing that seemed to be missing from her life was restraint. When Becca did something, she did it wholeheartedly.

"How're the kids?" Tina asked as she sank onto a white sofa that curved around about one-third of the room.

Becca sat down next to her. "I have to think they're fine. Summer camp, you know."

"Ah, I forgot. I wouldn't mind it if someone sent me to Colorado this time of year."

Becca leaned forward and touched Tina's arm. Her eyes were bright and alive. "I'm dying to tell you something. Guess who stopped by day before yesterday on his way through town."

"I can't imagine."

"Paul!"

Tina's heart lurched. Her lips narrowed into a tight line. "Are you referring to Dr. Paul Michaels, my former husband?"

"Oh, you know I am. He looks wonderful, very prosperous, and he asked about you."

"Splendid. Becca, please, if there's one thing I don't want to talk about, it's Paul."

Tina had met Paul Michaels at Texas Tech, where she had been majoring in agriculture. They had hit it off immediately, but months passed before their relationship grew into a full-scale romance. She had fallen in love the way young, blossoming women do—with all the intensity and passion she could give. He was two years ahead of her, so when he graduated, she dropped out of college without a second thought. By that time she had realized she wasn't learning half as much in school as she was every day on the ranch, and agriculture hadn't seemed a prerequisite for the role of wife of a big-city orthodontist.

So she'd happily followed Paul to Dallas, where she'd worked for a veterinarian while he attended dental school. And after graduation, he had been invited to join an established practice in Fort Worth. It had been a good marriage, she'd thought. They'd had a lot of fun together and were sexually compatible. They both had wanted a couple of kids "someday." Paul declared that Tina could work or not; it was up to her. Tina, at least, had been ecstatically happy... until the day she'd returned home early from visiting her father and found Paul with Mazie. From that time on, whenever she allowed herself to think about it, she wondered if Mazie had been the only one. Tina doubted it. The debacle had left her with more than pain, anger and feelings of rejection. She now seriously questioned her own instincts and judgment.

"I'll swear, I don't understand you—really I don't," Becca was saying. "How could you let a man like that get away?"

Tina smiled knowingly. "There's an awful lot of Mom in you, you know. What you mean is, how could I let an orthodontist get away."

Becca studied a fingernail. "Don't knock it, Tina. You could have had all this." Her arm made a sweep to indicate the room as a whole. Her eyes almost caressed her possessions. "So he fooled around a little. You could have at least given him another chance."

"Please tell me that the two of you didn't discuss the reasons for the divorce!"

"Not really. He just said he'd made a mistake and you wouldn't give him a chance to prove he was sorry. I'm not stupid. What kind of mistake could a husband make that would cause his adoring wife to walk out on him. I daresay it was a wee bit more serious than using the grocery money to play the horses."

"You're right. Horses weren't what Paul liked to play with. Listen, Becca, I don't want to talk about Paul. I have far too much on my mind these days even to think about him." Which was a lie. When the loneliness got to her, she thought about him.

"Yes, I know," Becca said with a sigh. "How's Dad?"

"Some days are better than others."

"But he's no better?"

Tina felt a flash of irritation. Sometimes she suspected her sister of not listening to half of what she said. "No, Becca, I told you. He's never going to get better, only worse."

"Honestly, Tina, I hate to say this, but shouldn't he be put in a place where there are people used to taking care of—"

Tina interrupted her with a vigorous shake of her head. "No, not yet. Not until it's absolutely necessary. But I'm glad you brought it up. Dad's been talking about you a lot lately. I really think you should come to see him. Even if it gave him a lift for only an hour...well, that's about the best we can do for him."

Becca looked away. "Oh, Tina...it just depresses me so."

"Of course it depresses you. It depresses me. Something like dementia can't be expected to make you feel good, for God's sake!"

"But the last time I was there, he behaved as if he didn't know me."

"And he's forever asking me how I'm related to him. We can't let that kind of thing bother us."

Becca clasped her hands and stared at them. "You were always better at handling difficulties than I was. I just fall to pieces. I don't know what to do or what to say when I'm around him."

"It's really not so difficult," Tina said. "Just talk to him about ordinary things. The kids, for instance. And if he asks you ridiculous questions, answer them truthfully. He's apt to ask you who you are. Just say Becca. Talk to him about the past. Ask him about the war. World War II was the biggest event in Dad's life, and he loves to talk about it. The strange thing about Alzheimer's is that long-term memory is pretty good."

"Oh, why did this awful thing have to happen to Dad?"

"I don't know," Tina said tiredly. "No one wishes it hadn't more than I do."

"It's ruined your life."

"No, it hasn't."

"You never go anywhere or do anything. You never buy pretty clothes or have any fun. I don't know how you stand it."

If you realize that, Tina wanted to say, *why not offer a little help?* "Becca, the day is coming when I'll be perfectly free to come and go as I please. Except for visiting Dad, there won't be a damned thing I'll have to do. But until then, I want to make his life as comfortable and pleasant as possible. It's all I can do at this point."

THIRTY MINUTES LATER, Tina left, having extracted a hesitant promise from Becca to visit Ty soon, and drove to the apartment complex where her mother lived. It consisted of four five-storied buildings grouped around a landscaped courtyard. The grounds received plenty of tender, loving care. Tina rarely had been there when the sprinkling system wasn't on. All the apartments had balconies, and flowers spilled from most of them. The entire effect looked less like West Texas than any place imaginable.

Joan Webster was waiting for her. Tina noticed that the table on the balcony was set for lunch. "I thought I'd take you somewhere," she told Joan.

"The kitchen here does wonderful things. I wanted you to sample it. Did you see Becca?"

"Yes, I just left."

Joan appraised her younger daughter from head to foot. "You look sweet, dear."

Joan invariably told her she looked sweet, and invariably told Becca she looked smart. Tina wasn't sure, but she had a feeling that smart outranked sweet any day.

"Come in, Tina, and tell me all your news."

The apartment was done in blues, grays, pinks and mauves—all elegant and feminine, a great deal like Joan herself. Tina would never understand how Ty had ever rated so much as a second glance from a woman like her mother. He had been much older than Joan, so perhaps that was the initial appeal, but Ty was a third-generation Texas rancher; therefore macho and slightly sexist. Joan liked to organize, control and manipulate. There was no question in Tina's mind that her mother could have been governor of Texas had she put her mind to it. She certainly could have handled the job. How frustrating it must have been to find herself married to a man as inflexible as steel pipe.

Of course, she'd had her daughters' lives to orchestrate, but Tina, having been a tomboy, hadn't cooperated. So Joan's boundless energies had been directed at Becca, who'd assimilated all her mother's values, thrived and grown into a "lady."

Tina also didn't know how her mother lived as well as she did; but, then, it wasn't any of her business. She did know that Ty had given Joan a healthy divorce settlement, and her mother might have invested it wisely. Personally, Tina suspected Becca and Derek helped Joan. It wouldn't reflect well on Derek to have his mother-in-law living in too modest a home. Again it was none of Tina's business.

"Sit down, dear," Joan said. "Not there...over there."

Tina sat on the print sofa her mother had indicated, and Joan pulled up a side chair. "Now, your news."

"My news is mostly of the bad variety these days."

"Yes, your poor father. It's so dreadful. How is he?"

"He isn't well. He'll never be well again."

"I'm so sorry. And I'm especially sorry that it's so hard on you. Can't you get help? If it's money..."

"No, no. Thanks, but we're fine, honest." Which was true, up to a point. Financially they were fine now, but if her father had to go into a home for ten or twelve years, that could change. However, she could work then. She really didn't anticipate any money problems; nevertheless, she was frugal. "Mom, I want you to do a favor for me. I want you to encourage Becca to come to see Dad. He's been talking about her lately, and I think it would do him a world of good."

Joan looked uncertain. "You know, Tina, I hate to say this, but... Becca doesn't handle life's little hills and valleys very well."

"Because she's never had to. And this is no little valley. This is a yawning abyss. He's her father, too, and I'd like for her to see him occasionally while he's still lucid part of the time."

Joan twisted the ring on her right hand. "I'll...do what I can, of course."

"Thanks. I'd appreciate it." Tina didn't press further. It was obvious that her mother badly wanted to change the subject. "So, what's been going on in your life?"

"Did Becca tell you that Paul paid them a visit?"

"Yes, she told me."

"He called me while he was there. I thought that was very nice."

"Charming. He's a real prince."

Hearing the bite in Tina's voice, Joan made a disapproving sound. "Really, Tina. Becca said she got the impression Paul would welcome some dialogue between the two of you."

"Oh, Mom, it's been more than two years. I don't in the least want to talk to him." She didn't, did she? Tina honestly didn't know how she would react to seeing him or talking to him again.

"I don't understand you, Tina. You can look and see what your sister has made of her life, and—"

"She married a rich guy."

"Yet you could just toss away a perfectly good husband—"

"He wasn't perfectly good."

"Like an old shirt, a man who will have a brilliant career and give you all the things Becca has—"

The doorbell's ring mercifully interrupted them. Joan got to her feet and admitted a waiter, who rolled in a cart. At her mother's request, he set out lunch on the balcony table before leaving. For the remainder of Tina's visit, they talked about the food, which was dainty and unfilling, the weather, which was too hot for June, and Joan's friends, who numbered in the scores. When it was time for Tina to leave for her meeting, Joan pressed last month's issue of *Vogue* on her daughter. "I'm finished with it. You might want to look through it."

Tina smiled. "Thanks, Mom." It was her mother's subtle way of telling her she really should do something with herself.

TINA ALWAYS WELCOMED the monthly support-group meeting. It gave her a chance to talk with people who were in the same boat. And since it always came on the heels of her visits with her mother and sister, it somehow soothed the sting of Becca's and Joan's eternal preoccupation with her divorce.

The meetings were held in a private conference room at a branch library. In the center of the room was a circle of comfortable chairs. A soft-drink machine stood against one wall, and on a folding table was a coffeemaker. When Tina arrived, Hollis Reed, whose wife suffered from Alzheimer's, was measuring coffee into a filter-lined cup.

He turned when the door opened. "Hello, Tina."

"Hello, Hollis. It's nice you could get away."

"Mildred's sister came in from Albuquerque for the week."

"How wonderful for you."

"It helps."

Slowly the room began to fill up. Fifteen people comprised the group. They came from dissimilar backgrounds and economic circumstances and had varying interests, but all of them had loved ones diagnosed with incurable diseases. And all of them were primary caregivers. They accomplished a lot at their meetings or nothing at all, depending on the way one wished to look at it. They certainly couldn't nurse their loved ones back to health, but they could help one another by sharing experiences and offering suggestions.

They stood clustered in small groups, talking about almost everything but their problems. There would be time for that later, when Kathryn Parker, their counselor, arrived. The weather got its usual going-over, as did a miniseries that had aired on television the previous week. Finally Kathryn arrived, and the talk died as everyone took a seat.

Kathryn was a large, handsome woman in her late forties. She seemed to genuinely care about everyone in the room. "Well, I'm glad to see almost everyone could make it. Shall we begin? Who wants to be first?"

Hollis was the first to speak. "I've about decided it's time to put Mildred in a convalescent home. I'm not a young man, and I don't have the sheer physical strength to take care of her any longer. But... I don't know how I'm going to do it."

That got the ball rolling, and for the next forty-five minutes, they all talked, some at length, some only a word or two. And if Tina had been asked to describe in one word the prevailing feeling among the group, that word would have been *guilt*—guilt that they hadn't noticed symptoms earlier, guilt that they sometimes felt resentful, guilt that they couldn't do everything that needed doing, guilt that they would someday have to turn a spouse or parent over to someone else to care for. Only these meetings gave them any respite from the ever-present guilt. One could see the tension leave a person's face after he or she had poured out worries to the group of sympathetic listeners.

When it was time for the meeting to end, Kathryn put down her notebook, and her eyes swept over the gathering. "I want all of you to do something for me before our next meeting. Will you?"

The group responded with nods and murmurs of agreement.

"I want you to promise that when the going gets really rough, you'll sit down and say to yourself, 'I am a wonderful person. I'm doing the best I can under terrible circumstances. But I'm only human. God didn't endow me with the ability to do the impossible.' Say it as many times as necessary. Please. For your own sakes."

IT WAS ALMOST FOUR when Tina walked through the back door. She hated being gone so long, but sometimes it was slow going getting out of the city. The kitchen was in a state of temporary calm and tidiness, and Ruby was nowhere to be seen. The blue sedan, the Yearwoods' car, hadn't been parked at the side of the house, so that meant the older woman had probably gone into town. Tina did, however, hear voices, so she headed in their direction.

A card table had been set up in the middle of the living room, and Russell and Ty were seated at it, playing some kind of game. Tina had bought dozens of games designed for people suffering from memory loss. Sometimes they interested Ty; sometimes he ignored them. Right now he seemed to be having a good time. She didn't immediately announce her presence but stood in the foyer and watched . . . and listened.

Ty was staring down at the table. One never knew if he was genuinely concentrating on the game or simply staring.

Suddenly he looked up at Russell. "What'd you say your name is?"

"Russell."

"Were you with me in the Solomons during the war?"

"No, that was a little before my time."

That seemed to satisfy Ty. He looked down at the table again, but he made no move to get on with the game.

After a few seconds had passed, he again looked up. "How did all my things get here?"

"What things, Ty?" Russell asked gently.

"Everything. All this." He waved his arm around, apparently indicating the room's furnishings.

Russell pursed his lips. "Well, I'm not sure, but isn't it nice that they're here? Now we can all enjoy them."

Ty frowned, then nodded. "You're right."

Tina's heart caught in her throat. What an absolutely superb answer Russell had come up with. It had taken her months of trial and error, reading literature and talking to Kathryn before she'd learned how to handle her father's often foolish questions. But Russell had come up with a response out of the blue. She crossed the foyer and entered the living room.

When Russell spied her, he got to his feet and smiled. "Hello."

"Hello." Tina walked to the table, put her hand on Ty's shoulder and bent to place a kiss on his cheek. "Hi, Dad. You look like you're having a good time. I saw Becca this morning."

"Who?"

"Becca."

"Oh."

Tina could see that her presence had caused Ty to lose interest in the game. From force of habit, she scolded herself. *You know how easily his concentration slips. Why didn't you wait?* Then she remembered all the things she had heard at the meeting, especially Kathryn's admonition to stop blaming oneself for every little thing. *He never gets all the way through a game, interruption or not. Forget it.*

"I'm tired of this," Ty said. "I want to take a nap."

"Sure, Dad."

Russell rounded the table and slipped a steadying hand under Ty's elbow while the older man got to his feet. "Chair or bed?" he asked.

Ty merely pointed to his worn, comfortable easy chair. Less than a minute after sitting down, he was asleep. Tina and Russell left the room quietly.

"He'll be all right there for a while," Tina explained. "When he wakes up, I'll go for a walk with him before supper."

"Tina, I hope you don't think I was goofing off, but Jake asked me to keep him entertained while Ruby went to the dentist."

"You do anything Jake asks you to, and I'll be happy."

Russell followed her into the kitchen. She took a pitcher of tea out of the refrigerator. "Want a glass?" she asked.

"Thanks." Russell guessed he had drunk more iced tea in the short time he'd been at the ranch than he had in all the rest of his life put together. These people lived off the stuff. But he had to admit that when the outside temperature felt five degrees cooler than Hades, it sure hit the spot.

"You know, Tina, Ty told me the damnedest story this afternoon."

"Oh?"

"Yeah, something about putting a refrigeration system in on an island in the South Pacific during World War II."

Tina rolled her eyes. "So the navy could land and establish a base. His outfit got some sort of commendation for it. He was with the Seabees."

"Did that really happen?"

"It must have. I've heard the story about eight-dozen times in my life."

"But the detail was so vivid."

"Oh, Dad remembers the past pretty good. He just doesn't remember that I'm his daughter half the time."

"It's so... crazy, and sad," Russell said. "When I was getting that game out of the cabinet, I came across some literature on Alzheimer's. I'd like to read it if that's okay."

"It's fine, but... why?"

"I just thought that if I knew more about the disease, I'd be of more help with Ty."

Tina set her glass on the counter, folded her arms and studied him. She had become used to having him around in a very short time. And Jake liked him, which said a lot for Russell's character. Jake might come across as a plain ol' country boy, but he was the most astute judge of human nature that Tina had ever known. If he liked someone, it was a safe bet that said someone was pretty okay. "May I confess something to you?"

"Sure," Russell said.

"I really didn't expect you to keep working after that first day."

He grinned. "Neither did I. I planned to get a ride into town and hole up in a motel until my car was ready."

"Why didn't you?"

Russell had to forcibly restrain himself from reaching out and tracing the outline of her mouth with a fingertip. The sight of Tina this afternoon was particularly unsettling. It was the first time he had seen her in a dress, and she looked beautiful, very feminine. She also had a fine pair of legs. "I'm not sure. Maybe it's because I'd never had a chance to work for anyone so pretty before."

Tina didn't know if he really thought she was pretty or was just indulging in some male thing. At the moment she didn't care. Even if they were only so many words, they still were nice to hear. "I take it you're not referring to Jake."

"You know I'm not."

A minute of palpable silence ensued. Then Russell recovered, drained his tea and set his empty glass on the counter next to her full one. "Guess I'd better go see what Jake wants me to do now." He felt an urgent need to get the hell out of there before he made a complete ass of himself.

He'd reached the door, when Tina's voice detained him.

"Russell?"

He turned. "Yes."

"Any word on your car?"

"Yeah. Seems that's a special paint job. Leon can't get the paint for at least a week."

"I know you're disappointed."

"Oh . . . I checked, and California's still there." Grinning, he opened the door and left.

Tina frowned. That meant the car wouldn't be ready for two more weeks. She wasn't sure how she felt about that. It was great having him with them, and he'd been a lot of help to Jake, but every day he stayed would make saying goodbye all that much harder. Shaw's Garage might be as slow as molasses in January, but the car would eventually be ready. Then Russell would be off. Before long he'd be settled in that pretty Eden of his dreams. He'd think about all of them now and then for a while, then not at all. She hated that. She was going to miss him.

Tina uttered a disgusted sound and pushed herself away from the counter. She needed to check on Ty. She had enough real problems without borrowing more. While Russell was with them, she would enjoy him for what he was—a diversion—and diversions had been in short supply in her life for a long time.

CHAPTER FIVE

RUSSELL WAS A DIVERSION, all right. He was male, single and attractive, and Tina was no more immune to that than any woman. He often made her think of things she hadn't allowed herself to think about since her divorce.

And there was another, more subtle reason that having him around was often hard on her. He brought to the ranch images of a world much broader than Tina's limited one. He made her long for some freedom of her own, and that was the last thing she should be thinking about. Ty controlled and measured her days and would for years to come.

Still, she listened to Russell's tales of the road and daydreamed. It was laughably obvious that he didn't belong on the ranch, doing the kind of work he was doing, but neither did she really. The difference was, he could leave and she couldn't.

Yet she couldn't help admiring him for sticking with the work, although she couldn't imagine why he did. But she was pleased he did. He was great fun to talk to. He even had the ability to turn her into something of a conversationalist, drawing her out and making her talk about herself. She told him about her family, her childhood on the ranch, even a little about her marriage. Tina soon thought Russell possibly knew her better than anyone ever had, including Ruby.

When he talked about himself, which he did only under Tina's persistent questioning, he had a thousand interesting anecdotes from his years of driving to share, and California's North Coast was never out of his conversation for long. That alone intrigued her. She'd never had a dream to pursue, so it wasn't easy for her to understand how a man could save his money and think about a place for ten long years, then actually go in search of it. She only hoped he wouldn't be disappointed when he finally got there.

"OKAY, DAD," Tina said, "we're going to get dressed now." She indicated the items of clothing on the bed, all laid out in the order Ty was supposed to put them on. "Shirt first."

This was the way all her days began. To anyone unaware of her father's illness, the clothing would have seemed rather strange. Everything was slip-on, from his shirt to his shoes. There wasn't a buttonhole or shoelace in sight, and Ruby had replaced all the zippers in his trousers with Velcro. The entire process of getting him ready for the day usually took twenty-five minutes, and he had to be talked through each step. If she stopped talking, he stopped dressing. Tina knew she could have cut the time in half by dressing him herself, but she refused to do that. Whatever shred of his dignity could be salvaged had to be.

At last he was ready. She patted his shirtfront and smiled cheerfully. "There! Don't you look handsome."

"I'm hungry," Ty said.

"Are you? Wonderful. I'll bet Ruby has breakfast ready for us." At that moment she heard Ruby calling to her from the bottom of the stairs. Tina stepped out into the hall.

"Becca's on the phone," Ruby said.

"Okay, I'll take it in my room." Returning to Ty, she led him to the edge of the bed. "Dad, I have to get the phone. I want you to just sit here and wait for me. Then we'll go down for breakfast, okay?"

Ty nodded and sat down, as docilely as a child, folding his hands in his lap.

Tina hurried across the hall to her room and picked up the bedside phone. "Becca?"

"Hi, Tina. Listen, I seem to have a free afternoon, and I...well, I thought I'd come out and see Dad if it's all right."

Joan must have worked on her. Silently Tina thanked her mother. "All right? It's great! Love to have you."

"I'm pretty apprehensive about this. I wish you would give me some guidelines. What should I talk to him about?"

Tina recalled how long it had been since Becca had seen Ty—months and months—and their father had been changing almost daily. Her sister, she feared, was in for a rude awakening. "Becca, the best thing I can tell you is to keep it simple. Don't try to explain things and don't correct him when he says something completely off the wall. Most of all, let him do the talking if he will, and try to be patient if he tells you a story you've already heard a hundred times. If he won't talk, then you tell him very simply what you did last week. He might respond—he might not. Just keep talking...and don't be offended if he falls asleep while you're in the middle of a sentence. Dad doesn't always respond appropriately to what others say or do."

There was a long minute of silence before Becca said, "I think you're trying to frighten me. You're exaggerating, right?"

"I wish I were. I'm not trying to frighten you. I'm trying to prepare you."

"Maybe today's not such a good day. Maybe I should come another time."

"There'll never be a good day, never again. Please come. A new face might do wonders for him. Not over the long haul, of course, but for an hour or two."

"Well . . . all right. But I can't stay long."

I thought you said you have a free afternoon, Tina said to herself sourly. "Sure, I understand."

"See you around two."

"I'm looking forward to it." And, dear God, she did so hope the visit went well—for her sake, for her dad's and for Becca's, too.

Tina hung up the phone and went back to get Ty. Entering the room, she stopped dead in her tracks, thunderstruck. He was standing in the middle of the room, stark naked except for his socks. His clothes lay in a heap on the floor. Tina put a hand to her forehead and stared at him in disbelief. "Dad, why on earth did you get undressed?"

"I had to go to the bathroom."

Tina slumped against the doorjamb as slow laughter bubbled in her throat. The laughter, she realized, was tinged with hysteria, but at least it kept her from crying. Pushing herself away, she went to pick up his clothes, then laid them out on the bed in precise order. Then she took a deep breath. "Okay, Dad, we're going to get dressed now. This time we'll start with your undershorts."

THE AFTERNOON did not belong in the moments-to-remember category. Too late Tina recalled that her father usually napped at two o'clock, so she had kept him unusually busy after lunch, which wasn't a good idea.

Becca was punctual, arriving at precisely two. After greeting Tina at the door, she sailed into the living room, where Ty was sitting in his easy chair. "Dad! How wonderful to see you." Bending over the chair, she placed a kiss on his cheek.

Ty stared at her for a second or two, then said, "Hello. How's the family?"

Becca straightened, shot a glance at Tina, then looked at her father with a frown. "Do you mean Derek and the kids? They're fine."

Tina stepped forward. "It's Becca, Dad. She's come for a visit."

"You're late," Ty snapped at Becca.

Her cheeks flushed. "No, I'm not. I said I would be here at two, and it's exactly that now."

"I told you to be home by eleven. No nice girl stays out until two in the morning. I don't know what's gotten into your mother, letting you run wild."

Becca was so flabbergasted she couldn't speak.

Tina nudged her arm and indicated the sofa. "Have a seat. I'll get us some tea." Becca gave her a pleading look, but Tina said, "Becca and Derek are going to the Bahamas soon, Dad. Wouldn't you like to hear their plans for the trip?"

Ty addressed neither woman in particular. "Did I ever tell you about the time I was in the Solomons during the war?"

Becca rolled her eyes toward the ceiling.

Tina forced back a smile and said, "No, I don't think you ever did. I know Becca would love to hear about it. I'll be right back."

She slipped out of the room just as Ty was saying, "Shorty Gordon and I enlisted right after Pearl Harbor, and we shipped out together... San Francisco, April 17, 1942..."

Out in the kitchen, she bustled about, fixing two tall glasses of tea for Becca and herself, a small glass of water for Ty, who probably wouldn't touch it. She was sure Becca was not enjoying herself, and maybe it had been a dirty trick, but her sister needed to spend some time alone with their father. She needed to realize the extent of his illness. Then perhaps she would at least sympathize with Tina's frustrations.

She placed the glasses on a small tray and carried it out of the kitchen, but before entering the living room, she paused to listen. Ty was still talking, which was encouraging, but then she realized he no longer was talking about the war. His voice sounded very agitated.

"Did you come to take me away from this place?" he was asking Becca.

"Well... no, I..." she said, searching for words.

"I hate it here. They never feed me. No one pays any attention to me. I don't know anybody. I want to go home."

"But you *are* home. You've lived in this house since before I was born."

"I want to go home to Sutter Street."

"You haven't lived on Sutter Street since you were a boy." Becca sounded close to tears. "You moved out here with Grandma and Grandpa when you were... like ten or something."

Oh, God, Tina thought, *I've told her and told her not to try to explain things to him.* She hurried into the room. Her hands shook as she placed the tray on the coffee table. "Here we are. Is everybody thirsty?"

"No, I'm hungry," Ty said, fuming, slumping back in his chair. "I didn't have breakfast, and no one gave me lunch."

Tina didn't argue with him. He always picked at his food, so maybe it did seem to him he never got fed. "You hardly touched your tuna salad at noon. I'll fix you a sandwich. How's that?"

"I'd certainly appreciate something," Ty said.

Tina motioned to Becca to come with her, and her sister looked as though she might faint from relief. In the kitchen the two women faced each other.

"What is he trying to do to me?" Becca asked in a shaken voice.

"Believe it or not, he's not being deliberately argumentative. He really can't help the confusion."

"Then what are you trying to do to me? I simply can't take it."

"I wanted you to see it firsthand. Until you did, you couldn't possibly know what it's like."

"Is he always like this?"

"No two days are the same. I can't plan for tomorrow because I have no idea what tomorrow will be like. And worrying about tomorrow takes energy I need for today." Tina made a move for the refrigerator. "I guess I'd better make that sandwich. Any time Dad shows the slightest interest in food, I'm thrilled. By the way, he does get fed. He just doesn't eat much."

"I didn't for a minute think you were withholding food from a sick old man. But, Lord, he's thin." Becca went to sit at the kitchen table. "I don't know how you

stand it. I couldn't. I think living with that would make
me act as crazy as Dad does. Tina, why don't you put
him in a place where there are trained professionals to
take care of him?"

"No." She removed the tuna salad from the refrigerator, carried it to the counter and put together a
sandwich. "He isn't that bad yet."

"Not that bad?" Becca cried. "How much worse
can he get?"

"He's still ambulatory. And with supervision, he can
still do some things for himself. I just feel so damned
sorry for Dad. Everyone feels confused from time to
time, and it's a feeling I hate. Think what it must be
like to be disoriented in time and place every minute of
every day. No, as long as he can stay here, he stays."

Becca shook her head in disbelief, then grew
thoughtful. "Do you suppose Alzheimer's is hereditary?"

Tina glanced at her sister over her shoulder. "Now
there's something I'm not going to worry about."

"But what if it is?"

"Becca, it's much too late for us to choose other
parents."

Just then the back door opened, and Russell entered the house. Seeing the two women, he stopped.
"Sorry. Am I interrupting something?"

"No, nothing," Tina said. "Come in, Russell. I'd
like you to meet my sister."

Introductions were made and politely acknowledged.

"Jake has had me running all over the county today, picking up this and that," Russell explained. "I
thought I'd stop in and see Ty before heading back to
the salt mine."

"Good," Tina said, placing the sandwich on a plate and handing it to him. "He's in the living room. Please take this to him."

"Will do. See you ladies in a minute."

Becca stared after him, and when he was safely out of hearing range she looked at Tina. "Who is that?"

"Russell? Well, he's . . . oh, it's a long story. He got stranded here, and . . . he's just someone who's helping Jake for a while."

"That man is a hired hand?"

"Not exactly. We're paying him, but he's not your average hired hand."

"I'll say. Where'd he come from?"

"Arkansas." Tina didn't particularly want to discuss Russell with Becca, who would then discuss him with Joan. And that would leave her wide open to an extensive grilling the next time she visited her mother.

Their conversation was interrupted by Russell's return to the kitchen. The plate holding the sandwich still was in his hand.

"No takers. He's asleep."

Tina sighed. "So much for getting him to eat something."

Russell set the plate down on the counter and looked at Tina with real concern. In a surprising move, he reached out and touched her cheek. "You look tired."

"I am tired. It's been one of those days."

"Couldn't you get some rest while your dad's asleep. If Jake doesn't need me right away, I'll sit with Ty while you get some rest."

Tina was touched by his caring. One of the most appealing facets of Russell's personality was that he noticed everything. For a minute she was intent only on him, almost oblivious to Becca's presence. Then she remembered her sister and snapped out of her reverie. "Thanks, but I'm fine . . . really."

Abruptly Becca got to her feet. "Tina, since Dad's asleep I'm going to be on my way. I'm not accomplishing a thing here. He doesn't know who I am, and he probably won't even remember I was here."

"Probably not," Tina said frankly. "He rarely remembers anything that happened ten minutes ago, yet he can remember the exact date he shipped out of San Francisco in 1942. I'm sorry it didn't work out better, but . . . thanks for coming, anyway."

"It all just seems so pointless. I still think Dad needs professional care." Becca's shoulders rose and fell in a gesture of helplessness. "I left my handbag in the living room. Don't bother seeing me out."

But Tina followed her. "No, I'll walk you to your car." Over her shoulder she said, "Get yourself something to drink, Russell. I'll be right back." It was her way of asking him not to leave yet.

"Sure. It was nice meeting you, Becca."

Thoroughly distracted, Becca nodded and said, "Thanks. It was nice meeting you, too."

The sisters left the kitchen. Russell went to the refrigerator for the ever-present pitcher of tea. So that was Becca. Tina had told him her sister was beautiful, and he guessed she was, in a flashy sort of way. Tina, however, was prettier.

He had to assume that Becca's visit had not been a roaring success. That was a shame. If ever anyone could have used a supportive sibling it was Tina, but nothing she had thus far told him about her sister had indicated Becca would be a comfort in a crisis.

He carried his glass to the table and sat down thoughtfully. By now he had read all of Tina's literature from the Alzheimer's Association, and he felt he could be of real help to her. Nothing he'd read frightened him that much. He really liked Ty, and every once in a while he saw vestiges of the tough old bird he imagined Tina's father had once been.

And he really wanted to help Tina. He admired the no-nonsense way she tackled what was truly a tragedy. She worked hard every minute of the day, and almost everything she did was geared to making Ty's life safer, more comfortable, healthier. Russell found himself wishing he could have known them both before the dementia had struck. He imagined their father-daughter relationship had been quite remarkable. Why had this awful thing been visited on such nice people?

But it had, and he could help. He couldn't get too deeply involved, of course. He would only be able to give Ty his attention for a limited time, but the literature stressed over and over that any respite for the primary caregiver, no matter of what duration, was worthwhile.

Tina returned to the kitchen, her face a mask of weariness and resignation. Seeing Russell, she smiled ruefully. "So much for that. I don't think she'll be back soon. Another of my brilliant ideas down the drain."

"Didn't go well, huh?"

She crossed the room and sat at the table opposite him. "Oh, Becca's just...Becca. She means well. I guess if the situation had been reversed, if I hadn't seen Dad in months and had walked in on him today, I might have been a bit shaken, too. I wasn't using my head. I thought a new face might be good for him, but now I realize he doesn't want new faces or situations. He feels more comfortable with routine."

"That's probably understandable, don't you think?"

"A couple of days ago when I brought Dad back from his walk, he scolded me for sometimes taking him in the front door and sometimes the back. He said he couldn't remember where he was when I mixed him up that way. I should have known from the way today started that this wasn't the best time for Becca to visit."

"How did today start?"

"I couldn't tell anyone at breakfast because Dad was there, but…" She recounted the dress-strip-dress-again episode from that morning. They both chuckled, but the laughter was more sad than mirthful.

"Tina," Russell said, "I've heard you talking Ty through his morning routine. Why not let me do that while I'm here?"

She looked puzzled. "Why?"

He shrugged. "Well, you see, I'm a man …"

I've noticed, Tina thought.

"And as a man, I think the ultimate humiliation would be having my adult daughter dress me."

"I'll have to do it when you're gone."

"Maybe not. Maybe Jake should do it. But, please, let me while I'm here. As a matter of fact, I've read all that literature, and I think there's probably a lot I can do to help you out."

Tina wondered if that wouldn't be a mistake. Russell wouldn't be around much longer, and she knew how easy it was to begin to rely on others. She certainly relied on Jake and Ruby. Without them, Ty would have had to be put in a home; it was as simple as that. "I'm not sure you know what the morning routine involves, Russell," she said. "When Dad's in one of his stubborn moods, it can take forever. Sometimes he swears the clothes aren't his and wants to know who they belong to. You never know what he'll come up with."

"Just let me try. You'll have to coach me at first, and I'll be quick to admit it if I can't handle the job."

It would be nice, Tina knew. Dressing her father was the one task she hated above all, not because of its difficulty but because, as Russell had mentioned, it seemed such a humiliation for Ty. "All right," she said. "Thanks."

Russell grinned disarmingly, drained his glass and stood up. "Guess I'd better get back to work. See you at supper."

"Yes, see you then."

Tina remained at the table for several minutes after he left. Ty had still been asleep when she'd returned to the house from seeing Becca off, but her ears were instinctively cocked for any noise from the living room. She knew her father's sound patterns, much the way a mother knows those of her small child, and she was constantly alert for any variance in them. Since Ruby was in town doing the weekly shopping, the house was unusually quiet. Tina took advantage of that to think.

The afternoon had been yet another learning experience for her. Obviously she couldn't count on Becca for any real help. Certainly she'd never be able to go off for a day or two and leave her sister in charge. Russell was nice to want to help, but that would only be temporary. When all was said and done, she had only Jake, Ruby and herself, and that was not going to change. She wouldn't ask Becca to visit Ty again. If her sister came of her own accord, fine, but Tina seriously doubted that would happen.

And she would accept whatever help Russell wanted to give with gratitude, but she wouldn't ask for any. She seriously doubted he had any idea what a thankless task caring for Ty was, how fraught with emotional hazards. There were days when he was thoroughly unlikable. The only reason her relationship with her father had been successful was that it had been a close, loving one before illness had struck. A stranger might well want to throw in the towel. Russell didn't have any idea what he was getting into. Tina fully expected him to withdraw his offer in a day or two.

ACTUALLY, RUSSELL TURNED out to be a marvel with Ty, and no one was more surprised than Russell himself. Having lived a solitary life for a number of years, with no one but himself to look after, he wouldn't have thought he would be especially good with others. In the beginning, on that first morning when he'd undertaken to get Ty dressed, he had approached the chore with plenty of self-doubt, but everything had gone smoothly. Ty had seemed to welcome the masculine voice. In fact, he responded unusually well to everything Russell did for him or asked him to do for himself.

Russell discovered he possessed a wellspring of patience with the man. Nothing was too much trouble. He never got annoyed when Ty asked him fifteen or twenty times what day it was. All he could think about was how unsettling all that confusion must be. He didn't allow himself to become irked when Ty was at his most unlovable. Russell found, to his everlasting amazement, that he was an instinctive caregiver.

Watching from the sidelines, Tina experienced some mixed feelings over all this—astonishment, delight ... and jealousy. That was such a new emotion for her she was unprepared for dealing with it. What was she jealous of—Ty's response to Russell or Russell's effortless caregiving? She had worked so hard for so long with her father, searching for advice from all sources and attending the support-group meetings. And she had made plenty of mistakes along the way. Russell, it seemed, had merely walked through the door and established an instant rapport with Ty.

It's easy for him to be kind, patient and attentive, she told herself pettishly. *He isn't mourning the loss of a relationship that will never be the same again. He knows he isn't going to have to take care of Dad for ten or fifteen years.*

Fortunately for everyone concerned, Tina's resentment didn't last long. For one thing, no one could harbor ill-feelings toward Russell for long; he was too congenial, too easy to be around. And his help really was a boon. Not only did he get Ty dressed in the morning, he played games with him after supper and got him ready for bed at night. And he did it all with unflagging good spirits.

So Tina quickly went from feeling slighted to wishing Russell would never leave. She even briefly considered asking him to stay a little longer. Then she remembered all his enthusiasm for the green Eden out on the West Coast. Her problems were not his, and he had already done more for her than one could reasonably expect of a stranger. She would enjoy his help while she could, and when it was no longer available, she would cope.

Still, one nagging question persisted. What would Ty's reaction be when Russell actually left? The good-looking trucker with the nice smile had become the focal point of her father's days. Ty didn't remember Russell's name half the time, just as he didn't remember hers, but he always recognized Russell's voice and seemed to perk up immediately.

For once Tina was glad Ty's attention span was so short. She could only hope that when Russell was gone, her father would quickly forget him.

She hoped she did, too.

CHAPTER SIX

ONE THING RUSSELL THOUGHT to do with Ty that had never occurred to Tina was to take him for long drives. It was an inspired idea; Ty loved it. All Russell had to do was say, "Hey, sport, I'm on my way into town. Want to come along?" and Ty would be on his feet, raring to go.

On this particular morning, Jake had given Russell some errands to run, and as usual Ty tagged along. For more than a week, they had been visited by a spate of afternoon thunderstorms, and they were enjoying unseasonably cool weather, meaning mid-eighties instead of high nineties. The morning was bright and fresh, and Ty seemed to be in good spirits. Since riding in the pickup had a sort of tranquilizing effect on the elderly man, Russell had devised a roundabout route into Leatrice in order to give him a longer ride. This morning, instead of entering town from the north, they drove in from the west.

They were three blocks inside the city limits, when Ty suddenly straightened and looked around. "See that grocery store over there?" he asked in an excited voice.

Russell saw a building that had once been a corner grocery. He could tell that from the faded sign over the door, but the building was boarded up. "Yeah, I see it."

"Turn there and I'll show you the house I grew up in. That's Sutter Street."

Russell slowed at the intersection, then noticed that the street marker read Raleigh Street. "This isn't the street. It must be a block or so ahead of us, Ty."

"No, goddamn it, this is Sutter Street. I oughta know. I turned at this grocery store every blamed afternoon when I walked home from school. Turn here."

Russell shrugged and did as he was told. What difference did it make?

The neighborhood had probably once been fashionable, but it had fallen on hard times. Russell cruised along, noting that the markers at every intersection indicated they were on Raleigh Street, not Sutter, but he wasn't about to argue with Ty. He fully expected the man to lose interest in his boyhood home any second now.

"It's right up there in the middle of the next block," Ty said. "It has a big old cherry tree in the front yard. Shorty Gordon and I practically lived in that tree. I fell out of it when I was ten and broke my leg. There!" He pointed excitedly, then stopped. "Where's the tree?"

"Are you sure this is the house, Ty?" Russell asked as he stopped the truck.

"Yes, I'm sure, but... Where's the goddamn cherry tree? Where's the tree?"

Oh, Lord, this was a mistake, Russell thought. This wasn't turning into a trip down memory lane at all. Ty was becoming far too agitated to suit him.

Just then Russell spied a man in a rocking chair on the porch of the house next door. He looked to be an old-timer, so on an impulse, Russell turned off the engine and opened the truck's door. "Hang on, Ty. I'm going to see if I can find out something for you. I'll be right back.''

Getting out of the truck, he sprinted up the walk toward the man. ''Pardon me, sir, but my friend over there is looking for a Sutter Street. Can you tell me where it is?''

The man wore overalls and puffed on a cigarette. He didn't get to his feet, nor did he stop rocking. ''Ya found it. Least it used ta be. But when old man Raleigh donated the funds ta build us a new library, the city fathers decided we oughta do something nice for him, like name a street after him. This'un's the one they picked.''

Russell didn't know why he was so enormously pleased that Ty had been right. ''Well, thanks...thanks a lot. By the way, was there ever a cherry tree in that yard over there?''

''Yep. But once the Websters moved away, nobody took care of it proper, and the bugs got to it. Had to be cut down.''

''I see. Thanks again. Much obliged.''

''Don't mention it. Your friend has a pretty good memory. This ain't been Sutter Street for...must be thirty years now.''

Russell hurried back to the truck, climbed in and slammed the door. ''You're right, Ty.''

'' 'Course I'm right.''

''The bugs got the tree. It had to be cut down.''

''Goddamn bugs.''

For one awful minute, Russell thought Ty was going to cry.

''Those were the sweetest cherries God ever put on a tree.''

Russell could hardly wait to tell Tina this. "Okay, sport, now we're going to Shaw's Garage. I want to visit an old friend."

The garage was located on the eastern fringe of the town, which meant they had to drive the entire breadth of the community. Ty was in a particularly talkative mood, and Russell was treated to a pretty full accounting of the man's boyhood. He remembered the oddest things—who lived in that house and what had stood on that corner. But several times he stopped in midsentence, turned to Russell and asked, "Did you ever tell me your name?"

When the pickup rumbled into the yard of Shaw's Garage, Leon crawled out from beneath a dilapidated car, stood up and smiled. Wiping his hands on a rag, he advanced on them. "Well, hello, Mr. Cade. Nice to see you." He then noticed Russell's passenger. "'Morning, Mr. Webster. Nice to see you, too."

"'Mornin'," Ty said. "How's the family?"

"Fine, sir. They'll be pleased you asked about them." Leon looked at Russell. "Guess you want to have a look at the Thunderbird, right? Well, there she is."

He gestured toward a spot by the chain-link fence that enclosed the yard. The Thunderbird had been parked off by itself, away from any other vehicles. Russell winced when he saw the bare metal right front, but he could tell, even from a distance, that the body work was superb.

"The paint finally arrived," Leon told him, "so we're going to get started this afternoon. With luck, you'll be on your way to California this time next week. I know you're glad to hear that."

"Well, yes, I am."

"Sorry it took so long, but nobody's gonna be able to tell anything ever happened to that sweetheart, least of all you."

"That's good." Russell turned the key in the ignition. "Thanks, Leon. Be talking to you."

During the drive back to the ranch, Ty was strangely silent for a man who had been so talkative earlier, but Russell thought nothing of that. The old man's moods shifted like the desert sands, and he had learned to shift with them.

The silence inside the truck was total until a few miles south of the ranch gate. Suddenly Ty turned to him.

"So, you're leaving me, too, eh?" His tone was accusing.

Russell couldn't have been more startled . . . or dismayed. Why, when so much of what was said just passed over Ty's head, had he picked up on that casual remark of Leon's? "Ty, I'm not leaving *you.*"

"You're going to California. That fella said so."

"Well, yes, but . . . I've always been going to California. I thought you knew that."

"You gonna take me with you?"

"I can't do that," Russell said gently. "I can't take you away from Tina."

"I never see Tina anymore. She has a husband now. I guess he's all that's important to her."

Russell searched his brain for something appropriate he could say. Don't argue, don't correct and don't explain, so just what the hell did he do? "You're the one who's important to Tina," he finally said inadequately. "I'm sure you don't realize how much. We never do, do we?"

But Ty was through talking. He lapsed into a good case of the sulks, instead. When they got to the house and Russell had led him through the back door into the kitchen, he brushed past Tina and Ruby without a word. Naturally Tina followed him to see where he was going, while Russell sank into one of the kitchen chairs and put his head in his hands.

"What's wrong?" Ruby asked solicitously.

"I pulled a boner today."

"Don't be hard on yourself. We all do occasionally."

Tina was back in a minute or so, a worried frown creasing her forehead. "He's pouting like a little boy. What happened?"

As succinctly as possible, Russell recounted the details of their trip into town.

When he'd finished, Tina sighed. "I was afraid of something like this," she said. "He's just become so attached to you."

"God, I feel terrible about it," Russell told her.

He looked as though he felt terrible, Tina noticed. She didn't feel so good herself, and for once the feeling had nothing to do with her father. It had been something of a jolt for her to hear Russell would be leaving in a week, even though she had known the day would come soon. The time had just passed so quickly. She'd thought herself prepared for his departure, but now she knew she wasn't.

"Well, take heart," she said. "Chances are good Dad will have forgotten all about it in an hour's time. I'll go sit with him and try to divert his attention to something else."

Russell wished he could forget. Daily he had cautioned himself against forming a strong attachment to these people. He'd known all along he would be leaving. The Texas Panhandle was not the North Coast, not by a long shot, and he wasn't any fonder of the work he was doing than he'd been that first day. He'd never given a minute's thought to staying longer than absolutely necessary.

What hadn't occurred to him was the possibility that Ty would become too attached to him. He'd only been trying to help. In hindsight, he could see how foolish that had been. He should have stayed detached, kept out of their lives. Now it was going to be hard to say goodbye to people who had taken him in and treated him like a favorite relative. How was he ever going to walk away from that childlike old man?

"OH, TINA, you've got to come," Becca wailed over the phone. "I just won't take no for an answer."

"Becca, Dad takes so much time now. At the end of the day, I'm too bushed for parties."

Becca was giving a birthday bash for Joan because, in her sister's words, "we haven't given a party in ever so long." Tina had to smile at that one. "Ever so long" to Becca probably meant a few weeks. And if she admitted to its being a bash, that meant it would be a huge affair, attended by scores of her "dearest friends." Tina desperately tried to think of a way to beg off. She didn't know many of Becca's society friends and had nothing in common with the ones she did know.

"Mom will be crushed if you don't come," Becca insisted.

"Well...listen, I'll see what can be arranged, and I'll get right back to you."

"All right, but promise me you will arrange something. I absolutely insist that you be here."

"It's not that easy. Ruby wants to go visit her daughter, and . . . I'll just have to see. I'll be talking to you."

Hanging up the phone, Tina turned to Russell, who was sitting at the kitchen table. Supper was over, and the dishes were washing. During the meal, Ty mercifully seemed to have forgotten all about California. Now he was in the living room with Jake and Ruby, and Tina and Russell were having their coffee.

"Obviously that was your sister," he commented.

"Yes." Tina returned to the table. "She's giving a birthday party for Mom, and she insists I be there."

"I think you should go, too." He meant that. He couldn't imagine a beautiful woman Tina's age having to live the life she led. She handled it graciously, but it was an odd existence.

"I don't know, Russell. One, I feel utterly out of place with Becca's crowd, and with Ruby leaving for a few days, I—"

"Hey, Jake and I aren't helpless. You really should use me while I'm here. For once you can go somewhere and not worry about your dad. I can handle things."

She'd grant him that. He handled things better than she did. "Well . . . I guess . . . since it's for Mom . . ."

"Go. Go and have a good time. I'll look after your dad like he was mine."

Oh, Russell, Tina thought sadly, *whatever am I going to do without you?*

BECCA GAVE PARTIES the way she did everything else—with style and flair—and she had pulled out all the stops for Joan's birthday. It was one of the swankiest parties Tina had ever attended.

It also was a study in conspicuous consumption. There were a dozen or more lavish floral arrangements situated around the house. The buffet table was a groaning board of elaborate goodies, including what appeared to be at least a fourth of all the shrimp pulled from the Gulf of Mexico that day. The diamonds, pearls and emeralds worn by the guests could easily have stocked a small jewelry store.

All of which was rather puzzling to Tina. Always before on Joan's birthday, she and Becca had sent their mother flowers and taken her to lunch. Why such a to-do this year? And why were her mother and sister showering her with such extravagant compliments? It was totally out of character.

"Oh, Tina," Becca gushed. "You look absolutely gorgeous. Really, just beautiful."

"Well, thanks."

"Yes, dear," Joan agreed, "you do look chic."

"That color is wonderful on her, don't you think, Mom?"

"Yes, very flattering,. I'm delighted you chose that dress, Tina. It definitely does something for you."

Oh, come on, Tina wanted to say. She thought she looked pretty good... but her mother and sister didn't usually compliment her so much. She had given a lot of thought to what she would wear tonight, considering the well-heeled crowd she'd known would be present. She'd chosen a dress that was a holdover from her days in Fort Worth when her own social life had been active. It was a stunning creation in shimmering sapphire with a scooped neck and tulip hem. Russell's eyes had almost popped out of his head when he'd seen her earlier, and that had pleased her more than all the praise Becca and Joan were lavishing on her. She just wished she knew what was behind all the flattery.

"Honestly, Tina," Becca said, "you have the most exquisite figure. You should wear clothes like that more often."

"Where would I wear them?" Tina asked reasonably. "This dress would stop traffic in Leatrice."

"Indeed. You really should leave that depressing little hamlet. You're wasted there."

Tina gave up. Neither Becca nor Joan had the slightest conception of what her life was really like. She merely smiled obscurely and was relieved when Becca spirited Joan off to greet other guests.

Pivoting, Tina turned to look out over the throng. It seemed to have doubled in size very rapidly. Not seeing even one familiar face in the near vicinity, she threaded her way through the crowd, trying to appear as if she had a purposeful destination. She stopped at the buffet table long enough to place a few tidbits on a cocktail napkin, then found a relatively quiet corner where she could nibble and survey the scene. As she had feared, it had been a mistake to come. What she couldn't figure was why Becca had so insisted she did.

She had her answer a minute later. She had just popped a shrimp into her mouth, when she heard a deep masculine voice behind her say.

"I always loved you in that dress."

Turning, Tina found herself staring into the handsome face of her ex-husband. The room reeled for a minute, and her heartbeat accelerated. She chewed rapidly, swallowed and gasped. "P-Paul! What are you doing here?"

"I was invited to a party."

Oh, God, the past two years had only enhanced his good looks. Blond, tan and fit. And that smile! *Rakish* was a good word to describe it. There had been a time when that smile had melted her insides. Unfortunately it still caused a flutter or two. "You drove all the way from Fort Worth for this party?"

"What's six hours out of my life? Becca assured me that it would be worth my while. I see what she meant. How've you been, Tina?"

"How could I be?"

Paul's face sobered for a second. "Yes, it's a shame about Ty."

"A bad cold is a shame, Paul."

His rakish grin returned. Paul, Tina thought, would do well to stay away from funerals because he was incapable of looking sad for more than a few minutes. Seeing him for the first time since the divorce was such a shock. Wave after wave of conflicting emotions assailed her. She had loved him so much, and they had lived together many years. The strongest emotion, however, was the urge to throttle Becca. How could her sister not warn her Paul would be here? It left her feeling totally unsettled, completely out of control.

Then she forced herself to remember why she and Paul weren't still married. It helped.

"Aren't you going to ask how I am?" Paul prompted.

"Obviously you're fine. Obviously you've done well. I'll bet you spent more for that suit than you did for your entire wardrobe the first three years we were married."

"I'll bet you're right."

He reached for her arm, but Tina skillfully stepped back out of reach.

"Becca said you probably would be spending the night," Paul commented. "Is that right?"

Tina frowned. "I don't know what gave her that idea. I have to get back to Dad." Then something occurred to her. "Are you spending the night with Becca and Derek?"

"Yes. We all thought it would be a perfect time for us to talk."

We all? Who could "we all" include if not her sister and her mother? Tina couldn't believe Becca and Joan had instigated this cozy little reunion. "Oh, Paul," she said wearily, feeling much as she often did with her father—that she was beating her head against a stone wall. "There's nothing to talk about. Everything was said a long time ago."

"Did I ever say I'm sorry?"

"Many times. But I always got the impression you were mainly sorry you got caught."

"I made a terrible mistake."

"And boys will be boys—is that what you're saying?"

Paul made an impatient sound. "No!" He lowered his voice, and his smile disappeared. "Goddamn it, the thing I seem to do best is annoy you."

Tina lowered her voice, also, although it would have been impossible for either of them to be heard over the din of the crowd. "Annoy me? I'm trying to imagine any woman who could return home to the scene I did and not be a little annoyed." She took a deep breath. "Now, if you'll excuse me, I must go... powder my nose or something."

What she did, instead, was go in search of Becca. Finding her, she grabbed her sister by the arm. "I want to talk to you... now."

Becca followed her out of the room and down the hall to the first bedroom Tina came to. The sisters went inside, and Tina slammed the door.

"Tina, what on earth—"

"Don't give me that! You know what on earth. How dare you invite me here when you knew Paul was coming. What did you hope to accomplish?"

For a second Becca looked as though she might try to deny arranging anything, but apparently she thought better of it. "All right, I'll tell you what I hoped to accomplish. I hoped that if you saw Paul again, you might come to your senses."

"I came to my senses the day I realized I would never be the only woman in his life. Maybe there are women who can live with that. I can't."

Becca ignored Tina's answer. "I'm your sister, and I worry about you. You don't lead a normal life. You live out on that dreary ranch, doing nothing day after day but taking care of a sick old man."

Tina stared at her in disbelief. "That sick old man is our father. And I grew up on that 'dreary ranch.' It's home."

"Oh, come off it, Tina. Are you trying to tell me you find your life rich and rewarding?" Becca scoffed. "I know Paul would like to get back with you. He all but told me that much. Do you have any idea what your life could be like—"

"Yes! I'd spend half of it wondering whose bed he was in. Drop it, Becca. Just please drop it."

But Becca had no intention of dropping it. "I'll tell you something else that concerns me. When I was at the ranch the other day I saw the way that man...er, Russell, looked at you. And I saw the way you looked at him. You spend all your time with old people. No wonder that a stranger looks good to you. But who is he, where does he come from, what line of work is he in, what kind of people are his parents?''

"I don't believe this! He's a very nice man who has been a great deal of help when we needed it badly.'' Tina paused and heaved a deep sigh. "Look, Becca, I'm sorry. I know you're thinking of what's best for me, but please let me live my own life. And don't ever ask me to anything that Paul is also attending.'' She moved toward the door. "I'm going to try to find Mom and tell her good-night.''

"You're not leaving.''

Tina nodded. "It's been a grand party, but I've got a beaut of a headache. I'll talk to you later.''

Tina found Joan and expressed her regrets. "Oh, Tina, you're leaving so soon? Becca and I thought—''

"I know what you thought, Mom, but I've really got to get home. Have a wonderful birthday.''

She couldn't get out of the house fast enough. Fortunately she was able to do so without encountering Paul again. She was shaking all over, and she wondered how much of that was caused by her anger at Becca and how much by the shock of seeing Paul again.

The drive back to the ranch was a lonely one. Images flashed in and out of Tina's mind. First was the hateful one—the expressions on Paul's and Mazie's faces when she had unexpectedly walked into that bedroom. The second was of a party. Tina couldn't remember the occasion, but Paul had been in rare form—drinking too much and flirting shamelessly with half the women there, one flashy blonde in particular. Tina had been furious with her husband that night, furious and humiliated by his behavior. And that, Tina now recalled, was the first time she had admitted to herself that Paul might be something less than Mr. Wonderful.

Oh, stop thinking about it! It's over. Tina drummed her fingers on the steering wheel and stared out into the black night. Then something Becca had said came back to her. *Just how did Russell look at me?* she wondered.

TINA UNLOCKED the back door and crossed through the dark kitchen. She didn't hear a sound, but there was a light on in the living room. As she crossed the foyer she spotted Russell seated on the sofa, reading a magazine. When he saw her, he looked surprised and glanced at his watch.

"Aren't you home awfully early?"

"It wasn't much fun. Did Ruby get off?"

He nodded. "Right after you left. And Jake's gone into town."

"Did Dad eat much supper?"

"About the usual. Listen, Tina, something happened tonight that you ought to know about."

She kicked off her shoes, sat down on the sofa and tucked a foot beneath her. "Oh?"

"I put Ty to bed at the usual time and gave him his medication, then came downstairs. About twenty minutes later I heard some kind of racket, so I went back upstairs. He had gotten out of bed, come out into the hall and tripped over the lamp table."

Tina gasped. "Oh, Lord, did he hurt himself?"

"No, but it scared hell out of him, and he was totally disoriented for fifteen or twenty minutes. He's fine now. I just checked, and he's sleeping soundly."

Tina slumped back against the sofa. "It's something new every day. What if it happens again?"

"I've been thinking about that. What about an outside lock on his door?"

Tina considered it. "I don't know, Russell. I'm afraid if he ever tried to get out of the room and couldn't, he might panic. Anything even slightly out of the ordinary just rattles him so."

"Well, let's get rid of any obstacles in the hall upstairs, and I definitely think a baby gate at the top of the stairs is a good idea. In fact, this whole house should be baby-proofed."

"You're right. I should have thought of it myself."

"Tina," Russell said gently, "you can't think of everything. No one can."

She chewed her bottom lip. She was heartsick and scared to death. The disease seemed to be progressing at a galloping rate, so much faster than she had anticipated. Ty had never gotten out of bed before. The sedative was supposed to prevent that. She wondered if she would ever again get a decent night's sleep for fear that he would get out of bed and she wouldn't hear him.

So now what should she do? Heavier medication? She had to be careful there, for she'd heard that too high a dosage could cause the patient to slip into a depression.

Speaking of depression, she wondered if she wasn't heading for one herself.

Russell watched her, saw her anxiety and wished he could be of more help. Very soon, Ty would be all hers again. "You look beautiful tonight, Tina," he said. "I wanted to tell you that before you left the house, but...the sight of you seemed to render me speechless."

The cloudiness left her eyes, and a small smile lifted the corners of her mouth. "Why, thank you, Russell. That's awfully nice to hear."

"Did you eat anything at the party?"

"Well, let's see...three shrimp and a scoop of cheese dip."

"Good grief, you must be starved."

"I guess I could eat something."

Russell stood up. "Come on. There was plenty left from supper. In fact, Ruby left a stuffed refrigerator. Did she really think none of us would cook while she was gone?"

In the kitchen he produced dish after dish. Tina selected what she wanted, fixed a plate and heated it in the microwave. Russell made himself coffee and joined her at the table, watching as she devoured everything.

Glancing up, Tina saw the grin on his face, and she smiled back sheepishly. "I didn't realize I was so hungry."

"Tell me about the party."

"It was a party. Been to one you've been to them all. Dozens and dozens of people dressed to the nines, eating, drinking and gossiping."

"You can't have stayed long."

"I didn't. Becca thought it would be great, good fun to invite my ex-husband. I disagreed, so I left."

"You saw your ex?" Russell would have given anything to meet the man Tina had been married to. He'd like to see what kind of idiot would mess up his marriage to a woman like Tina.

She nodded. "My sister and my mother think we should get back together."

"What do you think?" Russell asked quietly.

"I think...I think that Mom and Becca should butt out of my personal life. Even if I was interested in getting back with Paul, I couldn't do it now because of Dad. I've heard too many horror stories in the support group from women who are trying to juggle a sick parent, a couple of lively kids and a husband who's rapidly losing his patience. Why can't my family understand that? Mom, especially, behaves as though Dad has this problem, but it'll go away and everything will be dandy again." Sighing, she pulled a face. "Sorry. I seem to be raving."

And who would she have to rave to when he was gone? Russell wondered. He was beginning to feel like a rat deserting a sinking ship.

Unfortunately Tina's thoughts paralleled his. She was so relieved Russell had been there tonight. *What if I had been the one alone with Dad? Russell just handles him better than I do.* She guessed that, in spite of better intentions, she had come to do what she had promised herself she wouldn't—rely on Russell. Too often lately she had wondered what she was going to do when he was gone. But whenever the thought formed, she was able to push it aside. She would do what she had done before she'd ever set eyes on him, of course. Just keep going.

She pushed her plate away, glanced across the table, and her eyes locked with Russell's. Up close she noticed how warm and intense his were with their thick fringe of lashes. And she saw the look on his face. She couldn't have begun to describe it. It conveyed a message of sympathy, understanding...and, yes, affection.

Was this the look? she wondered—the look that had so alarmed Becca she had felt it necessary to dredge up Paul?

CHAPTER SEVEN

PAUL MICHAELS WAS disappointed over Tina's indifference, but he wasn't discouraged. Never short of self-confidence, he was convinced he could wear down her resistance now that he had made up his mind to do so.

The decision had been two years in the making. For the first six months after Tina had stormed out of his life, he had told himself that her reaction to his "indiscretion" had been all out of proportion. Mazie had meant nothing to him. She certainly hadn't threatened or lessened his love for his wife. That's why Tina's uncompromising stand had so baffled him. Most women, it had seemed to Paul, would have cried, raged, threatened, given the cold shoulder and demanded reparation in a dozen ways, but they wouldn't have actually ended the marriage without giving it a second chance. Using some sort of twisted male logic, he had conveniently shifted at least part of the blame for the split to Tina.

Once he'd passed that stage, Paul had decided he probably would enjoy being a bachelor again. Mazie had not been his first extramarital dalliance. His first had been with a fellow student named Karen. Tina had been away from home, visiting her father, and Paul and Karen had gone out for a drink. Somehow they had wound up in her apartment, with the predictable result. He had never slept with Karen again, but he'd felt a strange lack of remorse over the episode. On the few occasions he'd thought about it afterward, he admitted that it had been fun . . . and incredibly easy.

After that there had been other women, some of whom he barely remembered, none of whom had been even nodding acquaintances of Tina's. That was where he had made his mistake with Mazie, he'd decided. She had been a neighbor and a casual friend of his wife's. If he had it to do all over again, he never would have bedded a neighbor.

Paul wasn't sure just when the thrill of bachelorhood had begun to pall, but it wasn't fun anymore. All his colleagues were married and didn't in the least envy him his single status. He was the extra man at too many parties. Being married, it seemed, was the in thing. And when he thought of marriage, he thought of Tina. He missed her. He began to remember why he had married her in the first place. She was pretty, intelligent and fun to be with, but it was what she wasn't that had so appealed to him. She wasn't a chatterbox or a gossip. She wasn't extravagant, and she harbored no lofty social aspirations. She wasn't a clinging vine, but neither was she a single-minded careerist. She had been an almost perfect wife, and he had been a fool to risk losing her by sleeping with other women.

These thoughts had occupied his mind for months, when he'd found himself driving through Amarillo one afternoon. Impulsively he'd phoned Becca, not from any real desire to visit the Jenningses but from the hope that he would pick up some information about Tina. What he'd discovered had given him encouragement. Tina's life seemed to have fallen into the pits. Stuck out on the ranch taking care of a sick old man had to have her feeling pretty wretched. If ever she would be receptive to the idea of starting over, he'd reasoned, it would be now. He would offer her everything, which he could now afford handsomely, and that would include a respite from being a nursemaid.

Attending the party had been Becca's idea, and it had turned out to be a rotten one. But Paul was undaunted. From now on he would come up with his own ideas. Perseverance was his middle name, and he could be every bit as stubborn as Tina was.

IT WAS LATE AFTERNOON of the day following Becca's party, when Russell came out of the barn in time to see a sleek BMW driving up the road toward the house. Curious, because they never had visitors, he slowed his pace and reached the back stoop just as the car slowed down. It stopped, and a tall, blond man got out. The visitor was dressed casually but expensively, rather like a Ralph Lauren ad in *GQ*. When he spotted Russell, he advanced.

"May I help you?" Russell asked.

The man glanced at him with curiosity. "Yes, I'm looking for Tina."

"She's inside. Come on in." Russell climbed the steps and opened the back door, then stood back to allow the man to precede him into the kitchen. "I'm sure she's with her dad, probably in the living room. This way."

"I know the way," the visitor said.

Russell nodded curtly but continued in the lead, out of the kitchen toward the living room. Tina was curled up on the sofa with a book, while Ty was seated in his chair, apparently only staring off into space.

Hearing the clomp of Russell's boot heels crossing the foyer, Tina looked up and smiled. Her smile, however, faded instantly when she saw the man behind him.

"You have company," Russell said.

She got to her feet, but her expression was anything but a welcoming one. "Hello, Paul," she said coolly. "What brings you all the way out here?"

Paul, Russell noted. So this was her ex. Now he studied the man with a great deal more interest. Paul was almost too good-looking, he decided, and self-assurance enveloped him like a cloak. Russell's gaze flew to Tina. There was a lift to her chin, as though she were steeling herself for whatever was to come. She wasn't indifferent to Paul. In fact, she looked pretty agitated.

"I'm on my way back to Fort Worth," Paul explained to Tina, "and I thought I'd stop by for a minute."

"Considerably out of your way, isn't it?" Tina asked, wondering how much of this impromptu visit was Becca's idea.

"I don't mind." Paul then turned to Ty. "Hello, Ty. It's been some time."

Not a flicker of recognition crossed Ty's face. "Hello," he said. "How's the family?"

"Mom and Dad? They're fine, sir. I'll tell them you asked."

"Was there something in particular you wanted, Paul?" Tina asked sharply.

"Yes, I wanted to talk to you." Paul glanced pointedly at Russell. "In private."

A second or two of heavy silence fell over the room. Then Tina moved forward. "Russell, will you sit with Dad a few minutes? I won't be long."

"Sure, be happy to."

"This way, Paul." She briskly walked out of the room and down the hall to the office. Paul followed. When they were inside, she closed the door and crossed her arms. "Well, what did you want to talk to me about?"

"Do you mind if I sit down?"

"Oh, no...of course not. Have a seat." She rounded the desk and sat behind it, putting some distance and a large object between Paul and her.

Paul sat across from Tina and pretended to study the room. "It's been a long time since I was in this office."

"Yes, it has."

"It hasn't changed much."

Tina sighed her impatience.

"Tina, that guy out there..." Paul jerked his thumb over his shoulder to indicate the front of the house. "Since when does the hired help have the run of the place?"

"Russell's a friend, not hired help. Can we please get on with this?" She couldn't understand why she was so nervous or why she wanted Paul out of the house so badly. Was she afraid he'd worm his way into her heart again? He'd done it so easily the first time, but a lot of water had passed under the bridge since then.

"Becca tells me you're having a rough time," Paul said.

"She noticed? Now there's a news bulletin."

"You know...I could help you if you'd let me."

Tina frowned. "How?"

"A lot of ways. Money, for one."

"I don't need money."

"You will when Ty has to go into a home, which Becca thinks should be soon."

Tina scoffed. "Becca knows less about what Dad needs than anyone. Dad won't go into a home until I decide he must."

"And then what?"

She shrugged. "I don't know. I'll think about that when the time comes. Right now, Dad takes all my time."

Paul wondered how much he should humble himself. Actually, he didn't feel particularly humble. Sorry, yes. Very sorry he had botched the marriage. Humility didn't come naturally to him, but he guessed a certain amount of it would have to be employed if he wanted to get to first base with Tina. "It doesn't have to be that way. If you were in Fort Worth, you could have around-the-clock help."

"Why would I be in Fort Worth?"

"We could be together again." He leaned forward and spoke earnestly. "Tina, I regret all that went before, and I want another chance. There, I've said it. Please, give me another chance. I want us to be a family again, and this time we'll do it right—kids, the works. And I will be an exemplary husband." His voice quivered.

That startled Tina. At first she thought it was an act, but when she looked at him fully she believed he meant what he'd said. She couldn't imagine what had brought this on. Whenever she had thought of Paul during the past two years, she'd imagined he was enjoying the bachelor life. "Paul, it won't work. I'm going to be honest with you. I don't think Mazie was the only one. Nor do I think she would have been the last one if I hadn't caught you with her."

"Tina, please..."

"I'm not censuring. The past is the past. But I do want to tell you one thing, Paul. Perhaps it will help you if you ever remarry." She carefully kept her voice controlled. "When a woman discovers her husband is unfaithful, she doesn't only feel betrayed, she feels rejected. And rejection takes a long time, if not forever, to forgive."

"I never meant to reject you!" Paul exclaimed. "Mazie didn't mean a thing to me."

"I know that. I doubt any of them meant anything to you."

"Then . . . why—"

"Don't you see? That's what's so sad. You just used them." Tina got to her feet. "I really must get back to Dad. Russell has things to do, and Dad can't be left unsupervised for long."

Paul was stymied for once in his life. When Tina stood, he did, too. "I could make life a lot easier for you, Tina. More than that, I know I could prove to you I can be trusted."

"Paul . . . no . . ."

Paul knew better than to argue with her. He had learned that a long time ago. One gave her time to think things out, then rediscussed the issue. "Do you mind if I stay in touch?"

"I'd rather you didn't?"

"Are you sure?"

"Yes."

"Well, if you change your mind, your sister knows where to find me. Please don't bother seeing me out. Goodbye."

"Goodbye, Paul." Tina waited until she'd heard the front door open and close before leaving the office. Paul's visit had left her feeling jittery, and she didn't understand that. She had been right to walk out of his life. Never once had she regretted her move, and she certainly didn't want to give their marriage another chance. So why this peculiar feeling? Was it because of what he'd said? "I could make life a lot easier for you." He probably could do that.

"Tina, are you all right?" Russell asked, concerned.

She had reached the living room without realizing it. Hearing his voice, she snapped out of her reverie. "Yes . . . yes, I'm fine." She glanced toward Ty. "Is he asleep?"

"Yes."

"Thanks for sitting with him. While he's sleeping, I'll see what I can come up with for supper. You ought to really appreciate Ruby after a couple of days of my cooking."

Russell followed her into the kitchen. "The man was your ex, right?"

"Right. Oh, good grief, I didn't even introduce the two of you. Well, so much for good manners."

He grinned. "That's all right. I figured I knew who he was."

"Russell, after your divorce, did you ever have second thoughts . . . or wish you could give the marriage another chance?"

So that was what Pretty Boy had wanted. Russell didn't know why that alarmed him, but it did. "No, it wasn't a good match to begin with."

Tina nodded, then dropped the subject, much to Russell's dismay. He was alive with curiosity. "Now, let me see what I can uncover in the larder. I wonder how Ruby's finding things at Connie's. The two of them talked on the phone almost every day last week.

I know Connie's finding being a mother more than she bargained for.''

WHAT RUBY HAD FOUND when she arrived at her daughter's house was one very harried mother, two adorable girls and one sullen ten-year-old boy. The girls, eight-year-old Maria and six-year-old Consuela, had greeted her shyly but warmly, and they'd even tried out their halting English on her. Alejandro, on the other hand, was solemn and uncommunicative. And Connie's house, which for years had stayed almost antiseptically neat and clean, looked as though a major hurricane had torn through it. All Ruby had to do was take one look at Connie to know her daughter was going through a very difficult time.

Ruby took over preparing dinner so Connie could help the children tidy up a little—John was teaching night classes—and after the meal she performed cleanup duty while Connie presided over English lessons at the kitchen table. By bedtime Alejandro still had not said more than half a dozen words, and those were in Spanish. Once the kids were asleep, Connie unloaded all her frustrations on her mother.

''Sorry about the house, Ma, but what with running to the dentist, the optometrist, giving the kids lessons and cooking three meals a day... well, everything's a mess.''

''Houses get cleaned sooner or later,'' Ruby said. ''What about you? How're you coming with the young'uns?''

''It's so much harder than I thought it would be. The kids are... well, I guess *primitive* is the word I'm. looking for. I've had to teach them the most basic uses of soap and water. The first time I shampooed the girls'

hair, they screamed and carried on . . . you never heard
anything like it. If the neighbors could have heard, they
would have been sure I was beating the poor things
within an inch of their lives.''

''What's with the boy?'' Ruby asked.

Connie shook her head sadly. ''I'm afraid I'm not
getting anywhere with Alejandro. According to Mrs.
Guerra—she's the woman with the international
agency that handled the adoption—he resents being
treated on a par with his sisters. It seems that in the
Andean village where they lived, male offspring have
status even above their mothers. He doesn't like living
in a house where a *señora* is in charge most of the
time.''

''He'll come around, honey,'' Ruby predicted. ''Kids
hate change more than anything. He'll meet other boys
whose mamas are in charge, so it won't seem so strange
to him.''

''I hope you're right, Ma. But so far, Alejandro
won't even try to learn English, and with my Spanish
as basic as it is, I wonder if I'll ever be able to communicate with him.'' Connie sighed. ''You know, I had
all these fantastic ideas about how it would be. John
and I were going to rescue these poor orphans from
squalor and poverty, give them a clean house, lots of
good food, medical care, an education and all that. I
imagined their faces shining with gratitude.'' She uttered an unmirthful little laugh. ''The first three days
they were here they just stared at me suspiciously, like
I meant to do them harm. They didn't like the food.
They slept on the floor because they'd never slept anywhere but on the ground—said the beds were too soft.
Alejandro still sleeps there. Maria and Consuela have

come around, and I think they're beginning to enjoy their new life, but not Alejandro.''

"Well, it's too bad John can't spend more time with the boy. Sounds like he might do better with a man.''

"I know. But John's getting an offer to teach adult-education courses at night was a godsend. Right now the kids are costing us plenty. I don't think either of us realized how much we would miss my salary.''

"That reminds me . . .'' Ruby reached for her handbag, withdrew something from it and handed it to Connie. "Your daddy and I want you to have this.''

It was a check. Connie gasped when she saw the amount it had been written for. "Ma, I can't take a thousand dollars from you and Daddy!''

"Sure you can. We won't miss it. Living out there on the ranch, Jake and I don't have much reason to spend money.'' Ruby grew thoughtful. "You know, if Ty wasn't so sick, I think I'd try taking Alejandro back to the ranch with me. Some old-fashioned hard work might do that young'un a world of good. But of course I can't do it, not with Ty being the way he is and all.''

"Is Mr. Webster worse?''

Ruby nodded. "Quite a bit worse, I'm afraid.''

"Poor Tina must be at the end of her rope.''

"So far she's holding up pretty good. We've had a fella helping out at the ranch, and he's been great with Ty. But he won't be around much longer, and when he leaves, I'm afraid Tina's in for a sinking spell.'' Ruby shook away the sobering thought. "Now don't you fret over Alejandro, honey. I'll be here to help for a few days, and I never yet saw a young'un I couldn't handle. We'll get this ship sailing on a smooth course, you wait and see.''

"TABLE!" Ruby barked.

"*Mesa,*" Alejandro returned stubbornly.

"Table. Say it. I know you can. Say 'table,' and I'll give you a cookie, provided there's a please and a thank-you in there somewhere."

Ruby had noticed the longing looks the boy had been casting in the direction of the chocolate-chip cookies she had been baking. She doubted a child psychologist would approve of her methods, but if bribery worked, so be it.

A few seconds of silence passed while Alejandro glared at her defiantly. Then Maria and Consuela bounded into the kitchen.

"Coo-kee...pleez," said Maria, the spokesperson for the duo.

"Sure," Ruby said, and handed each girl a cookie.

"Thank you," they mumbled in unison, and ran out the back door.

Ruby turned, put her hands on her hips and looked at Alejandro.

He lowered his eyes. "Table," he said.

"That's better. Anything else?"

"Coo-kee...pleez."

"Of course." Ruby handed him the biggest one in the bunch.

He started to walk away, then stopped. "Thank you."

"You're welcome."

Alejandro followed his sisters out the back door, munching happily. Connie had been watching the exchange between her mother and almost-son, marveling at how well Alejandro responded to Ruby's drill-sergeant manner. "I'll swear, Ma, you're a miracle worker. Look at this house—neat as a pin. The girls seem so comfortable with you, and now you even have Alejandro smiling."

"He knows more than he lets on," Ruby said. "Watch his eyes when you say something to him. I noticed yesterday when you asked if everybody wanted ice cream. He didn't say anything, but his eyes gave him away. He knew exactly what you were saying. How could he help it? At that age kids' minds are like sponges. Don't take any guff from him...and make him talk to you in English."

"Gosh, I hate having you leave."

"Well, honey, I wish I could stay, but Tina needs me, too."

"Do you suppose you could come back when Mrs. Guerra comes for her regular visit? Alejandro loves to act up when she's here. You know, the adoption won't be completely approved for several months, and Mrs. Guerra has the authority to take the kids away from us until then. Just thinking about it scares me to death. I'm already so crazy about them...even Alejandro when he's at his worst."

"I'll try, but so much depends on how Ty's doing that day. We never know from one day to the next."

"I don't know what I'm going to do without you."

Ruby didn't either. All Connie's life, whenever she'd been in a bind, Ruby had come running. And even though Ruby thought that the adoption of three kids had been a rash move, she loved her daughter and all her maternal instincts urged her to help all she could.

During the drive back to the Webster Ranch the following day, Ruby's warring loyalties were all she thought about. Jake had flatly declared that they couldn't leave Tina, and in all honesty, Ruby didn't think they could, either. But what about Connie? It

was awful to feel pulled in two directions. If she left the
ranch to be near Connie, Tina probably would be
forced to put Ty in a home much sooner than anticipated. If she stayed with Tina, Alejandro might prove
to be more than Connie could handle. He might even
botch up the adoption. That really might do her
daughter in.

Everything inside Ruby told her that family should
receive top priority, but Ty and Tina were like family,
too. Her mind wandered over the years she had known
the Websters, almost twenty of them now. Joan had
still been around, Ty had been strong and vigorous and
Becca and Tina had been cute teenagers when she and
Jake had first gone to work at the ranch. In the beginning, they had continued living in Leatrice and driving
out to the ranch every morning after Connie had gone
to school.

Later, after Ty and Joan had split up and Connie
had gone off to college, Ty had asked them to move in
with him. For the company, he'd said. The big house
had seemed cavernous with only Tina and himself in it.
But Ruby suspected he'd had something else in mind.
Connie's education had been financially taxing for the
Yearwoods. Being freed of the responsibility of main-
taining a house in town had eased the burden considerably. She and Jake had been enormously grateful.

So Ty was much more than their employer, and Tina
was like a second daughter. Ruby didn't know what to
do. She allowed herself a moment to wish Russell
would stay. He had been so much help with Ty, and
Tina was going to miss him. Ruby feared she would
miss him more than his help. She'd seen the way her
eyes lit up every time Russell entered the room. Lord,
there was a whole new set of problems for Tina to deal

with. Next week was going to be bad enough, Ruby thought. How could she leave, too?

There didn't seem to be a good solution. No matter what she did, she knew she was going to feel guilty.

"HOW LONG do you figure you're going to be able to keep doing this kind of work?" Russell asked Jake, who was having some difficulty getting into the Jeep.

"Whaddya mean?"

"You know what I mean. I saw you gulping those pills."

"They're jus' aspirin."

"It's your back, isn't it?"

Jake frowned and scratched his chin. "Yeah. Reckon I got a touch of arthritis down low."

"Good Lord, Jake, my mother gave up her rose garden because of a bad back. You're out here day after day doing the kind of work that's hard on a good back. I repeat, how long do you figure you can keep on doing it?"

Jake turned the key in the ignition, and the vehicle lurched forward. "Don't know. As long as Tina needs me, I 'spect."

"Or until your back goes out altogether?"

"Reckon. Say, Russell, you ain't gonna mention any of this to Tina, are you?"

"Not if you don't want me to."

"Appreciate it."

It was a long way back to the house, so Russell had plenty of time to think. Even without a bum back, a man Jake's age couldn't go on doing this slave labor much longer. Then what would Tina do? It seemed to him that her life was going to hell in a hand basket at an alarming rate of speed. Ty had been nearly impossible to handle the past few days. With Ruby gone, Tina had run herself ragged. Now there was Jake's back to consider. If it went, they could close up shop period.

What if Tina got so desperate she went back to her ex-husband? She'd never said that was what Paul wanted, but Russell got the distinct impression it was. A chilling sensation ran up his spine. Tina was a smart lady, but sometimes life could get so rough that even smart ladies made rash decisions.

Money didn't seem to be a problem. Tina wasn't exactly rolling in the stuff, but apparently she had enough. So to Russell the solution seemed ridiculously simple. She should sell the ranch, move into Amarillo, where she could hire help, and start putting together some kind of normal life for herself. Then Jake could quit working, and Ruby could move near her daughter, which is what Jake had told him she wanted to do. Everybody would be happy.

Russell thought it was time he had a talk with Tina, and tonight after supper would be as good a time as any. He wouldn't mention Jake's back or Ruby's desire to be with her daughter. That would be carrying tales out of school. He'd merely try to make Tina realize the futility of living out in the back of beyond with an ailing father who required almost constant attention. He'd try to convince her that she deserved some kind of life of her own. Maybe she would listen. He hoped so.

Of course, he didn't really understand why he was so concerned. He'd be long gone from here before any major changes could take place, so why didn't he just butt out and stop trying to plan the future for everyone?

He didn't know, but he couldn't seem to stay on the sidelines. He was as worried about Ty as Tina was. Now he was worried about Jake. And he worried about Tina all the time. Russell sure never meant to get so involved with so many people, but the fact was he cared about all of them.

He liked the ranch more and more—not the work, just the ranch. When the house loomed into view, he felt a certain sense of homecoming. Maybe it was foolish, but it was true nonetheless. He knew exactly what he would find when he walked through the back door. If Ruby had returned that afternoon as planned, she would be at the sink and Tina would be in the living room with Ty. If for some reason Ruby had been delayed, Tina would be at the sink and Ty would be safely seated at the table, where she could keep an eye on him. Some concoction, always delicious smelling, would be on the stove or in the oven.

Upstairs, after his shower, he would find a closetful of clean clothes. He had repeatedly told Ruby that he had been doing his own laundry for a lot of years and could certainly continue doing so. She'd looked at him as though he were speaking a foreign language.

"You might as well let her do it, Russell," Tina had said. "Ruby has an advanced degree in looking after people."

So he had given in and done his best to keep his laundry to a minimum.

Then later, after another marvelous meal, he and Tina would linger in the kitchen over coffee and talk. In the beginning he had wondered what they could possibly find to talk about night after night, but he didn't recall many lulls in the conversation. They spent a lot of time talking about Ty, of course, but there were other topics, chiefly their childhoods. They paralleled in many ways. Certainly they had not been easy ones, but they had been comfortable and full of family. After-supper had become Russell's favorite part of the day, what he knew he would miss most of all.

Damn it, he had sawdust for brains. How had he let this happen to him?

TINA HAD COME to dread the ringing of the telephone. Her heart was in her throat every time she answered it. This time the call was a solicitation for money to send the Leatrice High School Band to some sort of contest, but any day now, any minute now, the caller would be Leon Shaw. She had no idea how she was going to handle it.

Hanging up the phone, she glanced at Ty. He still was sleeping in his easy chair, so she took advantage of the moment to slip into the kitchen to set the table for Ruby. Tina couldn't believe how glad she'd been to see that woman that afternoon. Ruby's absence from the ranch had seemed to last weeks instead of days. Ruby just had a certain special way about her. She only had to step into a house and order was immediately restored.

Tina had just crossed the foyer, when Russell walked through the kitchen door and into the dining room. Seeing each other, they both stopped.

"Hi," he said.

"Hi."

"How was your day?"

"About the same as usual. Yours?"

"Definitely the same as usual," he said with a grin.

She grinned back and fervently hoped that the warmth she invariably felt in her cheeks when she saw him at the end of the day wasn't outwardly evident.

Russell advanced, but as he drew near, he agilely sidestepped her. "My shower awaits. I'll bet I smell like a goat. See you in a minute."

Tina watched him take the stairs two at a time. Ever since Becca's remark about the way Russell had looked at her, she had studied him whenever she thought she could do so discreetly, hoping to see something of what her sister had meant. She couldn't say she'd found anything. All the longing looks in this house seemed to belong strictly to her. Turning, she continued into the kitchen.

"Want me to set the table now?" she asked Ruby.

"Sure. This ought to be ready about the time the men are."

"How was Connie?"

"Those kids are a handful," Ruby said.

"I'll bet."

"Tina, she wants me to come back the next time the woman from the adoption agency visits. Is that all right with you?"

"Of course Ruby—you know that. Any special reason?"

Ruby hesitated. At some point during the drive back to the ranch, she had decided that Connie would just have to do without her mother until Tina had adjusted to having Russell gone. It was the best she could do, the fairest thing, so she didn't want to give Tina any inkling that Connie had a real problem with Alejandro. "Oh, the boy likes to act up some when that woman's there. He's ten and full of sass and vinegar. I seem to handle him better than Connie does. And get this—he doesn't like being treated on the same level with his sisters. Seems that where they come from, males have special status, even male children."

Tina uttered a derisive sound. "He ought to fit right in with some of the characters around here when he grows up."

"Any word about Russell's car?"

"No, but there will be any day now, I'm sure." Tina reached into a cabinet and withdrew five plates. "I didn't tell you what happened to Dad the night I went to Becca's party, did I?"

Ruby frowned. "No."

While she set the table, Tina filled Ruby in on Ty's accident. "So I've spent the past few days literally crawling through this house on my hands and knees, trying to see it from a baby's point of view. It's as safe as I can make it, but Russell thinks we ought to install burglar bars on the upstairs window."

"Burglar bars?"

Tina nodded. "To prevent ... jumping."

Ruby's eyes widened. "Oh, my God!"

By the time the meal was ready, Russell, Jake and Ty had come into the kitchen. For the next forty minutes or so, conversation was limited to the usual supper-time trivia—the food, the weather and such. Everyone was aware of the need for making mealtimes as tranquil as possible. If Ty became upset, he wouldn't eat. The trouble was, no one could predict what would upset him.

That night all went well. Ty didn't eat much, and once he picked up his meat with his fingers, another first. But Tina didn't scold or try to get him to use his fork, though she made a mental note to ask about such behavior at the next support-group meeting.

Once the meal was over, as if on signal, Jake and Ruby took Ty into the living room, leaving Tina and Russell alone. They almost always cleaned the kitchen together in the evening, and they had developed a smooth system. He cleared the table, and Tina rinsed the dishes and loaded them into the dishwasher. And while she tidied the counter, he took out the trash. Then it was time for coffee.

This evening, however, when he came back into the kitchen, he said, "It's nice out there tonight. Want to go sit on the stoop and watch the sun go down?"

"Sure. We'll have coffee out there."

For several minutes, they simply sat, sipping their coffee and watching as the setting sun washed the earth in a golden glow, bringing a softness to country that looked so harsh in the bright of day. Flashes of heat lightning winked at them from the distance. Tina knew there was no such thing as heat lightning, but that's what the old-timers called those faraway flashes.

"Tina?" Russell's voice cut through the silence.

"Hmm."

"What are you going to do when I'm gone?"

When I'm gone kicked her in the stomach. "I guess I'll do what I do now—take care of Dad."

"May I tell you what I wish you'd do?"

"Of course."

"I wish you would sell this ranch and move into Amarillo. You'd have your mother and sister there. You could hire help or maybe put Ty into one of those adult day-care centers I've been reading about. Then you could go back to work or do whatever it is you enjoy."

Tina shook her head vigorously. "I can't do that, Russell. It's a well-documented fact that dementia

sufferers who are kept in familiar surroundings as long
as possible do better than those who aren't. I'm afraid
to take Dad away from this place. My God, if he got
upset over the front-door/back-door business, what
would happen if I put him into a strange place?"

"Ty doesn't know where he is half the time," Russell said as gently as he could. "I'm sorry if that sounds
cruel, but it's true."

"We don't really know what's going on in his mind."

They lapsed into silence for a few more minutes before Russell said, "Just yesterday he asked me if I had
come to take him away from here. He said he wanted
to go back to where 'everybody' was."

Tina digested that. "That's the way he felt that
minute. Five minutes later it might have been something else. I wonder what he meant by 'everybody.'
Maybe...maybe he was thinking back to when this
ranch was a big operation. There were a lot of cowboys working on it then, and Mom and Becca still were
here. It did seem as though there were a lot of people
around all the time. Maybe that's it. Who knows?"

Russell drained his cup and set it on the stoop between them.

"Want another?" Tina asked.

"No, thanks. I've got to tell you that I'm not only
worried about Ty. I'm worried about you, too."

"Me? Why?"

"You look too tired too much of the time. You've
got to take care of yourself. You can't very well give
care if you're sick."

"Oh, I'll be all right. I sleep well most of the time,
and Lord knows, I eat well. I can count on the fingers
of one hand the times in my life I've been really sick."

"I'm not talking only about physical health," Russell persisted. "There's emotional health, too. Worry and exhaustion can make you as sick as any germ can. That's why I wish you would move into the city, where you could hire help and get out more often. You deserve a life of your own. That way...well, you'd never be tempted to...accept the wrong kind of help."

Tina set her cup beside his, then raised her knees and hugged them. She wondered if he was alluding to Paul. Russell was unusually perceptive. He might have guessed the reason for Paul's visit. On one hand, she didn't know when anything had pleased her as much as Russell's concern. On the other, there was a certain finality to his tone, as though he already was beginning to say goodbye. She felt the first tinges of melancholy creeping through her, but she fought them off. If she hadn't allowed her father's illness to steep her in melancholy, she was strong enough to keep Russell's departure from doing so.

This, too, would pass, she reminded herself. One day Russell would be nothing but a fond memory.

Turning her head, she looked at him. He was staring into the distance, so she was treated to a splendid view of his wonderfully masculine profile. She noticed that he needed a haircut, and she wondered if she should offer to give him one. She had gotten pretty good at that since she'd started cutting Ty's hair.

"Why do you care so much?" she asked softly. "After all, we're not your problem."

He didn't respond to that immediately, only continued staring ahead. Then he turned to her, and there was that look again, the one that made her heart pound.

"That's where you're wrong," he said. "I've made all of you my problem."

"We'll be all right. When you...get where you're going, send us your address. I'll...keep you posted if that's what you want."

"That's what I want." Even if a complete break was smarter, that was what he wanted.

He continued to stare at her, and Tina stared back at him, boldly, seemingly riveted on him, unable to glance away. Then he raised a hand and brushed it across her cheek before sliding around to her nape. Gently he urged her toward him. Bending his head, he placed his mouth over hers.

The kiss was light though lingering. Tina supposed that most eighth-graders kissed with more passion, but it was physical contact, and it affected her more deeply than pure passion would have. She loved the feel of the texture of his cheek against hers. Why now? she wondered. Why not weeks ago, when there had still been time for...

For what? A brief, wild fling before he hied off to California and she went back to being a twenty-four-hour-a-day nurse? That would have been smart, real smart. If she dreaded seeing him leave now, how would she be feeling if they had been lovers?

Still, when he broke the kiss and lifted his head, she felt abandoned, and she hugged her knees more tightly to preclude the possibility that she might reach for him. The air between them seemed to vibrate. It wouldn't have taken much for that simple kiss to escalate into something more profound...just a touch...

Tina gave herself a shake. Unclasping her knees, she picked up the cups and got to her feet. "I'll take these in. Sure you don't want more coffee?"

"I'm sure." Russell sighed. He guessed the kiss had been a dumb move on his part. Talk about lousy timing. Nothing could come of it. Yet kissing Tina was something he'd wanted to do since, roughly, his second day on the ranch.

Who was he kidding? On that second day he had been so caved in and worn out he couldn't have mustered the energy to kiss her. A lot had happened to him since then. His stomach was as hard as granite. He had muscles he hadn't possessed the day he'd driven out of Red Star's yard for the last time. He had the energy of ten men—

"Are you coming inside, Russell?"

He shoved himself up and off the stoop. "Yeah, I'm coming. I'll go sit with Ty and spell Jake and Ruby. They might want to go into town or something."

As it turned out, Jake and Ruby were thoroughly engrossed in a movie on television, so for the remainder of the evening, Tina and Russell pretended to be absorbed in it, too. What they mostly did, however, was try not to look at each other.

THE TELEPHONE RANG while they were having breakfast the next morning. Since Tina was closest to it, she answered the call.

"Hello."

" 'Mornin', Tina. This is Leon Shaw."

Tina was sure her heart had stopped. "Yes, Leon," she said.

Russell jerked his head around at the sound of the man's name.

"Tell Mr. Cade his car is ready, and she's a honey," Leon went on. "I took before-and-after pictures for the shop, and I had an extra set of prints made in case he wants them."

"Thanks, Leon. I'll tell him," she promised, irritated at how enormously pleased Leon had sounded. "I'm sure he'll be in some time this morning to pick it up." Hanging up, she returned to the table. "Your car's ready," she said unnecessarily.

Russell nodded. Ruby took one look at Tina's face and sighed.

Tina stared at the food on her plate, food that suddenly looked very unappetizing. "I'll drive you into town after breakfast," she told Russell without looking at him.

"Thanks."

Only Jake wondered why such a pall of silence had fallen over the room.

CHAPTER EIGHT

"WELL, THERE SHE IS, Mr. Cade. Whaddaya think?"

Russell thought that if Leon's chest puffed up any more, the buttons on his shirt would pop off. But the man had a right to be proud of his work. Russell had searched for flaws and found none. "You did a wonderful job, Leon. You're a true artist."

Leon beamed. "I treated her like she belonged to me."

Russell rubbed the car possessively. It seemed to him he should have felt more elation. This was what he had been waiting for, and it was good to see his car all in one piece, looking none the worse for its ordeal. But during the drive into town, realizing that today was probably the last time he would see Tina, a curious sadness had overtaken him, and it wouldn't go away. Now he had to go back to the ranch, pack his things and say goodbye to all of them.

Well, no, not to all of them. He wouldn't say goodbye to Ty. That was something he and Tina had agreed on. They weren't worried that Ty would remember Russell, but they did fear that a farewell scene might upset the old man.

Russell fought off his doom-and-gloom mood. "Are you satisfied with the way the insurance company handled things?" he asked Leon.

"Couldn't be more. By the way, I took the car for a test spin. She jus' purrs. A body'd think she jus' came outa the showroom."

Russell turned to look for Tina. She was standing some distance away from them, her arms crossed under her breasts. He thanked Leon profusely once more, then strolled over to her. "Today's going to be a hot one," he said inanely.

"They all are this time of year."

"Want to stop by the Dairy Queen for something cold to drink . . . for old times' sake?"

Oh, why? Tina wanted to ask. *Why don't you just pack up and leave? Let's get this over and done with.* "Sure," she said.

"You lead, and I'll follow."

At midmorning, the Dairy Queen's only customers were a few coffee drinkers.

Marge came out of the kitchen when she heard the tinkling of the bell over the door. "Hi, Tina."

"Hi, Marge. Iced tea, please."

"Same for me," Russell said, wondering if he, too, had become addicted to the stuff.

They carried their drinks to a booth by a window. "The first time I saw this place," he remarked, "I sure never thought I'd ever see it again."

"I can imagine. Sorry it took Leon so long to get your car ready."

"Are you?"

"No, I guess I'm not. It's been nice knowing you." That sounded terribly inadequate, even to Tina's ears. She sipped the tea and tried to think of a way to say all the things she wanted to say, then wondered if any of them actually needed saying. "Russell, I . . ."

"Tina, I . . ."

They stopped and chuckled.

"You first," he said.

"I just . . . want to thank you for all you've done for us while you've been here."

"I wish you wouldn't. Everything I did I did because I wanted to."

"I know, and that made it all the nicer. I know I speak for Jake and Ruby when I say that you made things a lot easier for all of us. I wish Dad could convey his thanks, too, but . . ."

"Please, Tina . . ."

He looked decidedly uncomfortable, so Tina thought she'd better drop it. Words were inadequate, anyway. "Now, what did you want to say?"

Russell wanted to say so much that he didn't know where to begin. If it hadn't been for Tina and the Yearwoods, he would have spent all these weeks in a motel in Leatrice, going stir-crazy. Instead he'd been busy, helpful, and he'd felt welcome.

As he lifted the cup to drink, he spotted a poster on the wall over the cigarette vending machine. He lowered the cup and gestured toward it. "Do you folks go to that?"

Tina swiveled her head to see what he was talking about. Turning back, she said, "The county rodeo? We always went when I was a kid. Dad loved it. There's a fair, too. Last year I let Jake and Ruby go, and I stayed home with Dad. I'm sure I'll do the same this year."

"Would you like to go?"

"Oh, I hadn't given it any thought. It's pretty amateurish, but great fun."

"It lasts two nights. Why not let Jake and Ruby go, say, Saturday night, and we can go Friday." Russell honestly hadn't known he was going to suggest such a thing until the words were out.

" 'We'?" Tina asked in surprise.

"Yeah, you and me."

"But, Russell...I thought you'd be on the road long before Friday."

"That's only a couple of days away, and I'm not in that big a hurry. If you think you'd enjoy going, we'll go."

He knew it wasn't the smartest move of his life. He didn't even know why he was doing it. True, he dreaded saying goodbye, but did he think that would be any easier later? He told himself he was doing it for Tina. Once he was gone, he feared she would have to wait a very long time to go out strictly for fun. Ty was deteriorating badly, more so than even Tina realized. The morning routine, for instance, was becoming more difficult and was taking much longer these days. Ty often couldn't distinguish between his shirt and his trousers. Russell knew there were some bad times ahead. Tina could use an evening of fun, and a few days' delay would make no difference to him. It was as good a rationalization as any.

"Well?" he prodded.

Tina knew what she should do—tell him she really didn't care much for rodeos, but thanks, anyway. Having him stay until the weekend would only postpone the inevitable farewell. The waiting was already almost unbearable. She was so tense it would almost be a relief when he was gone. Why prolong the torture?

"Thanks, Russell," she said. "If you're really sure you don't mind waiting a few more days, I think I'd like to go...very much."

"HE'S STAYING?" Ruby asked in surprise.

"Well, not for long," Tina said, "but he wants to go to the rodeo, so how about if we go Friday night, and you and Jake go Saturday?"

Ruby smiled knowingly. "He wants to go to the rodeo my Aunt Fanny. He's stalling."

"What?"

"Stalling. When a man doesn't want to do something—like leave a place or a person—he can think of all sorts of reasons to stay. Rodeo, indeed!"

"I think you're misreading him," Tina insisted. "Russell's never given me any reason to think he'd consider staying here longer than necessary."

"Tina, I've been around the track a few more times than you have. Has Russell mentioned California lately?"

Tina couldn't remember. "I'm sure he has, but mostly we talk about Dad these days."

"I thought so."

Tina refused to give any credence to Ruby's speculations, but in her heart she wished they were true.

Ruby, meanwhile, sent up a silent prayer that Russell Cade would prove to be the solution to her own dilemma.

"I FIGURED you'd be halfway to Tucumcari by now, pal," Jake said, recovering from the surprise of having his right-hand man show up for work that afternoon.

"Hell, Jake, I wouldn't leave without saying goodbye. Besides, I'm not leaving yet. I want to take Tina to the rodeo Friday night. We're leaving Saturday night for you and Ruby."

"Hmm."

"What's that supposed to mean?"

"Nothin'. Jus' hmm. She's pretty, ain't she?"

"Who?"

Jake cackled gleefully. "'Who?' Listen to him. Tina of course."

"Yes, she's very pretty."

"And nice."

"That, too," Russell agreed. "And while we're on the subject, I want to talk to you about Tina. I want to ask a favor of you."

"Ask away."

"I've been trying—without much success, I might add—to persuade her to sell this ranch and move into town, where she could hire someone to help with Ty. You say Ruby wants to move closer to your daughter, and your back is apt to give out on you any day. Tina would be in a hell of a bind. Besides, the rest of her family is in Amarillo. She might even commandeer her sister into service."

"Becca?" Jake snorted. "You met her. Does she strike you as the kind you'd want in your corner when the fight got tough? Born to the purple that gal was."

"Well, if her sister won't pitch in, Tina could at least hire professional help occasionally. She's got some bad times ahead of her."

"Yeah, reckon she does. So...what's the favor?"

"Stay after her about selling out once I'm gone."

"I'll try," Jake said thoughtfully. "Don't know as how it'll do much good, though. One thing you can bet on is that whatever Tina does, she'll do 'cause she thinks it's best for Ty, not her. She was always the apple of her daddy's eye, and she remembers that. But this life she's leadin' now sure ain't worth screw-all, so I'll try."

Russell slapped the back of the man he'd come to regard as a good friend. "I can't ask for more than that."

"Guess I'm gonna kinda miss you. It's gonna seem downright strange not havin' you draggin' your ass behind me all day. You turned into a pretty fair hand."

"Coming from you, that's a real compliment." Russell was amazed how much the praise from the older man meant to him.

"You plannin' on keepin' in touch or jus' ridin' off into the sunset?"

"Oh, I'll keep in touch," Russell said. And he would, even though he knew that keeping in touch would be really painful for him. He fully expected to miss all of them horribly; letters and phone calls would hardly lessen his pain. The smart thing to do would be to hold on to the memories and sever the ties.

But he knew he could never do that.

FRIDAY NIGHT'S RODEO was held in conjunction with the annual county fair, and since it was the biggest attraction between Amarillo and the Oklahoma border, attendance records were broken every year. A chili cook-off was being held, and there were contests for everything from homemade quilts to sweet-pepper relish. A carnival troupe had set up midway rides and game booths. Vendors supplied popcorn and nachos, hot dogs and hamburgers, soft drinks and beer. Country music blared from loudspeakers, and scores of Texas flags flapped in the wind. Candidates for county offices used the occasion to shake hands and pass around leaflets, but no one seemed very interested in politics. The mood was festive, and everyone just wanted to have a good time.

Tina and Russell strolled around the grounds, eating tacos and drinking beer, taking in the sights while waiting for the rodeo to start. Tina kept meeting people she hadn't seen in years, including Joe-Ben Carter, his wife, Peggy, and their two little boys. Joe-Ben, as Tina later explained to Russell, had been her first real boyfriend.

"He looks well and happy," she remarked. "So does Peggy."

"Do you envy her?" Russell asked.

"I don't envy her Joe-Ben, if that's what you mean," she said with a laugh. "I envy her that family."

Russell looked surprised. "I've never heard you express any burning desire for motherhood."

"Let's just say I envy her the freedom to have a family. Oh, Don..." She stepped forward to extend her hand to an aging, portly man wearing cowboy garb. "How wonderful to see you!"

"Hello, Tina." The man pumped her hand. "You just get prettier every year."

"You're sweet. Don, I'd like you to meet Russell Cade. Russell, this is Don Madison."

The two men shook hands and exchanged pleasantries.

Then Don turned to Tina. "How's Ty?"

She shook her head. "Not too good, I'm afraid."

"Damned shame. Damned shame."

"Is Beth with you tonight?" Tina asked.

"Nope. She's down in Galveston with our daughter and all those grandkids. She can't stand knowing they're doing just fine without her."

"Give her my regards."

"I'll do that. Listen, folks, I hate to run, but I've got some people I'm supposed to meet, and—"

"Sure, Don, that's fine," Tina said. "Don't let us detain you."

"Nice meeting you, Russell. Tina, you take care of yourself." Don hurried away and got swallowed up in the crowd.

Tina stared after him. "I haven't seen him in ... I don't remember when. He and Dad were best friends for forty years."

Russell frowned. "Then how come he never comes to see Ty?"

They resumed their strolling.

"Oh ... Dad's condition embarrasses his old pals. And who wants to drive all the way out to the ranch to visit someone who doesn't remember who they are? Now Don's embarrassed because he never comes by. You saw what a hasty exit he made. A few years ago he would have fastened himself to us like paper on the wall."

"You'd think family friends would come to visit you. They must realize you're stuck out there and would enjoy a little company."

"Probably not." Tina grabbed Russell by the hand. She positively wasn't going to spend the entire evening thinking about her father. What good was getting away if she took her problems with her? "Come on," she said. "Something just occurred to me. You don't have even one souvenir of Texas, and I've got just the thing for you."

Her destination was a booth where a man about Ty's age sat hand-tooling leather belts. On the wall behind him hung at least a hundred belts, all of them beautiful.

"Hello, Casey," Tina said.

The man looked up. When he saw her he smiled, and his eyes disappeared into slits in his face. "Well, hi ya, Tina sweetheart. How're ya doin'?"

"I'm fine, thanks. Casey, this is my friend Russell. He's on his way to California, and he needs a souvenir of Texas. I thought one of your belts would be perfect."

"You do beautiful work, Casey," Russell commented.

"Thank-ee, son. Pick out the one ya like, and I'll put your name on it for ya."

All the belts were works of art. It was difficult to choose one. Russell finally made his decision, and Casey put aside what he was working on. "Do they call ya 'Russ' or 'Rusty' or anythin' like that?"

"No, it's just 'Russell.'"

In the smooth space on the back of the belt Casey expertly penciled in Russell's name, then began cutting away the leather between the letters. "What part of California ya headed for?"

"The North Coast."

Casey shook his head. "Never got up there, but I lived farther south for a spell, down where all the fruits and nuts are . . . human kind, I mean."

Casey guffawed at that, while Tina and Russell exchanged amused looks.

"Now, if ya want a real fancy souvenir, ya oughta let me make ya a pair of boots. If I do say so m'self, I make the finest pair of boots in the state. Ever'thin' done by hand, no shortcuts. I've made 'em for movie stars and singers and Ay-rab sheiks. Ain't gonna find nothin' like 'em in any store, I'll tell ya."

"Boots, huh?" Russell mused, considering it.

"Yep. I can measure your feet right here. I also make saddles."

"I don't have much need for a saddle, but I've always wanted a pair of really fancy cowboy boots. How long would it take you to make them?"

"Oh . . . better part of a week."

Russell paused. Another week, another delay, another excuse . . . and this one was legitimate. Lord, he was tempted! Everyone would understand his wanting a pair of fancy handmade boots before leaving Texas.

Imbecile! For the past two days he had dreaded the arrival of the weekend. The dread was a constant knot in his stomach. And sometimes when the dread was at its worst, he would entertain the idea of staying for a little longer. He could always think of a reason. Tina needed his help with Ty. If he stayed a while longer, Ruby could go help her daughter. All perfectly good reasons.

Then he would ask himself: Was this where he wanted to be? Was this what he wanted to do? And as nice as Tina and the Yearwoods had been to him, had any of them even once hinted that they'd like for him to stay? No, no and no were the answers.

"Well, I guess I'll have to pass, Casey, sorry. A week's a bit longer than I can wait."

Tina's pent-up breath oozed out of her. She hadn't realized she'd been holding it.

IT WAS AFTER MIDNIGHT when Tina and Russell returned to the ranch. A light shone from one of the living-room windows, but the rest of the house was pitch-dark.

Russell eased the Thunderbird in behind the pickup and switched off the headlights. "Looks like everyone's turned in," he said.

"Oh, I'm sure...hours ago." She reached for the door handle, but before turning it, she said, "I had a wonderful time, Russell. Thanks so much for taking me."

"I enjoyed it, too. I'm glad we went. It's been a long time since I've been to a county fair."

He made no move to get out of the car, so neither did Tina. After he had purchased his belt, they hadn't mentioned California again, but now she wanted to know. "When...do you think you'll be leaving?" Her voice was deceptively casual.

"Not tomorrow, that's for sure. I haven't done a thing about packing." He glanced out the windshield. "Besides, I don't much like the idea of your being alone tomorrow night with Ty. I didn't realize how dark the country is at night."

She uttered a little laugh. "I'm sure I'll spend many a night alone with Dad out here, Russell. I'm not afraid."

"Just the same, Sunday's soon enough."

"How long do you figure it'll take you to make the drive?"

"Funny, I hadn't given it any thought. Let's see...I ought to make Albuquerque the first night, Flagstaff or farther the second. Four days if I push it—five if I don't." He didn't want to talk about it. He didn't want to think about the trip...or about Tina living in this isolated house, taking care of Ty, maybe without even Ruby for company.

Five days, Tina thought, and he would be half a continent away. "Do you...suppose you'll ever get back this way?"

"I don't know. I never say never."

"If you do, will you drop in to see us?"

"Of course...if you're still here."

She uttered a dry laugh. "Oh, I'm sure I'll still be here...or someplace close by. I have a feeling it will be a long, long time before I can go anywhere."

It was uttered matter-of-factly, without a trace of self-pity. What she had said was true—she couldn't go anywhere for a long time. Russell couldn't shake the feeling that he was deserting her in her hour of need.

But that wasn't the case and he knew it. Yes, she had a whole slew of monumental problems, but there was certainly nothing he could do to solve them for her. If he could help her, he would, but he couldn't. He reminded himself that she had gotten along nicely before she'd met him, and she would after he'd gone. Maybe that thought would sustain him during the weeks ahead.

He slid his arm along the back of the seat, and his fingertips brushed her hair. "Tina, have you given any more thought to what I said the other night?"

"About moving into town?"

"Uh-hmm."

"Some." Actually, the only thing about that night she'd given a lot of thought to was the kiss. It was sad testimony to the bleakness of her existence that such a brief, light kiss could have made such a lasting impression. "And I'll admit that the idea has its appeal. I won't lie to you. When I was married I got rather used to living in a city where there were museums to visit, shows to see, good restaurants and shopping. Before

you came, I used to long for someone near my own age
to talk to. I love Jake and Ruby to death, but they're
simple people from another generation. Sometimes I
think I would like going back to college, just to make
sure my brain's still alive. Or maybe work at an animal hospital again. I really enjoyed that." She paused
to sigh. "But I'm afraid my decision has to stay the
same. All my instincts tell me that Dad's better off here
as long as possible."

"Damn, I hate that."

Tina shifted in the seat so she could look straight at
Russell "You're nice to care, but this time next week
you'll be far from here, and what's going on at this
ranch will be the farthest thing from your mind."

"Do you really believe that?"

"Yes... I'm a realist. When you get to that place
you've dreamed about for so long, you aren't going to
waste your time thinking about us. We'll simply be
added to the long list of people whose lives briefly
touched yours while you were on the road."

"Oh, Tina," he said, "you're wrong. Very wrong."

"Why would we be any different?"

"You just are. You especially are... so different."

They stared into each other's eyes, and Tina knew
with certainty that unless she made a move to get out
of the car, she was going to be kissed. Denial waged a
battle with desire. *Remember,* her sensible inner voice
said, *day after tomorrow he is going to get into this car
and drive away from here forever.* Still, when she saw
Russell's head dip, she leaned toward him. *It's just a
kiss,* she thought, *something to remember.* His lips
covered hers.

It was nothing like the only other kiss they had
shared. This one was long and greedy. It was tortur-

ous and thrilling, agony and ecstasy all at once. Even though her mind cried for him to stop, she slipped her arms around his waist and returned the kiss measure for measure. She opened her mouth to allow his tongue entry. When he pulled her closer, she melted against him. Her flowering passion tugged at the pit of her stomach. She wanted to hold him all night. Finally it was Russell who ended the kiss.

Neither of them spoke for a minute. Tina nestled her head in the curve of his shoulder and felt him press his cheek to the top of her head. She laid a hand on his chest and felt the steady thumping of his heartbeat. *Oh, I wish I could go to California with you,* she thought, *even though you've never given me any reason to believe you'd want to take me.*

Damn, I don't want to leave her, Russell thought. *I don't want to stay here. I don't want her problems. But I don't want to leave her. What's wrong with me?*

More than most people, Tina knew the futility of railing at fate. She had done some of that in the early days of her father's illness, and it had only served to make her feel more helpless. But now she indulged in a little resentment. Why had Russell shown up in the first place, bringing visions of a world of freedom? Why had he come at a time when she wasn't able to even hope for more than friendship with him? It wasn't fair.

Tina's good sense returned by degrees. Where was it written that life was supposed to be fair? One played the cards one was dealt. "This is silly," she finally said. "I'm not very good at goodbyes to begin with. This . . . sort of thing will only make it harder."

"I know. I'm sorry. I meant . . . I thought it would just be a simple good-night kiss."

Tina groped for the handle, found it and pushed open the door, flooding the car with light. "We really should go in."

"I know that, too," Russell said with a sigh. Getting out of the car, he followed Tina, who almost sprinted toward the house, as though searching for a safe harbor.

AT SOME POINT during a restless night, Russell made up his mind. His qualms about leaving the ranch were absurd. He had allowed himself to get so wrapped up in Tina and Ty, Jake and Ruby, that he had lost sight of his own goal. He recalled one of his mother's favorite adages: it's not the things you've done in life that you'll regret one day; it's the things you haven't done. He had thought and dreamed of California for ten years. He knew he would regret it if he didn't go. He would always wonder. He told himself he had over-dramatized Tina's plight. She would do fine without him. She was the type.

Of course, he admitted, it was easier to come to that momentous conclusion when he wasn't looking into Tina's beautiful, tired eyes. He had the courage of his convictions when he wasn't faced with the affection he sometimes saw in Ty's expression, or when he wasn't wolfing down Ruby's peerless cooking or trading gibes and tall tales with Jake.

Saturday promised to be difficult, a long day, his last day in this place that had been his home for weeks. But his future was not here. Come Sunday, he was getting into the Thunderbird and heading west . . . no matter what.

CHAPTER NINE

THE FOLLOWING MORNING, the sound of the vacuum cleaner reverberated through the house. Tina attacked the carpet in Ty's bedroom as viciously as if she were killing snakes.

She had spent a miserable night, so she wasn't in the best of spirits, and the day so far showed no sign of brightening her mood. She'd all but had to spoon-feed Ty his breakfast, and Russell had reported having a terrible time getting him dressed. Then her father had started in on wanting to "go back to where everyone was." Cleaning house was a good way to work off her frustrations.

For as long as she could remember, certainly for as long as Ruby had been at the ranch, Saturday had been cleaning day. Why Saturday she didn't know, but it was such a firmly entrenched part of their routine that it almost was an article of faith. Until seven or eight months ago, even Ty, seeing Tina and Ruby scurrying about the house, mopping, polishing, sweeping, would say, "This must be Saturday."

The predictability, the sameness, the sheer boredom of it all. *Why do we bother?* she wondered. It wasn't as though someone were apt to drop in unexpectedly. The only people who ever saw the inside of the house were the ones who lived in it.

Downstairs, Ruby was keeping a watchful eye on Ty while she dusted and polished brass. Outside, from the distance came the sound of Jake hammering away on something. In the guest room across the hall, Russell was packing. He'd told them he wanted to get an early start tomorrow morning.

Switching off the vacuum, Tina moved an uphol-stered chair so she could sweep under it. Then, at the touch of her finger, the machine roared to life again. Somehow its racket served to reassure her that her world was not coming apart, no matter how she some-times felt. People could drift in and out of her life, but Saturday cleaning would remain.

God, she was in an awful mood! She couldn't seem to shake it. Maybe it was the previous evening out with Russell that had her feeling so out of sorts. She had had such a good time, but it was the one and only date she'd ever have with him. Her first thought upon wak-ing that morning had been that this would be the last time she heard Russell's soothing voice talking her fa-ther through his routine. Her second had been that she wished Russell would leave today. Her third had been that she wished he'd never come here in the first place.

Turning off the vacuum, Tina unplugged it and pushed it out into the hall. Normally when she fin-ished her father's room, she headed straight for Rus-sell's, but he still was in there, and she didn't particularly want to talk to him. So she pushed the cleaner on down the hall to her bedroom. Then she heard Ruby calling to her.

"Becca's on the phone, Tina."

"Thanks." She took a deep breath before lifting the receiver. Given her rotten frame of mind, she wasn't sure she could take Becca's all's-right-with-the-world cheerfulness. "Good morning, Becca," she said as brightly as she could manage.

"Hi, Tina. What are you doing?"

"Cleaning house."

"I thought Ruby did that."

"She can't do everything."

"Oh . . . well, I guess not. Listen, I just wanted to touch base with you before we leave."

"Leave? Where are you going?"

"To the Bahamas, of course."

"Good Lord, is it that time of year already?"

"Actually, we're leaving a teeny bit early this year. Derek's folks are taking the kids to Tahoe, so we're going to sneak in a few extra days of fun in the sun."

Tina felt her entire body sag. "Have a wonderful time."

"Oh, we always do. There's a whole gang of us who hook up in Miami, then positively invade the islands. By the way, how are you doing?"

How could I possibly be doing? Tina wanted to yell. "Fine," she said.

"That's good. Well, I've got a million things to do, so I won't keep you any longer. Mom knows how to reach us if you need to."

Why in hell would I need to? Tina thought sourly. "Great. You guys have a safe trip."

Hanging up, it occurred to her that Becca hadn't even inquired about Ty. Irritation swept through her for an instant, then she brushed it aside. She knew she shouldn't let Becca get to her. Any other day she probably would have dismissed the call with only a modicum of envy. Becca didn't mean to be inconsiderate and thoughtless. She just . . . was. Tossing her head impatiently, Tina switched on the vacuum and went back to work.

Somehow the morning passed. She cleaned house as though it were going to receive a white-glove inspection when she was finished. Then she spent some time cleaning up herself. Mostly she tried to avoid Russell, which wasn't difficult since he seemed to be avoiding her, too. He made dozens of trips between his room and his car, all the while making sure Ty wasn't aware of the nature of the activity. Immediately after lunch, he announced that he was going into Leatrice to gas up his car and run some errands. He expected to be gone quite a while. Tina was sure he was just killing time.

Tonight would be a lot of fun, she thought. With Jake and Ruby gone and with a good four hours to pass between supper and a reasonable bedtime, they would have to talk. What in the devil would they talk about? They had barely exchanged three sentences all day. They couldn't discuss his trip, not until Ty went to bed. What she was going to do tomorrow or next week or next month would no longer be of interest to Russell, and she knew she couldn't stand a bunch of reminiscing about the time he had spent with them. So that pretty well left them with the weather.

Yes, it ought to be a lot of fun.

RUSSELL STROLLED up and down the aisles of Foster's Drug, hoping to get hit with an inspiration. He wanted to buy Tina a gift, but he didn't have the slightest idea what it should be. She liked to read, but how did he know what she'd read and what she hadn't? Besides, a book was too impersonal. He stopped briefly at the perfume counter, then recalled something his mother had once told him. "Unless you know a woman's particular favorite fragrance, perfume isn't a good choice." Scratch that. He wasn't sure Tina even wore perfume. She always smelled sweet and clean, but not of cologne.

The drugstore's gift shop was full of nice things, but he didn't want to get her something for the house. He wanted a gift for her alone.

Finally, not finding anything that really hit him as appropriate, he paid for his own purchases and went out into the hot afternoon. As he walked along the sidewalk to his car, he passed a jewelry store. That struck a chord, so he went inside. A dapper salesman accosted him immediately.

"May I help you, sir?"

"Well . . . I'm not sure. You see, there's this woman who's been awfully kind to me, and I'd like to get her something. She doesn't wear much jewelry, but she always has little gold studs in her ears, so I was wondering . . . maybe earrings?"

"A good choice. Were you considering diamonds?"

"I . . . I don't think so," Russell said uncertainly. "I'm afraid a really expensive gift would embarrass her."

"Cultured pearls, perhaps? They're always in exquisite taste."

Russell shrugged. "Okay, you're the expert."

He was shown dozens of pairs of earrings, but in the end he chose the simplest—one perfect pearl for each earlobe. The salesman had the present gift-wrapped, and Russell tucked the little package in his shirt pocket. That done, he drove back to the ranch.

He had thought that buying Tina something would make him feel good, but he felt like hell. As he parked the Thunderbird in its customary spot at the side of the house, he noticed Jake was tinkering with the tractor again. Russell often wondered if the machine really needed all the work or if Jake just liked to putter with it. Instead of going into the house, he crossed the backyard and joined his friend.

"Hi ya," Jake greeted Russell, squinting up at him. "Listen, I've been thinkin'... when that combine gits out here next week..." He stopped and stood up. "Ah, I forgot... you ain't gonna be here next week."

A team of contractors would be out the following week to harvest their wheat for them. It was on the tip of Russell's tongue to say, "If you need me, I can stay." He had to forcibly bite back the words. He was going to California, and that was that. "Yeah, sorry, Jake. I won't be here next week."

JAKE AND RUBY LEFT for the fairgrounds at five o'clock. Tina didn't think she'd seen Ruby look so animated in years. She was wearing a simple cotton dress, but it was new, and Jake had risen to the occasion by exchanging his jeans for gabardine trousers. Once they were gone, Russell took charge of Ty so Tina could prepare supper.

Mealtime was strained. Tina felt agitated from having spent the day keeping her emotions in check. She forced banal conversation for Ty's sake, but to her own ears her voice sounded nervous and high-pitched. Again Ty ate little and was even quieter than usual. Did he sense that something was up? The one thing she wanted above all was for Russell to get on the road without Ty's being aware of the departure.

When the meal was finally over, she shooed the men out of the kitchen so she could clean up. She managed to stretch a fifteen-minute job into forty-five, but the time came when she had no choice but to join them in the living room.

The card table had been set up, and they were engaged in one of her father's games. The television was on, but the sound was off. Russell looked up and smiled when she entered the room, but he quickly turned back to Ty lest the elderly man lose his concentration.

Tina crossed the room and plopped on the sofa, picking up the paperback novel she had been reading. It was the kind of story she normally loved—pure, preposterous fantasy designed to make the reader forget there was any such thing as real life. Tonight, however, its magic wasn't working. Tina read four pages, realized she didn't have any idea what she had just read, so put the book aside. Then there was nothing for her to do but focus her attention on the silent screen or on the men. She chose the men.

Russell was absolutely amazing, she thought. Ty's games were simplicity itself, so she knew they had to bore Russell out of his mind, yet he would sit there as long as her father would, pretending to be fascinated. Tomorrow night, if Ty wanted, she would have to be the one to sit there and play with him. Unfortunately her patience with the games was not as limitless as Russell's seemed to be.

A disturbing thought occurred to her just then. Her father liked habit and repetition, and playing the games with Russell after supper had definitely become a habit. What if he balked at having her for a partner? What if he asked for Russell? Should she tell Ty he was gone for good or pretend he had merely stepped out for a minute?

What she should do, Tina decided, was stop borrowing trouble. Sighing, she reached for a magazine and began leafing through it.

"Ah-ha!" Ty suddenly cried.

Tina started, and she glanced over immediately at her father.

But Ty was looking at Russell, a cat-got-the-cream smile on his face. "I've been cheating, and you haven't caught me once," he said.

Russell chuckled and rubbed his chin. "Well, I guess you're just too sharp for me, sport."

Ty always cheated, and Russell always pretended not to notice. Tonight, however, he really hadn't noticed. The game required absolutely no concentration on his part, so he'd been entirely too aware of Tina sitting on the sofa, trying to read but too fidgety to do so. She hadn't looked him in the eye all day, but in another half hour he would take Ty upstairs and put him to bed. Then she would almost have to look at him, talk to him. What would they talk about? Perhaps he should say goodbye tonight and get on the road before any of them got up tomorrow. It would make things easier... maybe.

He looked across the table at Ty and felt a twinge or two. *I love this old man,* he realized, and the thought was so startling it shook him. He didn't dare hazard even a glance in Tina's direction. Even if he couldn't see her, he would have known where she was. The unique fragrance that was her filled the room. It reminded him of corny things like freshly mown hay, clover and honeysuckle.

Ty sat back in his chair, taking his eyes from the board on the table, which meant his concentration was slipping. It was time to get him ready for bed. "Have you had enough for one night?" Russell asked.

"Yeah, I guess so."

"Ready to go upstairs?"

"I reckon."

Russell stood and rounded the table to place a steadying hand under Ty's elbow. Gently he helped him out of the chair and led him to the stairs.

"Good night, Dad," Tina called after them.

There was no reaction from Ty, so Russell nudged him slightly. "She means you, sport."

"Huh? Oh...good night." The two men started up the stairs. "Who was that?" Ty asked.

"Tina."

"Oh. Does she come here often?"

"Yes, quite often." Russell felt so deeply for Tina—stuck in this lonely house, taking care of a man who didn't know who she was and couldn't appreciate all she did for him. It was a hell of a life.

"Here we go," he said, guiding Ty into his bedroom to begin the familiar routine. It was much the same as getting a child into bed—wash your hands, now your face, brush your teeth, here are your pajamas. But Ty was worse than a squirming child. He was lumbering and awkward, and sometimes when he was being stubborn he turned to a lead weight. The worse occasions were when he insisted that his pajamas weren't his and refused to wear them.

Tonight, however, he was cooperative. Once Russell finally had put him to bed, given him his medication and satisfied himself that he was settled for the night, he eased out of the room and crossed the hall to his own. Tucking Tina's gift into his shirt pocket, he went downstairs to face the ordeal of telling her goodbye.

She had put away the table, the chairs and the game. "Would you like coffee?" she asked.

"Sure, if you'll have a cup with me."

She nodded distractedly and headed for the kitchen, Russell right behind her. "Did Dad give you any trouble?"

"Not really, but I don't know how you ever managed. He doesn't help a bit."

Tina took cups and the instant coffee out of a cabinet. "I'm stronger than I look."

"Apparently. You don't look very strong at all."

She made the coffee and started to carry her cup to the table, then thought better of it. Their cozy evening chats could end right now. "Let's have this in the living room," she said, and without waiting for his okay, she left the kitchen.

She settled on the sofa and, much to her dismay, so did Russell, sitting too close to her. "I hope Jake and Ruby are having a good time," she said pointlessly.

"I'm sure they are."

"She doesn't get away from this place any more often than I do."

As much as Russell liked Jake and Ruby, he wasn't particularly interested in talking about them. He reached into his pocket and withdrew the little package. "Tina, I know this isn't much, and it doesn't begin to repay you for everything, but...it's a little token...." If he wasn't very good at buying gifts, he was worse at giving them. Turning up his palm, he thrust the tiny item toward her.

Tina stared at it as though she'd never before seen a gift-wrapped package. "Oh, Russell...please tell me...you didn't buy me a present."

"Go on, take it, open it. It's not all that much."

Tina took the package and noticed the gold sticker in the right-hand corner. If he'd bought it at Gresham's Jewelers, he'd paid too much for it. Why, oh, why hadn't she thought to get him something?

Carefully she unwrapped the package, and when she saw the earrings her eyes filled with tears. "Oh... they're beautiful. I...could...kill you."

"Do you really like them?" He knew he sounded like an eager little boy. "You can exchange them for something else if you want."

"Exchange them? I should say not! I'll cherish them the rest of my life." She removed the gold studs from her lobes and replaced them with the pearls. "There! How do they look?"

Not a whole helluva lot like a hundred dollars, he thought. "Pretty. I'm glad you like them."

"I love them, and I thank you so much." Leaning forward, she gave him a social kiss, rubbing her cheek against his. If she gave him a real kiss, she would break up completely and make a total fool out of herself.

Russell clasped his hands in front of him and studied them a minute. "Tina...if I write, will you answer?"

She hesitated. She didn't know if she wanted letters. They would only serve to keep his memory alive. But, then, he probably wouldn't write more than once or twice. "Of course."

"I'm going to be very anxious to know how Ty is. You, too."

"Oh, I'll be all right."

"You probably will be...but just all right isn't good enough. I'd like to think things are going to get much better for you."

"We'll see. As you know, I can only take things one day at a time." She lifted the cup to her mouth and sipped.

"I know. I'm . . . really going to miss all of you."

Oh, God! Tina's eyes stung. She vowed that if so much as one tear fell, she would go to her room, lock the door and not come out until he was twenty miles down the road. "I'm sure . . . all of us will miss you, too. More than you'll miss us. After all, you're going on to a new place, a new adventure. The rest of us will just keep doing what we were doing before."

"Yeah, I . . ." Words failed him. It was harder than he had expected, and he had expected it to be very, very difficult.

Tina set her cup on the coffee table and clasped her knees. "Have you ever given any thought to what you'll do if California doesn't turn out to be what you want?"

"Truthfully, no."

"You're that sure of it?"

"I was when I left Red Star."

"Well, I hope it's everything you want and more."

Russell set his cup beside hers and turned to her. "Do you really?"

No, I hope you hate it. But even if he did hate it, did she think for a minute he would return to this place? What was there to return to? A ranch that had known better days and was becoming more and more difficult to keep up? A sick old man and a woman who was so burdened with responsibilities that she was as much fun as strep throat? "Yes," she said with a lift of her chin, "I hope everything turns out well for you."

"You could help make it easier for me you know."

"Me? How?"

"By agreeing to move into town and hire help for Ty."

"Oh, Russell ... please don't start that again. I've told you why I don't want to do that."

"I know, but it doesn't wash. Listen, Tina ..." He took her hands in his and gave them a shake for emphasis. Earnestly he beseeched her with his eyes. "I just feel so damned bad about leaving you."

"You feel sorry for me, but you'll get over that."

"I don't think so. I know I'm going to worry about you."

"None of this is your problem."

"Surely you don't think I'm going to be able to drive away and never give another thought to what's happening here." He felt almost angry.

"No, I don't think that. I know you'll miss us for a while. But one of these days your stay here will just be a dim memory."

"Do you honestly believe that?"

"Stands to reason, doesn't it? Isn't that the normal progression—out of sight, out of mind?" Tina wondered who she was talking to—him or herself.

Russell seemed to be staring directly at her mouth. She wondered if he was thinking about kissing her. She was certainly thinking about kissing him.

They were so intent on each other that it was a minute before the noise penetrated their preoccupied minds.

But suddenly Tina cocked her head, and her eyes widened. "What was that?"

"What was what?"

"I heard something."

Another noise came from upstairs, right over their heads—a loud thud, as if something had fallen. Ty!

Russell and Tina were on their feet instantly, heading for the stairs.

The baby gate was firmly shut, and Ty was not in the hall. They bounded up the stairs, swung open the gate and ran to his room. When Russell threw open the door and flipped on the light, the sight that greeted Tina's eyes made her heart pound. Ty was standing in the middle of the room with a lamp in his hand. His eyes were wild, like those of a trapped animal. The bedside table that the lamp had been sitting on was over-turned.

"Dad!" she cried, forgetting she was never supposed to raise her voice when her father was upset.

Russell hadn't forgotten. Quickly assessing the situation, he eased into the room as casually as if nothing unusual was transpiring. When Ty saw him, he threw the lamp, missing Russell's head by inches. The lamp hit a dresser, broke into several pieces and fell to the floor. Russell continued advancing slowly, being careful to make no quick movements. To Tina's horror, her father lunged and swung at Russell with his fist.

The blow caught Russell right over his eye. Tina moved forward to help, but he turned to her. "Stay back," he said in the same tone he would have used if he had been asking her to pass the salt.

"Where is it?" Ty yelled. *"Where is it?"*

Russell put a hand on his shoulder. "Easy, sport. Everything's just fine."

Ty swung again; Russell skillfully ducked. Tina stepped back against the wall and clutched her throat.

"Where is it?" Ty repeated.

"Now, Ty, easy does it," Russell said, "I'm going to move around behind you. Everything's just fine." Slowly he stepped sideways until he was behind Ty. He put his hands on the old man's upper arms and stroked. "See, everything's fine. Relax ... just relax."

Ty's face was so flushed that Tina wondered if he was in danger of having a heart attack. Then his body sagged. He screwed up his face as if he was going to cry.

"Where is it?" he whimpered.

"Where's what, sport?" Russell asked calmly.

"The thing ... you know, I sit on it. Where is the goddamn thing?"

Tina was thoroughly perplexed. Her father obviously was talking about his chair, and it was right over th—

Her gaze fell on the piece of furniture, and a slow dawning overtook her. Now she understood. Slumping against the wall, she began crying softly.

Russell patted Ty reassuringly. "You mean your chair, don't you? It's right over there ... see?"

Ty stared at the chair. "Oh," he said.

Russell continued patting, stroking and crooning until he was sufficiently satisfied that Ty was calm enough to be put back in bed. The exertion had exhausted the old man, so sleep came quickly, but Russell wasn't taking any chances. He stood by the bed until Ty's breathing became even and shallow. That was when he first became aware of Tina's crying. Looking across the room, he saw her slumped against the wall.

"Don't cry, Tina. He's all right now."

She straightened and wiped at her eyes. Then she walked to the lamp and picked up the pieces, carefully feeling around for shards. "Now he's all right," she said sorrowfully, "but what will he be like in an hour ... or tomorrow?"

"He's sleeping soundly. I probably left him too soon when I put him to bed earlier. Here . . . give me that." He took the broken lamp out of her hands.

"Russell, you have a nasty scrape over your eye."

"Yeah, he got me good."

"Come across the hall and let me put something on it."

"It'll be all right."

"No, let me clean it with peroxide."

In the bathroom, as she daubed the spot over his eye, he asked, "What do you suppose brought on that outburst?"

Tina looked as though she might start crying again. "The ch-chair," she sniffed. "He must have gotten out of bed and wanted to sit in it. I moved it when I vacuumed this morning, and I f-forgot to put it back in its usual spot."

"Jesus! Do you mean that's what started all this?"

"I'm afraid so." Screwing the lid on the peroxide bottle, she sniffed again and wiped her eyes. "The sedative doesn't work anymore. Monday I'm going to have to call his doctor and ask him to give Dad something stronger. Then I can start worrying about what kind of problems that will bring on. Just when I think I can't stand one phase a minute longer, I don't have to because a new phase comes along to take its place." She put the bottle back in the medicine cabinet, and they left the bathroom. "I've heard about this sort of thing with dementia patients. It's called 'catastrophic reaction.'"

"That's pretty catastrophic, I'll agree," Russell said.

"I had about decided it wasn't going to be part of Dad's pattern. Everything's moving so fast . . . too fast."

Russell was worried about her. She looked very sad, which was understandable, but there was a defeated tone in her voice he'd never heard before.

They reached the bottom of the stairs.

"Where do you want me to put this?" he asked, indicating the lamp.

"In the trash out back, I guess. I'll buy something unbreakable Monday."

"Okay... and then I want to talk to you."

After depositing the lamp in the trash, he went into the living room, where Tina sat slumped on the sofa, the very picture of dejection.

She glanced up when he entered the room, and from the look on his face she thought she knew what was coming.

"Please don't start in on me about moving to Amarillo."

Russell knew there was no gentle way to say what he felt he must say. "What do you suppose would have happened if you had been here alone with Ty tonight?"

Her shoulders rose and fell. "I...don't know. You certainly handled it beautifully, but I forgot everything I'd ever learned. All I felt was panic."

"Of course. He's your father. Well, I'm telling you—there's no way you could have handled him. He looks frail, but when he's agitated he packs a mean wallop. If he had hit you the way he hit me, he might have knocked you down. He might have knocked you out. If I hadn't been here..." Russell shuddered at the thought. "He could have hurt you. He could have hurt himself. He was totally out of control."

"Well, I..." Tina spread her hands in a gesture of helplessness. She wished she could allow herself the luxury of losing control. She was just so tired of... everything. "I'm s-scared," she admitted aloud, and tears splashed down her cheeks.

Russell hurried to sit beside her and put a comforting arm around her shoulders. "You'd have to be. You have something to be scared of. Tina, I know you don't want to hear what I'm about to say..."

"Don't, please..."

"And I hate like hell to have to be the one to say it, but..."

"I don't want to hear any more about moving!"

"It's gone beyond that," Russell said as gently as he could. "You've got to put Ty in a place where he'll be safe, where he'll be taken care of around the clock. It's time. You can't do it anymore."

"Maybe we're overdramatizing an isolated incident," Tina said hopefully.

"What if we aren't?"

Tina looked off into space, lost in her private thoughts, so Russell waited. When she turned back to him, she said the last thing he would have expected to hear.

"Did I ever tell you why the Websters settled here in the Panhandle in the first place?"

Russell made a groaning sound. "What on earth does that have to do with anything?"

"My great-great-grandparents were from Alabama," she went on, as though he hadn't spoken. "They were about wiped out after the Civil War, so they decided to go to Oregon and start all over again. They planned and saved and dreamed about it for a long time, just the way you did with California. Finally they started out. But when they got this far, their youngest child died. They couldn't stand the thought of leaving the grave behind, so they unpacked the wagon and built a house not far from it. This must have been the loneliest spot on earth in those days.''

Russell rubbed his eyes tiredly. ''Tina, that's a touching story, but I don't see the point.''

''Family,'' she said simply. ''The Websters have always been high on family. The Crawfords, my mother's side, aren't like that at all. They're free spirits who go their own way and seldom see one another, but the Websters always think of family first. Guess I've got it in me. I can't stand the thought of Dad living with strangers, people who know nothing about him and don't really care.''

''But . . . Ty doesn't know who you are most of the time.''

''Maybe not, but . . . I know who he is.''

Russell sighed. He knew it was an agonizing decision and one only Tina could make. With affection, not passion, he drew her closer to him and guided her head to his shoulder. Wordless minutes passed, and they held on to each other. He felt a slight dampness seep through the fabric of his shirt, so he knew the tears were falling again. He wished he could cry. As it was, there was a lump in his throat the size of a Ping-Pong ball.

Lord, it was hard to believe that only weeks ago he hadn't known the Websters. Now he was so enmeshed with them that he found it impossible to extricate himself. They had plunged him into one of the greatest emotional upheavals of his life.

He wanted to know that Ty was safe and as content as a man in his condition could be. And he needed to know that Tina was safe . . . period. ''Will you admit it's

something you're going to have to do sooner or later?''
he asked.

"Y-yes."

"Is it going to be any easier, say, six months from
now?"

"N-no."

"You should at least investigate the homes near here
and know what's available and how much it's going to
cost."

"I will, I promise. I'll look into it."

Russell wondered. Without him here to keep after
her, would she? "I think we should start first thing
Monday."

Pulling back, she looked at him questioningly.
"'We'?"

"Ah, Tina, I can't leave without knowing what kind
of place he's going to live in."

"But...California..."

"I'll make it eventually. I have to know about Ty's
future. And tonight showed me that I can't go off and
leave you until he's no longer your sole responsibility."

"Do you realize I'll probably have to put him on a
waiting list?" Tina asked.

"Yes."

"And still you'll stay?"

"Yes."

Tina didn't waste her breath in feeble protest. The
relief and gratitude that flooded her prevented it. She
hadn't asked. She didn't think she had indicated in any
way that she wanted him to stay. She hadn't even
known how much she'd wanted it until he'd said he
would. "Russell, promise me something."

"If I can."

"If the wait turns out to be a lengthy one, if you start feeling restless and want to leave, please tell me. I'll understand."

"That's an easy-enough promise to make. I'm not one for suffering in silence."

It had been a tense, uncomfortable day and a frightening evening, but now life didn't seem so bleak. Tina felt as though she had just received a stay of execution. As she relaxed, a heavy weariness settled over her. "I'm so tired," she confessed.

"You look it. Hop on up to bed. Remember what I told you—you can't take care of your dad if you don't feel good yourself."

Numbly she nodded and got to her feet. "I don't know how to thank you."

Russell stood, too. "Thanks aren't necessary. I'm doing what I want to do."

"You're really fond of Dad, aren't you?"

He bent to place a light kiss on her cheek. "Yes, but it's not only Ty I'm fond of. I think you know that."

It was odd, Tina thought. She really didn't know this man well. Certainly she hadn't known him long. Yet he had come to represent everything she'd longed for during the past two years—strength, comfort, companionship and protection. "Good night, Russell."

"Good night, Tina. Sleep in tomorrow if you feel like it. I'll be here."

I'll be here. Tina thought those might possibly rival *I love you* as the most wonderful three words in the English language.

CHAPTER TEN

TINA SLEPT LATE Sunday morning, so by the time she was fully awake, Russell was in the middle of getting Ty ready for the day. She slipped on her robe, opened the door to her room and inched out into the hall to listen. From where she stood she could see her father sitting on the bed and Russell standing in front of him. She didn't have to hear more than a couple of sentences to know things were not going smoothly.

"Someone's stealing my clothes," Ty complained.

"What makes you think so, sport?" Russell asked.

"Those aren't mine. Someone's taking mine and leaving all that junk."

Tina watched Russell pretend to seriously study the shirt he was holding. "Well, if that's true, we're going to have to get to the bottom of it. But, fortunately, this shirt is your size. Until we find your own clothes, this will have to do. Here we go."

Ty refused to help, so Russell ended up dressing him.

"What's today?" Ty demanded at one point.

"Sunday."

"Why aren't we in church?"

"I don't know. Do you want me to ask Tina?"

"Who?"

"Would you like me to ask the lady across the hall why you aren't in church?"

"I think you should, don't you? We always used to go."

Tina hurried back into her room to dress quickly, thinking that Russell was going to need all the help he could get. But in the unfathomable way of Ty's illness, he was as docile as a lamb all during breakfast. Afterward, Jake took him into the living room to read the Sunday comics to him. Ty laughed in all the wrong places, but what difference did that make? He seemed to be having a good time.

Russell took advantage of Ty's being occupied to ask Tina a question. "Why don't you take him to church anymore?"

She rolled her eyes. "Because he started singing hymns all the way through the sermon. You can imagine the twitters and finger pointing. I could stand being embarrassed myself, but I couldn't stand his being the object of ridicule. It's a shame, really. Dad loved going to church, but I'm afraid it's not a good idea for us." She added with a smile, "The minister agrees with me."

"Church, huh?" Russell murmured thoughtfully. Pivoting, he went into the living room, where Jake was finishing with the comics. "How about church, sport?" he suggested.

"Good! Good!" Ty boomed.

Russell turned on the television and flipped the dial until he found a church service. Sure enough, Ty sang lustily through most of it, but he sat through the entire thing, his eyes glued to the screen.

Such a simple thing, Tina thought, her admiration for Russell growing by leaps. Why hadn't she thought of it?

There were a lot of things she wished she'd thought of. She wished she had had the foresight to start keeping a diary the day she'd learned the nature of her father's illness. Perhaps that would have helped her see patterns and learn what brought on fits of pique or temper or whatever.

Last night's episode, for instance. It had obviously been triggered by the misplaced chair, but what had precipitated other temper fits? And why was Sunday usually Ty's best day of the week? Was it because she, Russell, Ruby and Jake stayed inside, thereby filling up the house and staying close to him?

Maybe her father really did need to go "back where everyone was," she mused. Maybe he actually did need more people around him. There was so little for him to do here in the house. In a convalescent home there would be activities and people around from morning until night. Maybe he would be happier there.

Or maybe she was rationalizing.

Naturally, Ruby was bursting with curiosity about Russell's last-minute change of plans, though not especially surprised. "I figured he'd come up with something. Sure took him a heck of a long time, though."

She sobered, however, when Tina described Ty's behavior the night before and her decision to at least start thinking about a nursing home. Nobody knew better than Ruby what a heart-wrenching experience placing her father in a home would be for Tina. "What do you think you might do... afterward?"

"That's something you, Jake and I are going to have to talk about," Tina said. "Maybe... sell this place. That's certainly what Russell thinks I ought to do, and I know he has a point. It's impossible to find help, and

I feel guilty that Jake has so much to do. I can't afford to get sloppy and sentimental just because my great-great-grandparents dropped anchor here."

Ruby turned back to the sink. "Tina, did you remember that this Friday is when the lady from the adoption agency will be at Connie's?"

"Sure."

"I'd about decided not to go, but now that Russell will be here..."

"Go. Ruby, don't you ever let anything that's going on here keep you from your daughter. I seem... to be having a thing about family these days."

THAT NIGHT after supper, while Ruby and Jake kept Ty company, Tina and Russell once again enjoyed their coffee out on the back stoop. A curious sort of relaxation had taken hold of Tina. She had to assume Russell was the source of it. For sure the day itself hadn't been appreciably different from countless other Sundays, and it seemed to her she should have been upset and apprehensive about tomorrow. Actually searching for a home to put her father in was something she had dreaded since the day the doctor had given a name to Ty's peculiar behavior, and who could predict how she would feel tomorrow after wandering in and out of those places? She might be depressed down to her toenails. Tonight, however, she felt strangely peaceful.

"Russell, have you ever felt content and happy when there was almost nothing to be happy about?"

Russell looked at her, a small smile on his face. She had been in a fey mood all evening; he'd noticed it at supper. There was a light in her eyes, a bit of a sparkle he hadn't seen before. In masculine fashion, he hoped he'd had a hand in putting it there. "Is that the way you feel now?"

"Uh-hmm. I wonder what's wrong with me."

His smile widened. "That reminds me of something I read once, can't remember where. It went something like...if you can keep your head while all about you are losing theirs and blaming it on you, you might not fully understand the situation."

Tina chuckled. "Oh, I think I understand what's going on. Maybe...maybe I've just decided not to think about it for a couple of hours."

"Lord, Tina, if you feel happy, don't analyze it. Just enjoy it."

"You're right." She closed her eyes and breathed deeply, enjoying the evening air.

Russell watched her, thinking how nice it was to look at Tina when she was happy. What a delight she must have been in earlier, more carefree days. All day he had speculated on what might have happened had they met in another place, under different circumstances. By now they probably would have been lovers. He fancied that she was attracted to him, and he knew damn well he was attracted to her.

This was not the first time he had thought about making love to Tina, but he'd never considered it seriously because of the tenuous nature of their relationship. From the night he'd first kissed her right here on this stoop, he had repeatedly reminded himself that the last thing Tina needed was another emotional involvement at this difficult time of her life.

But that was then and this was now. He was here for an extended, unspecified length of time...weeks or months, who knew? Without the prospect of his leaving hanging over their heads, a lot could happen between them in that amount of time. The prospect was unbelievably exciting. He studied her more intently.

Tina didn't seem aware that she was under scrutiny. In fact, she seemed a million miles away, deep in thought, and that was the last place he wanted her to be. Russell tipped her chin up with one finger, grinning at her. That brought her back to the here and now.

"What are you thinking?" he asked.

The corners of her mouth lifted, and she smiled a winsome smile. "Oh... it's silly..."

"Everyone should have the right to be silly occasionally."

"I was thinking—wishing, really—that right now, this minute could last forever."

"That would be nice, wouldn't it?"

He continued to study her face for a second or two before bending his head to kiss her. And this time, instead of merely accepting his kiss, she leaned into it. Her arms slid up his chest and her hands locked behind his neck. He pulled her closer, until they were hip to hip, thigh to thigh. Without breaking the kiss, they maneuvered until they fit together perfectly, like two coiled snakes.

Had anyone told Russell that something as simple as a kiss could shake him to his toes, he would not have believed it. It wasn't even their first kiss. But this one was different.

Lifting his head, he looked down at Tina, and the wonderment he saw in her face pleased him more than anything in his life ever had. His heart thumped so loudly he was sure she could hear it. For the first time in years he genuinely desired a woman, not simply lusted after her. Instead of hurting, the desire felt good.

It was nice to feel something special for someone special. The moment was magical.

Was tonight too soon? Many times he had lain awake in his room and thought of her sleeping next door, in a bed as lonely as his. Once Ty was asleep and Jake and Ruby were in their downstairs bedroom next to the office, it was as though he and Tina were alone in the house. He wondered if similar thoughts had ever crossed her mind.

"Tina, I..."

"Russell, I..."

They stopped and exchanged smiles. Then Tina's arms dropped from his neck and slid around his waist. Squirming to just the right position, she snuggled into the circle his arms made for her and pressed her cheek against his chest. Russell heard her utter a sound of the utmost contentment, like the purring of a cat. It was enough for a minute simply to hold her.

The doorknob behind them rattled noisily. Breaking apart, they turned to find Jake staring at them with a sheepish grin.

"Sorry, folks...but, Tina, there's a fella on the phone name of Hollis Reed. Says he had a message to call you."

"Oh...yes. He's a man who attends the support-group meetings. I called him this afternoon."

"Want me to tell 'im you're busy?"

"No, I'll take the call. He's so hard to get hold of." Tina glanced at Russell, wondering if he regretted the interruption as much as she did. "I really need to talk to him before tomorrow. I'll...be right back."

"I'll be here," he assured her.

Tina hopped up and followed Jake into the house. She used the phone in the office where she could easily take notes. "Hollis, thanks so much for returning my call."

"Don't mention it, Tina. How can I help you?"

"I've about decided to start looking for a long-term care center for Dad."

"I'm sorry. It's not an easy decision to make. I know."

"Is Mildred doing all right?"

"As well as can be expected, thanks."

Tina opened the middle drawer of the desk and withdrew a sheet of paper. "I wrote down a list of places out of the phone book."

Hollis asked her to read the list. She did, and there were three he told her to forget.

"The rest are okay, some better than others," he added. "I'm not one hundred percent satisfied with the place Mildred's in, but it was the best I could afford. God, it's expensive, Tina."

"I expected it to be. My friend and I are going to start investigating tomorrow, and I don't really know what to look for."

Hollis first mentioned the obvious—a clean facility, cheerful staff, plenty of activities. "But when I was shopping for a place for Mildred, I noticed some things I wouldn't have thought of. If you see a bunch of old people sitting around in their pajamas and robes in the middle of the day, find out why. If the staff discourages visitors at mealtimes, be suspicious. The food's either lousy or indifferent. And there's another thing…harder to describe. You want a place where the staff treats the patients with a certain…oh, *dignity* is the word, I guess. If you hear the nurses and orderlies using baby talk, look somewhere else. And you don't want a hospital atmosphere, either. Mildred doesn't

need a hospital. She needs a place to live where she can
be cared for properly."

Tina scribbled down everything, thanked Hollis
profusely and hung up. So many considerations, she
thought morosely. Pray she made the right choice.
Then she remembered Russell waiting for her. She
hurried through the house and out the back door to
rejoin him.

Russell glanced up when the door opened, and his
soaring spirits plummeted. There would be no romance tonight. He had no idea what the call had been
about, but her worry lines were back. The slump of her
shoulders as she sat down next to him told him that the
magic was gone.

But that was all right, he told himself as he took her
hand. It had come once. It would again.

BY MIDAFTERNOON the following day, Tina was so
discouraged she was near tears. She and Russell had
been looking at homes since ten that morning. They
had been in and out of half a dozen care facilities, and
she had seen everything Hollis had warned her about
and more. She didn't think she was being overly picky.
Russell had agreed with her on all counts. If anything,
he was more particular than she was.

There was one more name on her list, but Tina was
about ready to call it a day.

Russell, however, was adamant. "Let's not leave a
stone unturned. Besides, I like its name. Fairhope.
Nice."

Fairhope Manor was not located in Amarillo proper
but in a small community south of the city, quite a
drive from the ranch. Tina didn't mind the drive, but

she held out little hope that a small town could offer something she couldn't find in the city.

Actually seeing the place did not encourage her, either. Though the grounds were beautifully landscaped and well kept, the structure was anything but imposing. Unless Tina missed her guess, Fairhope Manor had once been a motel.

But when she and Russell stepped through the entrance doors, she gasped. What once had been a lobby was now a charming reception area furnished in bright, cheerful prints. Huge windows looked out over an enclosed courtyard. There were plants and flowers everywhere. She even heard music and laughter. "It's lovely," Tina whispered to Russell.

He agreed. "For sure it doesn't look like a nursing home."

The friendly, fortyish woman who greeted them introduced herself as Edna Lowell. "My husband, Collin, and I own Fairhope Manor. Collin's a gerontological psychologist, and since we live here, he's always on duty. Come on and I'll show you around."

Thirty-five minutes later, Tina couldn't believe her good fortune. Everything about Fairhope Manor was what she had dreamed of—wide halls, spacious rooms, cheerful colors, smiling faces. The dining room smelled like the kitchen at home. The bulletin board listed dozens of weekly activities, from arts-and-crafts lessons to church services and singalongs. She was sure there were many very sick people behind closed doors, but the ones she saw in the public rooms were occupied and seemed reasonably content. The overall atmosphere was pleasantly serene.

But the most amazing thing to Tina was the presence of children. She saw three, one of them not over four or five.

"Ours," Edna explained. "They have full run of the place. You'd be surprised how many of our residents respond favorably to them. Of course, not all do, but kids are smart. They gravitate toward the people who like them and stay away from those that don't. By the way, would the two of you care to stay for dinner? The first seating is at six."

Tina and Russell exchanged pleased looks. "I'm afraid not," Tina said. "But thanks—thanks a lot."

Once the tour was over, Edna invited them into her office. "I'll want you to tell me all about your father. We need an extensive history in order to evaluate the kind of care he needs."

When Edna had said "extensive," she had meant it literally, including as much about Ty's childhood as Tina knew.

Finally it was time to ask the difficult questions. "I suppose there's an incredibly long waiting list."

"Well, there is a waiting list, but not all our residents are here for long-term care. Many are here because they temporarily need more intensive care than they can get at home. The turnover is greater than you might think."

The cost was also greater than Tina had thought, but it was worth it. She knew she would never be satisfied with any of the other places now that she had seen this one. She asked Edna to place Ty on the waiting list. It was the most traumatic experience of her life.

"PLEASE TELL ME I did the right thing," Tina pleaded as they drove away from Fairhope Manor.

"Believe me, you did the right thing," Russell said. "You did the only thing. But...can you afford it?" He hated to ask about her financial circumstances, but he'd almost choked when he'd heard it would cost more than two thousand dollars a month to keep Ty there.

"Yes, I think so. Just. Dad's money will be what pays for his care. I have very little of my own. There was no divorce settlement since children weren't involved, and I haven't been able to work in more than two years. I pay myself a small salary for keeping the books, and the ranch just about breaks even. Dad lives off the interest of investments he made in the flush days, and that ought to just about take care of Fairhope...with a little bit left over."

"Enough to take care of yourself?"

"Uh-huh. Remember, once Dad moves, I can go back to work."

They drove in silence a few minutes, Tina staring out the window. She had done all the driving that day since she knew her way around, but now Russell was behind the wheel. He didn't want to pressure her into conversation, but there was one thing he simply had to say to her.

"Tina, I've got some money...."

She jerked her head around. "Oh, Russell, no!"

"I'm perfectly serious. I saved a bundle while I was on the road."

"California money?"

He shrugged. "It would be better spent on Ty if you need it."

Tina reached over and patted his shoulder. "That's awfully sweet of you, but if I needed money, I'd hit Becca up first...or Mom." The words were no sooner out of her mouth than she uttered a little groan. "Something just occurred to me. I really should stop in and see Mom...just for a minute. She doesn't live far from here. Would you mind terribly?"

Russell didn't mind at all. For the first time in recent memory he was wearing a coat and tie, and he was rather curious about Joan Webster. Whenever Tina talked about her mother, it was with an odd mixture of admiration and exasperation. "That's fine with me."

"This is a good time, since Becca's out of town. I'd never be forgiven visiting one and not the other, which is ridiculous. I don't think they're that anxious to see me. Stop at that convenience store on the corner. I'll give Mom a call first to make sure she's home."

Joan was home and was delighted that her daughter and a friend wanted to stop by. Tina's mother turned out to be exactly what Russell had expected—proper and elegant, from her widow's peak to the toes of her expensive shoes. She reminded him a great deal of Becca, but not at all of Tina.

After ushering Tina and Russell in and offering them something to drink, she addressed her daughter. "What brings you into town today, dear?"

Tina told her, and the color drained from Joan's face. "Oh, Tina, you mean...is Ty really in such a bad way?"

Russell thought it strange, even disgraceful, that apparently neither Joan nor Becca had taken the time to learn anything about Alzheimer's. He looked at Tina.

"I've been trying to tell you that for months," she said. "Dad is demented."

"Tina!" Joan gasped. "What a hideous thing to say!"

"That's the name for it," Tina said quietly. "Dad is suffering from a dementia."

"Well...there must be a gentler way to describe him. To call him 'demented' sounds so... brutal."

Tina could see that she had thoroughly rattled Joan, and she regretted that. She would be careful in the future. She was so accustomed to discussing her father's condition with Russell, who by now knew as much about Alzheimer's as she did. They used the words the medical people used. She guessed those words would sound cruel to her mother. There had been a time when Tina had wished Joan would visit Ty. She no longer did. Let her mother remember her father the way he used to be. She changed the subject.

"Have you heard from Becca?"

Joan's face brightened. "Yes. She says they're having a glorious time."

The rest of the conversation was limited to small talk, and Tina deliberately kept the visit short. She could tell her mother was impressed with Russell, and she herself was a bit surprised at how smooth and urbane he could be. He looked wonderfully handsome in a business suit, though he'd confessed to despising such attire and never wearing it unless an occasion absolutely demanded it. The expression on Joan's face clearly indicated that she was pleased her daughter had found such a "suitable" young man.

When it was time to leave, Joan walked them to the door. Extending her hand to Russell, she said, "It was a pleasure meeting you, Russell. Please come again."

"Thank you, Mrs. Webster. I'm happy to have met you, too. Tina talks about you so much."

"I suppose I've really been remiss. I didn't ask you what line of work you're in."

"Until recently, I was an over-the-roader."

Joan frowned. "I beg your pardon."

"I drove an eighteen-wheeler."

Her mother's poise never failed her, Tina noticed. Joan barely flinched.

SOME TIME LATER, Russell eased the Thunderbird in behind the pickup at the side of the house and switched off the engine.

"I wish we didn't have to go inside," Tina said wistfully.

"So do I."

"I wish we could turn around and drive off, just drive anywhere and not come back until we were good and ready."

"So do I."

A long sigh escaped Tina's lips. "But we can't."

"No, unfortunately we can't."

Tina slung her handbag over her shoulder and reached for the door handle. "Thanks."

"For what?" Russell asked.

"For...everything. For just being there."

He understood. His presence had given her the courage to do the hateful thing she had to do. He was glad he had been of help. He wished there were more he could do. "You're welcome," he said, and opened the car door.

In the kitchen Ruby was just finishing cleaning up after supper. "I didn't know whether to wait on you two or not."

"I'm glad you didn't. Russell and I will heat up something. How's Dad?"

"Not too bad. Didn't eat much." Ruby hesitated before asking, "Did you do it?"

Tina nodded, and Ruby sighed sadly.

"It's really a nice place," Russell offered. "Better than I . . . than we had hoped for."

"There's no such thing as a nice . . . one of those places," Ruby muttered.

Russell followed Tina into the living room, where Ty and Jake were watching television. At least, Jake was watching, Ty was staring at the wall. Tina sat down and faced her father squarely. "Dad, Russell and I saw a wonderful place today," she said gently.

Ty looked at her blankly. "Oh?"

"Yes. It had great big windows and lots of beautiful flowers. There were people everywhere and many things to do. There even were children." She swallowed away the lump in her throat. "It was very pretty."

"That's nice," Ty said. "Maybe someday you can take me there."

CHAPTER ELEVEN

WHEN JAKE AND RUBY finally ambled off to bed after the ten o'clock news, Russell turned out the lights and checked the front door. Tina had gone upstairs perhaps twenty-five minutes earlier, looking as beaten as a whipped puppy. He imagined she was long asleep by now, but when he reached the top of the stairs and fastened the baby gate, he saw that her door was ajar and her light was on. She had looked so tired earlier; maybe she had fallen asleep without turning off the light. He first checked on Ty, then peeked into Tina's room.

The light came from a small lamp atop a chest of drawers. The four-poster bed had been turned down— she slept on blue-and-white check sheets, he noted— but Tina was standing across the room at a window, staring out at the black night. Her arms were crossed, and her head was resting against the molding. She was wearing a white floor-length robe that fastened under her breasts and fell in soft folds.

She's so lovely, Russell thought. Pensive and sad, but very lovely. Softly he rapped twice on the open door.

Tina turned. She wasn't surprised to see him. In fact, she would have been bitterly disappointed if he had merely gone to his own room. She had deliberately left the lamp on and the door ajar, hoping he would come to check in on her.

It amazed her that she wasn't more nervous and unsure about what she intended doing. A premeditated seduction was totally uncharacteristic of the woman she normally was, but it was very in keeping with the way she felt tonight. Without Russell she would have felt alone. As wonderful as Jake and Ruby were, they did not give her the sense of being-in-this-together that Russell did. In the past, she had accepted his willingness to help—shamelessly, she sometimes thought. Well, tonight she needed him in a different way.

She wasn't entirely without qualms, however. Having never instigated a seduction, she wasn't sure how to proceed. How would he interpret her wanting him to make love to her? Being honest, she supposed there was a chance he would turn her down. He'd do it graciously, of course—so skillfully and gently she would hardly know she was being rebuffed...until she thought about it later.

That was a chance she would have to take. "Hi," she said. "Has everyone turned in?"

"Yes. I just checked on Ty, and he's sleeping soundly."

"Thanks. Your patience with him never flags, does it? I'm afraid mine does much too often."

"That's because you remember him when he was wise and strong and took care of you. I've only known him the way he is now." Hesitantly Russell stepped into the room. "Would you like me to get you something to help you sleep?"

"No, I'll sleep eventually."

He advanced another step or two, watching her carefully. If the slightest hint of disapproval crossed her face, he would beat a hasty retreat. But she behaved as though it was perfectly normal for him to come into her room at bedtime.

"What are you doing?" he asked.

"Thinking. Feeling sorry for myself, actually. And for Dad...and for all those people living at Fairhope."

Russell stopped when he got within a few feet of her. "Don't ponder it too much, Tina. You did what you had to do. He'll be in a place that's a lot better than most."

Now that he was so close to her he could see that the robe had intricate embroidery at the neck, which scooped low enough to reveal the gentle swell of her breasts. Her face was free of makeup, and she looked fresh, clean, very vulnerable and incredibly desirable. A sharp sensation stabbed at his groin.

"Do you know what I've been wondering?" she asked.

"What?"

"I've been wondering if I'll ever want to have children."

Russell stiffened. So that was what she had been thinking about. She had been in such a mood all evening, withdrawn, lost in some private reverie. "Good Lord, I don't like that kind of thinking."

"I'm serious, Russell. Maybe I waited too long. I'll never be a twenty-three-year-old mother...I'll be, at best, a thirty-something mother. So when my child is fortyish, I'll be old enough to be 'a problem.' I'm not sure I want a child of mine to ever have to agonize over what to do about Mama."

Russell quickly closed the space between them and gathered her into his arms. "Tina, Tina...this alarms me—it really does. Now stop it. Thinking along those lines can't help but make you blue, and you sure don't need that right now."

She slipped her arms around his waist and melted against him. Russell tried to remember that all she needed was to be held. Most people did when they were upset. But he found it impossible to hold Tina without wanting much more. He stroked her hair and let her cling, while trying his best to keep his more erotic thoughts in check.

Several long silent moments passed before she said, "You feel good."

"That's nice to know."

She clutched him a little tighter. "You feel strong, like a . . . a harbor of refuge, a port in a storm."

Russell didn't know what to say. He wasn't sure he could say anything. He thought he was strangling. The reality of Tina's delectable body pressed against him rendered rational thought almost impossible.

"Do you know what else I've been wondering?" she murmured.

"Wh-what?"

"I've been wondering if I want to be alone to-night."

Blood rushed to Russell's head; he heard it drumming in his ears. "And . . . have you reached a decision?"

Tina took a step backward. Her eyes dipped, then lifted and looked at him boldly. "I don't want to be. Please stay with me." That said, she stepped back into his embrace.

Only two very flimsy layers of cloth separated his palms from her flesh. She felt pliantly warm and dainty, while he suddenly felt huge and clumsy. Exhilarated to the point of mindlessness, he still managed to caution himself. This was the time to exercise control. The motive behind her invitation was simple—she wanted comfort and solace, not passion. He had to remember that, to keep his own lust reined in and his touch gentle. If he handled this right, the all-consuming heat would come later.

"Tina." Taking her face in his hands, he rained a shower of light kisses over her forehead, cheeks and throat before closing his mouth over hers. He thought he felt her lips quiver when his touched them. So, she wasn't completely sure about this. All the more reason to proceed with care. He would have liked to kiss her savagely, but that would have spoiled everything, destroyed everything she'd hoped to gain from making love. He forced himself to keep the kiss thorough and deep, but sweet at the same time.

A shudder rippled through Tina's body, and her knees threatened to give way altogether. Russell felt her sag, and he quickly cupped her buttocks to steady her.

"Close the door," she whispered.

He released her and crossed the room in long strides to close and lock the door. Fleetingly he considered turning off the lamp, then decided against it. He would only if she asked him to. Turning back to the bed, he saw Tina's robe flutter to the floor to lay in a puddle at her feet. What she wore underneath was white and skimpy and revealed a body that to Russell's eyes was perfection itself—full high breasts, small waist, taut belly and slender, shapely legs.

She knelt on the bed and opened her arms, beckoning to him. Russell's feet seemed to weigh ten pounds each as he walked toward the bed. Impatiently he

tugged his shirt free of his waistband. As he reached for
its top button, Tina said, "No! Let me do that."

He let his hands drop to his sides, and advanced to
the edge of the bed. Her fingers deftly freed the shirt
buttons from their holes and pushed the garment off
his shoulders. Then she laid her cheek in the clump of
hair on his chest.

Maleness is so fascinating, Tina thought. *Wonderfully wide shoulders, all those beautiful muscles, that
taut, tanned skin. Adonis could not be more beautiful
than Russell is.* She could hardly wait to see the rest of
him, to feel the rest of him. With the tip of her tongue
she teased his flat brown nipples, while her hands
roamed over his chest, his arms and down his back.

Gritting his teeth, Russell clutched the bedpost and
allowed her to stroke, pet and discover until he could
stand it no longer. He stepped back, quickly divested
himself of the rest of his clothes, then joined her on the
bed. With one fluid motion, he pulled her nightgown
over her head. They knelt, facing each other, and luxuriously caressed. He filled his hands with her breasts.
Tina closed her eyes, and a sound escaped—part sigh,
part moan.

Since his divorce, all the lovemaking Russell had experienced had been of the casual variety, demanding
only his body, never his mind, certainly not his heart.
But this was different. Tonight every fiber of his being
was involved. He kissed her once, twice, three times,
each kiss a little fiercer, a little deeper than the one before. He moved slowly, touching all the right spots and
giving her the opportunity to savor the sensations he
was arousing in her. He watched her face, gauging her
responses—heavy lidded eyes, parted lips, quick
breathing. Her luscious breasts strained against his

palms. He had only to look at her face to know he was doing the right things. She was completely aroused, held captive by desire. Now she wanted and needed him.

Tiny eruptions went off inside Tina, and fueled by Russell's masterful touch, the shower of sparks soon became an inferno. The volcanic response brought every part of her to life, tingling, throbbing, aching. Her body began to sway involuntarily to some primitive beat. The desire had become almost unbearable. "Russell . . . please . . ."

He moved over her and slid her beneath him. She arched toward him, searching for the fulfillment she knew he would bring her. As their bodies united, they quickly found the rhythm most pleasing to them both. They kept it up until they both jerked convulsively in completion. Russell was surprised to realize that the loudest cry of ecstasy had come from his own throat.

TINA HAD EXPERIENCED good sex before. But what she had once considered good paled by comparison with Russell's lovemaking. Often during her marriage she had silently accused Paul of caring twice as much about his own satisfaction as he did hers. Somehow she knew that Russell would have been deeply disappointed had she not exploded in that mind-shattering orgasm she was only now recovering from. His technique bordered on being courtly and worshipful, yet he had brought her to heights of blazing passion that had almost been unendurable. She wondered where such a solitary man had so expertly learned the art of pleasing a woman. Then, on second thought, she decided she never wanted to find out.

"Tina, are you awake?"

Russell's voice sounded as if it were coming through fog.

"Uh-huh. Half. Don't ask me to do anything vigorous, like move. I think all my bones have melted."

He rolled over and kissed her tenderly. "Do you want me to go to my room?"

"No! Why would I?"

"I only wondered if you would be embarrassed if Jake or Ruby came upstairs..."

"They wouldn't, not in the middle of the night, not unless I called. But even if they did... Ruby's always telling me I lead an unnatural life. She'd probably be pleased as punch to know that we're up here frolicking in my bed. What's more natural than that?" She giggled, then sobered. "Russell, do you think I'm terrible for wanting...this from you? I mean, the same day I put my father's name on—"

Russell quickly silenced her with another kiss. "Yes," he growled. "Disgraceful. I'm filled with remorse over having been a party to it. Oh, Tina...of course I don't think you're terrible. You needed comforting. Lovemaking, done right, should be a comfort...and that, love, was done right."

Tina stretched and purred. "I know. It was wonderful."

The words were no sooner out of her mouth than a dispiriting thought occurred to her. *And it will be one more thing to miss when he leaves.*

Oh, she was a hopeless case! She had forgotten how to enjoy life's pleasures for fretting over its ifs. She had known when she'd enticed him into her boudoir that what she would get was an interlude, a memory. But such a welcome one. She had promised herself she would enjoy, seize the moment and worry about tomorrow tomorrow, and that was precisely what she was going to do.

Turning her head on the pillow, she looked at the magnificent male body stretched out beside her. He smiled at her enigmatically—a male version of Mona Lisa's smile. She would have given anything to know what he was thinking.

Russell was thinking that Tina was the most exciting person alive. She also was the easiest to be with, even with all her problems. She was intelligent, thoughtful, caring and sweet. Now he could add sexy to the list of adjectives. She had stirred his senses as no other woman ever had. He would have liked to tell her he loved her and to hear her say she loved him. But the word *love* implied a commitment that neither of them could possibly be ready to make. Yet at that moment he did love her...very much.

He slid his arm beneath her shoulders and pulled her to him. Her light, delicate body found its niche and settled against him.

"I guess by now you've figured out that I planned every bit of this," she said.

Russell frowned. "What?"

"Come on. Don't try to tell me you don't know why the door was open, why the lamp was still on."

It slowly dawned on him what she meant. He raised on one elbow to look down at her. "I don't know when I've felt so flattered."

"You don't think I'm a wicked, wanton, shameless hussy?"

"Hussy? Where in the hell did you hear a word like that?"

"Hey, I read."

He grinned. "Oh, yes. I've seen some of your books lying around. The covers are very interesting. There always seems to be a bare-chested guy trying to rip the dress of a very well-endowed woman."

"Why do you think they're called bodice-rippers?"

He kissed her soundly. "You've made me very happy. This night has been magical."

"I'm so glad. You've made me happy, too."

"Tell me something...what if I hadn't nibbled at the bait?"

"I'm...not sure. I suppose I would have gone to your room." Once again Tina felt her body begin to stir. She pressed against him insistently, and within seconds she felt his turgid response. Why was he so exciting? Actually, they were two very ordinary people. Yet when they were together, they seemed extraordinary.

His mouth was on her ear. His warm breath stoked the fire. "I want you, Russell."

"God knows, I want you, too."

"Tell me what you like, what I can do to please you."

A guttural sound came out of his throat. He rolled over on his back and pulled her on top of him. "You," he said. "You please me. Anything, Tina...anything. Please yourself and you'll please me...I promise."

DURING THE following week, Tina felt herself falling in love. Having been through the process before, she had no trouble recognizing the signs. Her heart was on a roller coaster. When Russell touched her, no matter how casually, it stopped altogether. Her cheeks flamed whenever he looked at her, for now there was intimacy in his gaze. When they talked, the simplest subjects took on an air of monumental importance. Sometimes it seemed she lived only for night and their time together.

There were differences between her marriage and her infatuation with Russell. The first time she and Paul had made love they had known each other a long time and had mapped out their future. She had been completely comfortable and sure of herself from the beginning. She certainly couldn't say that now. She was very uncertain about what her and Russell's affair meant to him. Was it a meaningful experience ... or a delightful romp, a fling? It was the one thing she couldn't talk to him about.

As for the future ... well, Tina wouldn't let herself even dwell on that. The future for them was as cloudy as a storm-filled day. Realizing that, she often asked herself some pertinent questions. Was she really falling in love or simply having a wonderful time? Was she only lonely and starved for affection, or was Russell truly the most exciting man she'd ever known? If their relationship ended tomorrow, would she be heartbroken or merely regretful? If becoming romantically involved with him wasn't the smartest thing she'd ever done, was it the dumbest? There were no answers, only questions.

Still, considering everything, Tina was happier than she had been in a long time. If either Jake or Ruby noticed the stars in her eyes or the look of pure contentment on Russell's face, they were careful to keep it to themselves.

Ruby certainly never mentioned that Tina came down to breakfast each morning looking excited and expectant, or that she appeared to be doing more with herself, not simply throwing on whatever was handy, brushing her hair and swiping on lipstick. She and Jake, in private, might smile knowingly and wonder aloud if Tina and Russell really thought they hadn't noticed love in bloom, but on the surface they pretended everything was the same. If it hadn't been for Ty, Ruby thought, her darling Tina might have found life pleasant, indeed.

TINA HAD LEARNED to expect the unexpected from her father, and he rarely disappointed her. So when he began wanting to take his afternoon naps in his bedroom instead of his living-room chair, she didn't attempt to subtly change his mind. Though it was easier for her to keep an eye on him in his chair, she went along. She simply had Russell go into town and buy a room monitor, the kind parents keep in an infant's nursery.

Of course, a nap in his bed also meant adding another undress/dress-again session to the daily routine, and she received varying degrees of cooperation from Ty. And once she had him tucked in, she had to wait at his bedside until she was sure he was asleep.

On Friday afternoon, however, she discovered she had something else to contend with.

"There's a black dog sleeping at the foot of my bed," Ty grumbled irritably. "I want him gone."

Tina, busy hanging up his clothes, threw a glance at the foot of the bed. "Do you remember Ebony, Dad?"

"Who?"

"Ebony, the little Scottie I had. You loved for him to sleep at the foot of your bed. You said he was a lot of company."

That apparently satisfied Ty. He laid his head on the pillow. "Well, he could at least not take up so damned much room."

Tina adjusted the blinds on the windows, then walked to the edge of the bed to stare fondly and sadly at her father. As his breathing became even, she leaned over to smooth the covers, and her foot hit something under the bed. Getting down on her knees, she saw that it was a shoe box. She pulled it out and inspected its contents. Then her shoulders heaved, and her eyes filled with tears. She waited until Ty was sleeping soundly before carrying the box out of the room and down the stairs to the kitchen.

Russell was backing out of the refrigerator. In his hands was the pitcher of tea. Hearing her enter the room, he turned with a grin, but the grin faded the minute he saw her crestfallen face. Tina viciously slammed the box down on the table, plopped in one of the chairs and put her head in her hands. "I hate this disease, hate it!" she cried. "It's a maniac!"

He frowned his concern. "What now?"

"This!" She thumped the box and began removing its contents one by one. "Used tissues, a worn-smooth emery board I threw away after giving Dad a manicure. Three pennies, a plastic spoon, a handful of bobby pins, some rubber bands, two used paper napkins, a cuticle stick... Oh, oh, that's no good. He could poke himself in the eye with that." She shoved the stick aside.

"I... I don't understand," he said. "Where'd you get that junk?"

"From under Dad's bed. He probably put the box there for safekeeping. I'll bet he doesn't even remember it's there."

Russell set the pitcher on the table and sat across from her. "Well, is... is there anything really wrong with Ty's gathering up all that stuff? It looks pretty harmless to me."

"Oh, it's not dangerous, but it's hoarding, and that means he's going through another of dementia's phases. It's so crazy, like Dad's reading a textbook on Alzheimer's and imitating the behavior patterns step by step. Now he's begun hallucinating. There's a black dog sleeping at the foot of his bed. I wonder how long the dog will be with us." She ran her fingers through her hair. "I hope I handled that one right. I know you're not supposed to go along with the hallucination. I knew I shouldn't say, 'Oh, what a cute doggie.' Other than that ... I'm never sure ..."

Russell reached across the table and took one of her hands in his. "Tina, please don't analyze every move you make. I think you do damned good. So Ty thinks there's a dog in his room. As long as it doesn't upset him, what difference does it make? Personally, I hope the dog sticks around. He might make a perfect companion for your dad."

"I guess you're right, but ... Do you know what really worries me?"

"Everything in the world apparently."

"In support group we were told that there's often a straw-that-broke-the-camel's-back aspect to caregiving. A person will put up and put up with the most maddening behavior, then one insignificant little thing will happen and ... ping! Off the deep end."

"You're not going to go off the deep end ... because I'm here. I'll step in long before you crack."

Tina laid his palm against her cheek and pressed. "I know. What on earth would I do without you?" Immediately she regretted having said that. Half the reason he still was with them, she suspected, was that he'd felt guilty about leaving. She didn't want guilt or pity to have a hand in keeping him there.

Shaking herself out of her depressed mood, she began putting Ty's "treasures" back in the box. "I'd better stick this under the bed again, just in case Dad remembers where he left it. And all of us are going to have to be damned careful about what we throw away or leave lying around from now on."

"Agreed." Satisfied that she was all right for the time being, Russell stood up. "I'm going to get back to Jake now, unless you need me in here."

"No, no... go on."

"What are you going to do this afternoon?"

"Take the monitor in the living room and read until Dad wakes up, I guess."

"Will Ruby be back tonight?"

"I don't know. Probably not. So you guys are stuck with my cooking again." She gave him a lame smile.

"Keep your chin up, love."

"Yeah...sure." Tina stared after him until the back door closed behind him. There was one positive note to the hoarding and hallucinating, although she probably wouldn't have admitted as much to anyone, maybe not even Russell. She felt less guilty about putting Ty's name on that waiting list. If his condition continued to deteriorate at its present pace, she wouldn't be able to handle him in a few months. There was so much ahead—delusions, maybe. Then apathy, depression, loss of motor control. For his own safety, she now knew he belonged at Fairhope. That made her feel a little better. Not much... but a little.

Tina folded her arms on the table and rested her head on them. *I am a wonderful person,* she chanted silently. *I'm doing the best I can under terrible circumstances. But I'm only human...*

RUBY LOOKED AT Connie suspiciously. "What are you trying to say to me, honey?"

"Ma..." Connie cleared her throat nervously. "Today's meeting with Mrs. Guerra was the best we've ever had. In fact, today's the best day I've had since you were last here... across the board. Alejandro was almost... pleasant. That can't be a coincidence."

"So?"

"Well... John and I were talking about it the other night, and... we want you and Dad to move in with us."

"What?"

"I mean it, Ma. We can take the back bedroom and the sun porch, and with some remodeling, they could be turned into kind of an apartment for you. Maybe we could add another bath and—"

"Wait a minute, Connie. Ever since you were born, your pa and I have vowed and declared we would never live with you. We've set aside money that's strictly to take care of us in our old age. No, baby. Jake would never go for it. I won't live in my daughter's house."

"But I need you. You live in a stranger's house, and that doesn't seem to bother you."

"Ty and Tina are anything but strangers."

"You know what I mean. They aren't family."

"Exactly why I don't mind living with them," Ruby said stubbornly.

Connie chewed her bottom lip and studied a fingernail. "I casually mentioned to Mrs. Guerra that I was going to suggest this to you, and she said she wouldn't have any qualms at all about finalizing the adoption if you were living in the house. She said it's remarkable how Alejandro warms to you."

Ruby sighed. "I wish you hadn't done that, not without talking to me first. You know the problems at the ranch."

"Are Tina's problems more important than mine? I thought you said Mr. Webster is going into a home."

"We don't know when. We don't really know what's going to happen."

"What about that man who's at the ranch now, the one Tina's supposed to be so crazy about? Can't he help her?"

"For sure none of us knows what Russell's going to do. Right now, I'm needed there."

"You're needed here, too."

Ruby was no idiot, even though she had been foolish over her daughter since day one. She could envision what would happen if she and Jake moved in with Connie, John and the kids. At first they would merely "help out." But John was overworked and hardly had a minute to spare. All around the house Ruby could see things crying out for a handyman's touch. Jake wouldn't be able to stand that, so he'd take over. Then, as life settled into a comfortable groove, as it would if she and Jake were there, she could already hear Connie's reasoning: *There's really not much for me to do, Ma. I'm thinking maybe I should go back to work and let John give up that night job.* And next thing Ruby would know, she'd be in charge of a house and three kids—packing their lunches, being there when they came home from school, making them do their homework—just at the time of life when she and Jake should be thinking of getting a small place and taking life a little easier. No, thanks.

Besides, Jake would never go for living in his son-in-law's house. He and John had absolutely nothing in common except love for Connie, and that seemed more competitive than companionable. Even if the two men had been the best of pals, Jake wouldn't move in. He stubbornly reminded Ruby over and over that their daughter needed to lie in the bed she'd made. "We warned her a hunnerd goddanged times that she had no business adoptin' them three kids," he'd said. "Did she listen? 'Course not. Don't go bailin' her out, babe. I ain't sayin' you can't help her out ever once in a while, but give that gal an inch and she'll take a mile."

Ruby hated to admit it, but there was a lot of truth in what her husband said. Yet right now Connie really needed help. Maybe she'd brought her problems on herself, but they existed. And Ruby knew she would help, maybe a little less than Connie wanted and a little more than Jake thought she should, but she would help.

"Give me a little time, honey. I won't move in with you, but once Ty is settled and we know what Tina's going to do, I'll move closer to you. Will that do?"

"I guess it'll have to, won't it?"

Ruby had never talked to Connie about her deep feelings for the Websters, so her daughter would have no idea what difficult days these were for her. She thought she was prepared to say goodbye to Ty one day soon, not in words but in her heart. But she honestly didn't know how she was ever going to say goodbye to Tina.

CHAPTER TWELVE

LIFE WAS AS SLOW as it ever got on the ranch except in the dead of winter. The wheat was in, ending that phase of the yearly cycle. The yield had been slightly lower than the previous year's, as had the profit, but when one lived off the land, one became accustomed to such fluctuations. That's why they had diversified. If one crop failed, another, hopefully, would yield bountifully.

The corn harvest was a couple of months away, and the cotton wouldn't be picked until cold weather nipped at it. Most of the cattle were in feedlots, and the dog days were upon them. Russell and Jake did more tinkering than working. Had it not been for the demands Ty made on their time, the days would have been idle, indeed.

Sometimes in the early morning, when the air was cool and still and Ty was dressed and settled for the day, Tina liked to carry a cup of coffee out onto the back stoop, there to sit and stare at the far horizon. "This is wonderful country," her father used to tell her, "and do you know what the best thing about it is? There's not one thing here that would even remotely interest a tourist."

Of course that wasn't entirely true. The Palo Duro Canyon south of Amarillo drew plenty of tourists, and the city itself had many attractions. But Ty had meant

Leatrice and its environs. It was highly unlikely that anyone would drive five minutes out of the way to see it. Which, Tina thought, made Russell's advent in her life seem all the more improbable, all the more fateful.

Much to her surprise, she had received a long letter from Paul. She'd had misgivings about opening it, but it turned out to be chatty. He brought her up to date on some of their old friends and their old haunts. Paul's motives in writing it weren't entirely clear to her. Had he hoped to revive old memories, perhaps start her thinking about the good times? She even gave some thought to answering it, then decided that probably wasn't such a good idea. No sense in making him think something might exist that didn't.

But in the letter Paul said something that caught Tina's attention. He mentioned having received a phone call from Becca. Since when had those two become so chummy? Tina wondered. She had talked to her sister only once since the Jenningses' return from Bermuda. Naturally, the first thing she'd told Becca was about Fairhope.

"Tina, you did the right thing," Becca had said. "I know how difficult it must have been for you, but there was no alternative."

"I hope you realize that once Dad is actually there, we'll both have to visit him often." She emphasized "often."

"Oh, sure... of course. Then maybe you'll leave that depressing little community and move into the city... unless other things happen."

"Like what?"

"Who can predict? Things happen. But if you're here, we can see more of each other."

Tina wondered if living in Amarillo would make any real difference in the amount of time she spent with her family. It seemed she was always the one who instigated visits and phone calls. She hadn't seen or heard from her mother since the day she and Russell had stopped by after visiting Fairhope. Becca's and Joan's lives were so different from hers, and she couldn't see that changing no matter where she lived. Whenever she imagined living in the city, she saw herself working, attending the support-group meetings and visiting her father. Never did a busy social life enter the picture.

And always there was something vital missing from the scenario. Russell. She often tried very hard to imagine Russell and her together, strolling hand and hand through life, but nothing much came to her. Whenever Russell entered her mind's eye, he was dressed in jeans and boots, either tagging along after Jake or sitting at the card table with Ty. So if Ty was at Fairhope and the ranch was sold ... Her thoughts would brake and go no further.

Russell never mentioned California anymore, but neither did he mention putting down roots in West Texas. She longed to ask what he intended doing once Ty was in Fairhope, but the words would stick in her throat. She simply enjoyed him and their affair. He was a sensitive, accomplished lover, and she was, if not on cloud nine, then certainly happier than she had been in a very long time. She was going to savor every precious minute she was with him. If that was sticking her head in the sand, that was the way it had to be.

THE CALL from Edna Lowell came on a Wednesday afternoon while Ty was taking his nap. "Tina, one of our residents is moving back home tomorrow. He roomed with a man named Harve Chesterton, and in going through my applications, it occurred to me that your father and Harve might be well suited to each other. Do you have a minute to discuss this with me?"

Tina sank into a chair. Her chest suddenly felt constricted, and her eyes burned. So soon, she thought. "Yes, of course."

"Though Harve shows early signs of dementia, he still is a relatively healthy man. He's with us mainly because he has no family except for a sister in Phoenix, whom he refuses to go live with. He himself admits he shouldn't live alone, so he elected to move here. He's about Mr. Webster's age and is a retired navy man. I thought since they both are veterans, that might be a common interest. How does it sound, Tina? It might be some time before we have another opening."

Harve sounded as though he would be perfect for her father. Why, then, did her throat burn? Why were tears running down her face? "This g-gentleman . . . Mr. Chesterton . . . er, Harve . . . does he know about Dad, about his condition?"

"I wouldn't discuss Mr. Webster with him until I'd talked to you. But I've been at this for a lot of years, Tina, so I'll point out a few things to you. One, your father's transition from home to here will be easier if he has company with him most of the time. Two, Harve still has most of his faculties, so he can watch your father, and three, Harve likes being in charge of something or someone. Military, you know. Also, he's lived in this area ever since his retirement, which must have been . . . oh, goodness, twenty or so years ago. He has a wealth of friends who visit him frequently. Didn't you tell me that Mr. Webster expresses a need for more people around him?"

"Y-yes."

"He might rather enjoy Harve."

Tina swallowed away the lump in her throat. "Edna, thanks so much. Can you give me a few minutes? There's someone I want to discuss this with. I'll get right back to you."

"Of course, Tina. I know how difficult this is. I'll be waiting for your call. But I really can't hold the vacancy long. There are so many waiting."

"I understand. I'll get back to you in no time."

After hanging up the phone, Tina sat with her hand on the receiver, staring off across the room. It was odd that she wasn't better prepared for this. It was something that had been hovering in the back of her mind for weeks, but now it seemed to have come out of the blue. She had thought taking care of her father for the past two years was difficult. She had thought putting his name on Fairhope's waiting list was difficult. Nothing could touch this. The guilt was enormous. She felt lost, floundering in a sea of uncertainty, and she knew she couldn't commit Ty without talking to Russell. Perhaps it wasn't fair to drag him into this, and in the end she and she alone would have to make the decision, but she at least had to talk to him.

She carried the room monitor into the kitchen and set it on the counter. "Listen for Dad, will you Ruby? I have to find Russell."

The tone of Tina's voice instantly alerted Ruby to some kind of trouble. "Sure. He can't be far. All four vehicles are parked right outside."

"I won't be long."

Tina found Russell in the barn, the one place where it was possible to escape the worst of the afternoon heat. It had been years since any livestock had been housed there; the structure was dark, relatively cool and smelled of the hay, a shirtless Russell was pitching up into the loft. Seeing her, he stopped his work and smiled.

"I've got to talk to you," she said, sitting on a rung of the ladder leading to the loft.

He dropped the pitchfork. She looked positively gray. "What's wrong?"

"Edna Lowell just called."

"Who?"

"The lady at Fairhope. They have an opening."

Russell's chest heaved. He came to stand in front of her and take her face in his hands. "Oh, sweetheart..."

"It happened awfully fast, didn't it? But someone moved back home. Dad would have a roommate...." Haltingly she told him about Harve Chesterton. "Whwhat do you think?"

"What can I think? I don't want him to go, but...I know he must. Maybe this fellow Harve...well, he might be good for Ty. Here he seems to do nothing but sit or sleep. At Fairhope there are people and activities and..." The words trailed off. He couldn't think of anything really encouraging to say.

Tina pressed her cheek against his smooth, taut belly, and he held it there. Everything inside her trembled. "We're not talking about sometime anymore," she said. "Not months or weeks but...days. Maybe day after tomorrow."

"I know, but would it be any easier two, three weeks from now?"

"It's so peculiar. A month ago, I thought I was overburdened, that I couldn't possibly do all I needed to do. Now...I find myself wondering what in the world I'll do with my time when Dad is gone." Shoving aside emotions she couldn't afford, she slipped her arms around Russell's waist, gave him a squeeze, then stood up. "I'll go call Edna before I lose my nerve."

Russell watched her hurry out of the barn; then he returned to his work, pitching the hay with a vengeance. It was awful for Tina to have to make such a decision. He knew the guilt she must be feeling, and he wasn't entirely free of the emotion himself. He'd been the one who'd convinced her it was time to get serious about finding a home for Ty.

He viciously jammed the pitchfork into the haystack. Since the day he and Tina had found Fairhope, all of them had been primed for the day Ty would actually leave them. Ruby kept his clothes ready at all times; when a shirt came off, it was laundered immediately. In her bedroom Tina had a suitcase packed with toilet articles and other essentials, so there would be no need for a last-minute flurry of packing, nothing that might get Ty upset. So why did decision time seem to have hit like a thunderbolt?

Russell worked like a man possessed until he was out of breath. Then he stuck the pitchfork's tines in the dirt, folded his arms on its handle and pressed his forehead against them. It suddenly dawned on him that Tina wasn't the only one with a fateful decision to make. He had one, too, and it no longer could be relegated to one of these days. The realization left him stunned. Did he pursue his dream or abandon it altogether? He knew what he wanted to do. He just wasn't sure if Tina would cooperate.

ONCE SHE HAD TOLD Edna they would take the opening, Tina knew it wouldn't be wise to delay her father's actual move. Russell agreed, so on Friday morning they drove Ty to Fairhope.

"Is this where everybody is?" Ty asked as he got out of the car.

"Yes," Tina said.

"It doesn't look the same."

Tina had attempted to get Becca to accompany them. She had thought it was something they should do together. But Becca, as usual, had a rash of excuses. She had engagements that simply couldn't be broken. She was very sorry, but... So, also as usual, Tina was left with the hateful chore. This time, at least she had Russell to help.

Edna was waiting for them. She greeted Ty with the air of a hostess welcoming a dinner guest, and she immediately ushered him to his room. Tina had not tried to explain to Ty that he would be staying here. She didn't think it would have done any good. She was going to take it step by step, play it by ear and hope for the best. If Ty became fearful or agitated, Edna had assured her the staff knew how to handle it.

That such a thing didn't happen Tina attributed solely to Harve Chesterton. He was a hail-fellow type of man who didn't know the meaning of the word *stranger*. The minute Edna Lowell ushered them into the room, Harve was on his feet, glad-handing everyone.

"Come in, come in," he boomed. "I'm Harve Chesterton."

"Hello," Ty said. "How's the family?"

"Don't have anybody but my sister, and I can't say we get along all that good. She makes noises about wanting me to come to Phoenix, but I personally think that's so much b.s. You must be Ty. Glad to have you.

Been waiting for you. Sit down and take the load off your feet."

"Thanks," Ty said, plopping down in one of the room's two easy chairs. He glanced around. "Nice place you have here, Merv."

"Harve. Edna tells me you were in the war."

"Damned right I was."

Tina noticed that neither man clarified which war they were referring to. She supposed that as far as they were concerned there'd been only one.

"Were you in Europe or the South Pacific?" Harve asked, settling into the other chair.

"South Pacific," Ty said. "Seabees."

"Aw, you guys did a helluva job, helluva job. I was with the Third Fleet, old Bull Halsey's command."

My God, Tina thought, *we could have searched the world over and not found someone as perfect for Dad.*

Just then Harve looked up at her. "Well, aren't you a pretty thing!"

Tina smiled broadly. "Why, thank you."

"Isn't she a pretty thing, Ty?"

Ty looked at her as though he'd never seen her before. "Yeah, she is. Tell Herb here your name."

"Harve!"

"I'm Tina, Harve. Ty's daughter." She extended her hand, and Harve pumped it vigorously.

Ty leaned toward Harve, his expression eager. "Say, did I ever tell you about the refrigeration unit my outfit put in ..."

While all this was going on, Russell was unobtrusively slipping in and out of the room, carrying in Ty's things from the car and putting them away. That done, he snooped around, making sure Harve didn't have medication or other dangerous substances lying around. Satisfied that all was secure, he joined Tina.

Ty, obviously delighted with his new audience, seemed to have forgotten them entirely. Tina sent up a silent prayer that this would prove to be the best thing she could have done for her father. She also hoped that Harve was a man of limitless patience. The refrigeration story was winding to a close, but it wouldn't be the last time he'd hear it, she'd bet on that.

Harve had some war stories of his own to tell, and surprisingly he had Ty's full attention. Naval battles were apparently far more interesting than anything Tina had ever come up with. She and Russell listened patiently to the two men for another half hour or so. She hated to leave but knew she should, and in all honesty, her father didn't seem to know or care that she was there. Finally Harve gave her the perfect opening.

"Say," he said, slapping his knee, "you picked a perfect day to come, Ty. The kids come on Friday afternoon."

"What kids?" Ty asked.

"Some kids from one of the schools come and put on a show for us. But that's after lunch. By the way, they've got good food here, real good."

"They never fed me in that other place."

Harve stood up. "We've got everything here, everything. Do you want me to show you around? Do you like Ping-Pong?"

Tina wondered if her father was still coordinated enough to play. But, then, what difference did it make as long as he was occupied and had company? She stepped forward and placed her hand on Ty's shoulder. "I've got to go now, Dad. You stay here and visit with Harve, and I'll see you later."

"Sure, sure," Ty said with a little wave. He stood up and followed Harve out of the room.

Russell took Tina by the hand and urged her out into the hall. She cast a longing look at her father's retreating figure. She felt like a pressure cooker about to blow its lid.

"Are you okay?" Russell asked solicitously.

"I . . . I guess so. Oh, Russell, what's going to happen when he realizes I've gone, that he's going to have to stay here from now on?"

"He probably won't ever realize that, Tina. At least, not the way you or I would."

"I feel terrible . . . just walking away."

"It's best not to have a farewell scene, don't you think?"

"I . . . guess so. I don't know. . . ."

"Please try to relax. It had to be done, and now it is. He seems happy enough."

She nodded and sighed.

"Would you like to go see your mother or Becca?"

"Good grief, no!" Tina said irritably. "They're the last people I want to see today."

Russell understood. "Well, how about lunch in Amarillo? And we can go shopping afterward if you like."

"Men hate to shop with women."

"That, sweetheart, is a rather broad generalization. I don't hate to shop. We can do anything you want to do." The one thing Russell didn't think she ought to do was go home, not right away.

"We can, can't we?" she said with a touch of disbelief in her voice. For more than two years, whenever she had been away from home, she had been filled with a sense of urgency, an overwhelming need to get back.

Now... She glanced at the door to her father's room. "We don't have to hurry home, not anymore."

"Then let's not." Gently taking her by the arm, Russell led her to the entrance. "What sounds good for lunch?"

"There's a place near Mom's apartment that has the best green chili enchiladas."

"Green chili enchiladas, coming up."

Tina was amazed to discover she was ravenous. Ever since Edna's phone call, she had all but choked on food, but that afternoon she ate hungrily. She studiously avoided mentioning her father even once. After lunch, she and Russell spent hours at a mall. It had been a long time since she had enjoyed the luxury of leisurely shopping, and everything was a delight, everything but the prices. She saw dozens of things she would have liked to have, but mindful of the need to watch her money, she restricted her purchases to two blouses and some cosmetics.

It was late afternoon when they returned to the ranch. Russell had watched her intently all afternoon, looking for signs of a backlash from the tensions of the previous two days, and he thought she had handled the day beautifully. He'd even noticed some of the strain that had seemed permanently etched around her eyes was gone. But the real test would come when they went inside and she realized she didn't have to march straight into the living room to see how Ty was.

Ruby wasn't in the kitchen, but at the sound of the back door opening she came out of her room, glanced anxiously from Tina to Russell, then bit back all the questions she was dying to ask. Instead she motioned toward the table. "Tina, I found that under Ty's bed.

I didn't know if I should keep it or not. It doesn't look like anything very important."

The minute Tina saw the shoe box filled with her father's "treasures," she cracked. "Ohh..." she wailed, sinking into one of the chairs and letting the tears pour. She sobbed and sobbed noisily.

Russell walked to stand behind her, to stroke her shoulders sympathetically.

Ruby couldn't have been more alarmed. She looked at Russell with puzzled eyes. "Wh-what did I do? What is it?" she cried.

"The straw that broke the camel's back," he said sadly.

SHORTLY AFTER ten-thirty that night, Russell silently entered Tina's room and closed the door behind him. She was propped up in bed waiting for him, red eyed but no longer crying. He had thought she'd never stop, and Ruby had been at a loss, having never seen Tina break down. Russell now understood that instead of being controlled all afternoon, Tina had actually been tightly wound and ready to spring. Personally, he was glad she had gotten it out of her system.

"Headache?" he asked.

She nodded. "A granddaddy from all that crying."

"Did you take something?"

"Uh-huh. A couple of aspirin. I'm sure I look a fright."

"You look damned good to me. You always do. I've got something for you."

"Oh?"

From behind his back he produced some sort of garment that he held up for her inspection. Tina gasped. It was a dress she had admired while shopping that afternoon. Actually, she had fallen in love with it and had kept going back to finger it. But she'd decided it was much too expensive for the life she led. It was the kind of dress the fashion magazines referred to as "office-to-dinner," and she never went to either an office or out to dinner. "Oh, Russell . . ."

"Don't tell me. I shouldn't have."

"You really shouldn't have."

"I saw you casting covetous eyes on it, so I thought you should have it."

"It's very impractical."

"Must you always be practical?"

"You're sweet, always thoughtful. Thanks so much. Come over here and let me thank you properly."

He leaned over the bed, and she kissed him soundly. Then he straightened. "What do you want me to do with it?" he asked, indicating the dress.

"Just lay it over the back of that chair. It'll have to be pressed before it can be worn."

He laid the dress carefully on the chair, then proceeded to treat Tina to a delightful male striptease before joining her under the sheets.

"You're a very sexy man," she murmured.

"And you're a sexy lady. I guess we were meant for each other, huh?" Gathering her to him, he kissed and stroked, petted and primed, nipped and nuzzled, until he felt all the tension leave her body. Then he made slow, lingering love to her, until she was weak and sated in his arms.

"You're so wonderful," she murmured dreamily.

"So are you. Magnificent. Without question the most fantastic woman I've ever known."

Tina slithered against him, seeking the most comfortable position, curling one leg between his. She rubbed her cheek against the mat of hair on his chest and caressed his nipple with her fingertip. "Your body absolutely fascinates me."

"Good. I hope studying it becomes a lifelong interest. Sweetheart, I want to talk to you."

"Talk? What could you possibly want to talk about?"

There was a lengthy pause before he said, "California."

Tina stiffened in his arms. She tried to pull away, but he clamped his legs together, imprisoning her. "How...could...you?" she cried. "Tonight of all nights!"

"You don't understand," he said gently.

"You're certainly right about that. I've known we'd have to talk about it sooner or later, but your timing is lousy. If there's anything I don't want to talk about tonight it's California."

"Tina...sweetheart...please listen to me. What I mean is—you and me, let's go to California together."

"Wh-what?"

He gave her a little shake. "I can't bear the thought of leaving you. I love you. I want us to go to California together, and I want to do it right. Tina, I'm asking you to marry me."

CHAPTER THIRTEEN

TINA SPRANG AWAY from him, and this time he let her go.

"Russell!" she cried.

"Is it really that big a surprise?"

"I...I thought..."

"What? Surely you didn't think I was saying goodbye."

"I...I didn't know what to think." He had just told her he loved her. He had asked her to marry him! She should have been delirious with joy. Yet she felt like crying again. "Why are you doing this to me? You know I can't go to California."

"Why not?"

"A dozen reasons. Chiefly, Dad."

Naturally Russell had anticipated that. "He doesn't know you as Tina, his daughter, anymore. Sweetheart, as long as Ty has someone around, he really doesn't care who it is. I hate saying that to you because it sounds so brutal, but...it's the truth."

"But...I have to see him. I'd worry myself sick if I couldn't see him."

"You can come back as often as you like. You know Jake and Ruby will visit him often, and you'll have to tell Becca she must, that it's her responsibility."

"Oh, Russell, I don't know. Dad, the ranch...Jake and Ruby. And Becca is totally unreliable when it

comes to anything but what she wants to do.'' Her head
spun. There were so many considerations.

"Is the ranch really a big problem? I assumed that
once Ty was at Fairhope, you'd put it up for sale. You
can't run it, Tina. Why would you even want to try?''

"I don't know. It's been home for so long, but I
don't think that's it. Where would Jake and Ruby go—
what would they do? They've lived here a long time,
too.''

Russell was hamstrung by his promise to Jake. He
badly wanted to tell Tina that Jake's back gave him a
fit half the time and that Ruby wanted to move closer
to Connie. Those were things that would have made a
difference to Tina, but he couldn't use them. "They're
not getting any younger. They've reached a time in life
when they ought to be able to take it easy.''

Tina's breath fluttered out on a suspended sigh. She
laid back down in the circle of his arms. "I...just don't
know. I'm so confused.''

Russell said nothing for a minute, merely kissed the
top of her head and stroked her hair. Then... "Would
you like to go?''

"What?''

"Forget everything else for a minute. Pretend those
other considerations don't exist. Answer one question. Would you like to go to California with me?''

"Of course I would.''

"Maybe I got the cart before the horse. I probably
should have first asked if you want to marry me.''

"More than anything. I love you.'' That she could
say without hesitation.

"Don't you think you've earned the right to do
something you want to do for a change?''

Tina didn't know how to think about what she wanted to do. Even in her more carefree days she hadn't been a rash or impulsive person. She supposed the boldest move of her life had been to quit college and marry Paul while her father was begging her to finish her education. And look how that had turned out. "It's not that easy, Russell. It's never been that easy, not for me. I have to think about what I should do."

"Well, sweetheart, nothing can be done tomorrow or the next day or the next. Something like what I've suggested will require weeks of preparation. Now you know how I feel and what I want. So just sleep on it, hmm?"

Sleep came easily for Russell, but it proved to be next to impossible for Tina. The hours ticked by, and she hardly closed her eyes. What he was offering her sounded like paradise, but paradise came with a price. She would have to leave behind all that was familiar and begin a new life half a continent away. That she could handle, but what about visiting Ty? The only way she could see her father would be to hop on a plane. She knew Ty didn't seem to recognize her, but since no one was certain how an Alzheimer victim's mind worked, how could she be sure? Just thinking of her father sitting in his room, wondering where she was, sent cold chills through her. She had assumed she would visit him several times a week, that he would occupy large chunks of her time. The guilt that now seemed to be as much a part of her as the color of her eyes rushed over her like a wave.

Scrunching up her pillow, she stared at Russell's sleeping figure. The weeks since they had become lovers had been good for her. Instead of feeling tired and

dull and constricted all the time, she felt young and
feminine and alive. Could she go back to being that
tiresome other person, the one whose life had seemed
to be nothing but a series of lows?

And because she was in love and badly wanted what
Russell offered, she reminded herself of a few things.
She meant a lot to Russell; she meant nothing to her
father. It wasn't his fault or hers, just the result of that
hateful disease. She had done everything she could for
Ty. Now didn't she deserve her own happiness?

Gently Tina laid her hand on Russell's chest and felt
the steady thumping of his heart. He loved her! And he
wanted her to share his dream with him. Oh, it was
tempting!

Yet, one nagging thought gripped her and wouldn't
let go. She knew she shouldn't be so greedy, but she
wanted more. She wanted to hear him say that if she
didn't go to California, he wouldn't, either.

WHEN TINA FINALLY WENT downstairs the following
morning, Ruby informed her that Jake and Russell
would be in Leatrice most of the morning.

"They had a bunch of stuff to pick up, and Jake
thinks the Jeep's running a little ragged. He's going to
take it by Shaw's and see if Leon knows what's wrong
with it. Good Lord, Tina, you look awful. Bad night?"

"Very bad. It must have been after four before I finally fell asleep."

"Worrying about Ty?"

"That and three dozen other things." Tina made a
quick cup of instant coffee and carried it to the table.

"Let me get you some breakfast."

"Don't bother. I'll have toast or a muffin. It's too
late for breakfast."

Tina stared over the rim of the coffee cup, lost in thought. She had hoped the light of day would bring great flashes of insight as to what she should do. It hadn't. Her first thought upon waking had been of her father—what kind of night had he spent, how was he being cared for, had he eaten lunch, dinner and breakfast? Her second thought had been of Russell and what he so enticingly represented—love and freedom. She was as confused as ever.

Ruby watched her and waited a minute or two, thinking some explanation might be forthcoming. When Tina said nothing, she gave in to her curiosity. "Want to talk?"

Tina put down her cup and looked at Ruby. "I've got a big decision to make."

"I had hoped your days of big decisions were over."

"Wait until you hear this one. It's a lulu. Russell has asked me to marry him, and . . . he wants me to go to California with him."

Ruby's mouth dropped, and her eyes widened. "Are you going to do it?"

Tina took a deep breath. "Oh, Ruby, I don't see how I can. I've tried justifying it every way in the world, but I always come back to Dad. I'm afraid I'd worry about him all the time, and what kind of start would that be for a marriage?"

"Do you want to marry him?" Ruby asked sensibly.

Tina smiled wistfully. "Sure I do. In case you hadn't noticed, I'm nuts about the guy."

"Do you want to go to California?"

Tina's smile faded. "It sounds wonderful, but it's so damned far away. Why couldn't Russell's dream have

always been to settle down in Albuquerque or...
Lubbock?"

"Oh, Tina, you've done and done for Ty. You did
the hard part, the twenty-four-hour business. Let Becca
take over now. Let her get her butt over to sit with him
a few hours three times a week."

"You know how dependable she is."

"I'll personally haul her over to that place if I have
to."

Tina smiled. Ruby would, too.

"You have a chance to make a new life for yourself," Ruby persisted. "Grab it. I promise that Jake
and I will visit Ty every week, and I'll write and let you
know how he's doing."

Ruby's impassioned stance was something of a surprise for Tina. Since the day her mother and sister had
moved to Amarillo, Ruby had been her main maternal
influence, and a rather protective one at that. She'd
expected a few doubts, a bit of reluctance. "You know,
Ruby, it's not just Dad. I have to think about you and
Jake, too. This has been your home since I was a little
kid."

"Tina, please don't give us a thought. As a matter of
fact..." Ruby glanced away for a minute, then back at
Tina. "I should have talked to you about this before, I
guess. It's Connie. She's up to her eyelashes in problems with those kids, especially Alejandro, and she
really needs me, at least until the adoption is finalized.
As soon as Ty went in that place...well, I was going
to have to tell you I'd be leaving."

"Leaving?" Tina cried.

"Actually, Connie wants Jake and me to move in
with her, but my momma didn't raise a fool. I know
exactly what would happen if I moved in. Connie

would turn over the whole shebang to me and go back to teaching. No, thanks. But Jake and I have talked about getting a little house somewhere closer to her. He swears that as long as you're here, he's staying, but he shouldn't. His back just kills him some days, so he shouldn't be doing the kind of work he does."

Tina couldn't have been more astonished. "Where have I been all this time, in a cave? How come I didn't know any of this?"

"We didn't want to bother you with it, not with all you've had to worry about." Ruby reached across the table and squeezed one of Tina's hands. "You know, you've been just like my own kid. I wasn't about to leave while you still had Ty to take care of. I figured you didn't ask for any of your problems, and Connie took on hers with her eyes wide open. But...she has them, and I want to help. Believe me, leaving this ranch is going to be the hardest thing I've ever done."

"Oh, Ruby...everything's happening so fast."

"Go with Russell. He's a good man. He'll always look out for you. Don't miss this chance."

So she would be losing Ruby right away and Jake eventually. That knowledge should have made her decision easier. Obviously the ranch would have to be put up for sale. That would have had to happen even if she'd never met Russell. Why was she still so confused and uncertain?

Draining her coffee, Tina stood and carried the cup to the sink. "Let's not bother cleaning house today, okay? I think the world will survive if the dusting and vacuuming don't get done one Saturday. I'm going to see Dad."

"Tina, it's only been a day."

"I know, but I want to find out what kind of night he had, if he ate dinner and breakfast."

"Can't you call and speak to the woman who runs the place? You haven't had anything to eat."

"I'll grab something in town. I just want to see him." Tina took the pickup's keys off the hook beside the back door. "Don't wait for me for...anything."

Although she did want to see her father, she had another reason for going to Fairhope. She wanted to talk to Edna Lowell. Tina hated being so indecisive. All her life she had made decisions and taken her lumps when they turned out to be bad ones. She'd also never been one for pouring out her woes to whoever would listen. She'd often been amazed when people she didn't know well told her the most intimate details about their private lives. But the past two years had changed a lot of that. The support group had taught her that talking to an uninvolved third party could sometimes put things in perspective. Anyway, it couldn't hurt.

It was after ten-thirty when Tina arrived at Fairhope. All of the early-morning chores for the residents were over. Baths had been given, medication dispensed, everyone was dressed and the day's activities had begun. She first checked the game room and the television parlor for signs of her father. Not seeing him, she headed for his room. She had reached for the knob, when the door swung open and one of the young orderlies stepped out into the hall. He was grinning from ear to ear.

Tina inclined her head toward the room. "Are Mr. Webster and Mr. Chesterton in there?"

"Oh, yes, they're in there."

"How are they?"

"They're in fine fettle this morning. General MacArthur just promised to return to the Philippines."

Tina entered the room in time to hear Harve say, "MacArthur didn't have any choice. He had to go to Australia. Roosevelt ordered him to, and, goddamn it, he was the president!"

"Good morning, all," she said cheerfully.

Harve twisted in his chair. "Well, good morning, Tina. Come in, come in."

Unfortunately, Tina noticed, Ty looked a little put out that the conversation had been interrupted. Undaunted, she crossed the room and dropped a light kiss on his cheek. "Did you sleep well?"

"He slept like a baby," Harve answered.

"How was breakfast?" Tina still addressed Ty.

"He ate an omelet and two biscuits," Harve said. "I ate his sausage 'cause it didn't appear he was going to."

"Well, that's good. So, everything seems to be going okay."

"Fine, fine. Ty and I were just doing a little reminiscing, though he doesn't seem to think quite as highly of MacArthur as I do."

Then her father was simply being contrary, Tina knew. Ty Webster worshiped every place Douglas MacArthur had ever stepped.

"How about staying and having lunch with us, Tina?" Harve suggested. "Good food here, real good."

That might be a good idea, she thought. "I think I will, but first I want to go speak to Edna. Do either of you want something from up front?"

"No, we've still got some talking to do," Harve said. "Right, Ty?"

"Right," he grunted.

"Then I'll see both of you at lunch."

Out in the hall, Tina paused to think over what she had seen and heard. Her father was clean-shaven and dressed in slacks and a freshly pressed shirt. He had company; he wasn't just sitting somewhere alone. She did wonder if Harve's answering all her questions was a good idea, but at least she got truthful answers. Ty probably didn't remember whether he had eaten breakfast or not, and he certainly wouldn't remember what he had eaten. But her most lingering impression was of the way he had looked at her, or rather through her. He hadn't said one word to her, nor had he acknowledged her presence in any way. At home he had been forced to notice her, even if he didn't know who she was. At home she had still been part of his life. Now it seemed she no longer was.

I've got to stop thinking this way, she reminded herself. Squaring her shoulders, she went down the hall to the front of the building where Edna's office was located. The receptionist told her to go right in.

"Good morning, Tina," Edna said in greeting. "Have a seat. I didn't expect to see you quite so soon."

"I guess I feel like a mother who's just sent her oldest child off to kindergarten."

Edna smiled knowingly. "Your father's first day with us was very successful. He and Harve seem to be getting along famously."

Tina folded her hands primly in her lap. "I did want to see Dad, of course, but I actually am here this morning because I wanted to talk to you."

Edna gave her her full attention. "That's what I'm here for."

Now Tina felt foolish about baring all to someone she hardly knew, but there wasn't much she could do but start talking. As succinctly as possible, she explained the situation with Russell and California. Edna didn't have to ask what the problem was; she knew.

"And you want to know if it's conscionable of you to even consider going when your father is here, right?"

"Right."

Edna tapped a pencil against her chin and looked at Tina thoughtfully. "I don't have Mr. Webster's file handy, but I seem to recall your telling me that he lived a very good life."

"He lived exactly as he wanted to. I don't think he would have changed places with a soul on earth. I'm not sure how he felt about the breakup of his marriage. He-men like Dad don't discuss their innermost private thoughts with their daughters, but other than that...he did what he wanted when he wanted. He was so fiercely independent and individualistic that it was awesome."

Edna digested that. "You know, although Alzheimer's isn't associated with long life, it's entirely possible that your father may live another ten or twelve years...but sadly, they won't be good years. You've studied the disease. You know what's ahead."

"Yes, I know," Tina said with a sigh.

"The next ten years of your life, on the other hand, can be the greatest of all. The last two have taken a toll, haven't they?"

"Oh, boy!" Tina said with an unhappy laugh. "There have been times when I didn't even recognize myself."

"And didn't you say there's other family nearby, someone who could be contacted in case of an emergency?"

Tina wondered. Just how would Becca react to a phone call saying Ty was ill or had had an accident? "My sister lives in Amarillo. Her number is in Dad's file."

Edna pondered a minute, then said, "I, of course, can't tell you what you should or shouldn't do. I can only tell you that you've done all that's possible. Your father will be cared for here by people who know what they're doing. I can, however, promise you a few things. We never allow any of our residents to go long without visitors. We have a hard core of volunteers who come at staggered times during the week, just to sit and talk to those who have no family. Mr. Webster will be encouraged to do anything he can do. As long as he can walk, he'll walk. As long as he can feed himself, he will. He'll receive prompt medical attention if he needs it. Other than that..." She spread out her hands. "The ball's back in your court. However..." She smiled a bit impishly. "If I had to voice an opinion, I'd say go."

The two women talked a few minutes more, mostly about Ty's past. Then Tina thanked Edna warmly, left the office and returned to her father's room. By this time, Harve was up to the fall of Bataan. Save for a perfunctory nod from her father's roommate, her appearance went unnoticed. She picked up a copy of *Sports Illustrated,* sat on one of the hard-backed chairs scattered around the room and leafed through it until lunch was announced.

The food was excellent, a cold plate of chicken salad, asparagus spears, cherry tomatoes and grapes, but Tina could have gone off in a quiet corner and eaten it while reading a book for all she contributed to the conversation. She knew very little about World War II, and that's all the men wanted to talk about. Ty's responses weren't always appropriate or in context, but that didn't faze Harve. He just kept talking.

By the time lunch was over and Tina said goodbye to her father, she felt better in one way and worse in another. Having Ty ignore her completely was a terrible experience, but he seemed more content than he had in a long time. No longer would she worry that he might be missing her.

It was a bright, beautiful day, and she was anxious to get home, but as she drove through Amarillo, a thought occurred to her. If she expected to receive assistance or support from Becca, she ought to keep her sister informed. She'd make a nuisance of herself if necessary. She wouldn't let Becca go many days without being reminded one way or another of where their father was and what she should do about it.

Besides, in some perverse way, Tina missed seeing her sister if much time passed between visits, even though their meetings usually did little more than highlight their differences. At the first convenience store she saw, she pulled in and called Becca. The maid who answered the phone informed her that Mrs. Jennings was spending the afternoon at her mother's house. Splendid, Tina thought. She could see both of them with one visit.

And she supposed that both Joan and Becca ought to hear about Russell and California.

"WHY, TINA," Joan exclaimed when she opened the door, "what a surprise!"

"I'm not interrupting anything, am I?"

"Not a thing. Becca's here. Come in, dear."

Becca uncurled herself from the sofa when Tina entered the room. "Well, hi!"

"Hi, Becca."

"What brings you into town on Saturday?" Joan asked.

"Dad." Tina looked directly at her sister. "He's at Fairhope now."

Becca's expression altered. "Oh?"

"Yes, he moved in yesterday. I have a map showing its location. I want you to promise me you'll go to see him soon and introduce yourself to Edna." Reaching in her handbag, she withdrew the map, laid it on an end table, then sat down.

Becca glanced at the map but didn't pick it up. "I was in one of those places once. I was depressed for days."

"You'll just have to risk being depressed, I guess. You'll have to visit him. But I think you'll be surprised by the atmosphere at Fairhope. It's almost cheerful. And Dad has a wonderful roommate he's quite taken with."

Becca was carefully noncommittal. "Oh, Tina, the relief must be enormous."

Tina frowned. "Relief? Some of the pressure's off, yes, but I can't say I feel relieved at all."

"But you must, dear," Joan said. "That constant care must have been exhausting."

"If I feel anything, Mom, it's regret. Regret that I had to do it."

"So, you have your own life back. What are you going to do now?" Becca asked, dismissing the unpleasantness. "Sell that ranch, I hope."

"Yes, the ranch will definitely have to go."

"Then what? Move here?"

Tina clasped her hands and lifted her chin slightly. "Actually, a very tempting offer has come my way."

Both Becca and Joan leaned forward, eager and curious. "A job, dear?" Joan asked.

"No. Russell has asked me to marry him. If I do, we'll go to California."

An eerie silence descended over the room. It was so quiet that Tina would have sworn all the clocks had stopped ticking and the refrigerator had stopped running. Her mother and sister exchanged glances of utter disbelief, then fastened incredulous stares on her.

It was Becca who broke the silence. "Are you referring to that man who's been working for you?" she all but screeched. "That . . . that truck driver?"

"Why do you say it in that tone of voice?" Tina snapped harshly. "You make it sound like driving a truck is almost illegal. Why is it any less worthwhile an occupation than building houses or raising cattle or . . . putting braces on kids' teeth, for God's sake?"

"It *is* him! That's who you're talking about." Becca put a hand to her chest. Had she lived in another century, Tina thought, she might have swooned. "You could do so much better than that."

"How do you know? You don't know a thing about Russell. He's the kindest, most wonderful man I've ever known. He's been just great with Dad. He's given me more support and encouragement than—" She stopped.

"Oh, Tina, dear." Joan had a pained expression on her face. "How could you even consider such a thing?"

"For the most basic reason in the world, Mom. I love him."

Becca shook her head vehemently. "No, I refuse to believe that. You've just been stuck out on that ranch so long. This guy comes along and—"

"We've been through this before," Tina said. "I'm not that impressionable."

"But what about Paul?"

"Paul?" Tina cried. "What about Paul?"

"He said he went to see you."

"He did."

"He said he wrote to you."

"He did. Since when have the two of you started staying in such close touch?"

"I just thought . . . hoped . . ."

"Well, don't. I told you I'm not impressionable. I'm also not impulsive. Surely you don't think I simply walked out on him in a fit of pique. I adored the man, and he shattered my trust. I gave a lot of serious thought to how I feel about things like marital fidelity before I filed for divorce."

"Oh, God!" Becca exclaimed. "What man doesn't fool around a little? Tina, you're not that naive."

"I can't believe you said that."

Becca shot Joan a helpless look. Then she played her last card. "What about Dad?"

Tina felt as though everything inside her had shattered into a million pieces. "What about him?" she asked icily.

"Can you honestly just put him in that place and go off and leave him?"

That did it! Tina shot to her feet, as close to uncontrollable rage as she'd ever been. "Listen to me, Becca. For more than two years Dad has occupied almost all my waking minutes. I have shaved him, dressed him, fed him, cut his hair, taken him to the doctor, given him his medicine, answered countless questions three dozen times each and worried about him constantly. When I could no longer do what had to be done, I found the nicest place I could and put him there so he would be safe. And what were you doing for him all that time? Not a damned thing! You wouldn't even come to see him. Don't you ever, ever throw that in my face again!''

Becca and Joan sat frozen in shock.

Tina made a show of looking at her watch. ''Now, you must excuse me. I have to get home. Don't bother seeing me to the door. I'll be in touch.''

She was shaking so badly when she left the building that she had to circle the pickup a couple of times before she was in control enough to get behind the wheel. God, Becca had her nerve! she thought as she drove away from the apartment complex. Relief? Relief implied having wanted something to happen that finally did. Whatever she felt, it wasn't relief.

Tina drove back to the ranch in a fit of fury. *Why do I bother with them? Why? They exasperate me. Their supercilious attitude toward Russell was the final blow. Let them call me from now on. I won't call them.*

It dawned on her then that Becca hadn't mentioned money. Her sister was the one who'd said from the beginning that Ty needed to be in a home. Now that it had happened, she hadn't even inquired how their father's care was being financed. Tina thought if their situations had been reversed, that would have been the first thing she would have wanted to know.

Of course, Ty himself actually was paying for his own care, but Becca didn't know that. Then Tina reminded herself that her sister couldn't be judged by anything approaching normal standards. Having had money, lots of it, for so long, Becca didn't think about what things cost. That didn't sweeten Tina's sour mood a bit. For the rest of her father's life, she would have to think about money constantly.

She had calmed a little by the time she reached home. At least when Ruby asked, "What did you do all day?" she was able to tell her about her visit with Joan and Becca without ranting. Ruby was entirely sympathetic and properly disgusted, since she had little use for either woman.

"And Ty?" she asked.

Tina sighed. "It was sad in a way. He didn't even say hello to me. But on the plus side, he seems enchanted with his roommate and hangs on his every word. He certainly never gave me that kind of rapt attention. I'm just hoping it lasts." She sighed again, then glanced around. "Is there anything that needs doing around here?"

"Not a thing. It's pretty quiet. I must have gone in the living room half a dozen times today to check on Ty. Guess it's going to take a while to realize he's gone."

"I know. The first thing I did when I woke this morning was go to his room. It was a real shock, seeing that bed all made up. Are the men back yet?"

"Nope. Leon must have found something major wrong with the Jeep."

Tina glanced around again. She couldn't imagine what she was looking for. It just seemed so strange to have time on her hands. "Well, if there's nothing to do down here, I think I'll go upstairs and read for a bit."

"Which is exactly what I plan to do, too."

In her room, Tina kicked off her shoes and picked up the paperback novel she seemed to be having a hard time finishing. Lying on her bed, she propped one pillow against the headboard and opened the book. But the combination of little sleep the night before, the round trip to Fairhope and her fit of anger had taken a lot out of her. Within minutes she was sound asleep.

THE NEXT THING SHE KNEW, someone was gently shaking her. Her eyes fluttered open, closed, then opened again. She stretched and roused by slow degrees. Fully awake, she looked into Russell's smiling face.

"Hey, Sleeping Beauty. It isn't long until supper."

"What time is it?"

"Almost six."

"I can't believe I slept so long. Now I guess my schedule's really screwed up. When did you and Jake get back?"

"About an hour ago. The Jeep needed a tune-up. Sitting around Shaw's Garage for three hours isn't my idea of the way to spend a day. How was Ty?"

"He was fine. Very taken with Harve." Tina reached up and ran her fingers through his hair. "Don't I get a kiss?"

"One kiss, on the way."

He gathered her to him, and his mouth covered hers. His lips were warm and tasted faintly of salt. When he lifted his head, she made an almost imperceptible sound and gave him a look of pure contentment. "Russell?"

"Hmm?"

"Let's go to California."

CHAPTER FOURTEEN

TINA WASN'T SURE what had made up her mind for her. She guessed it was a combination of things. One, she was in love, which certainly helped. Two, all the components of her life seemed to be conspiring to get her to California. Her father no longer acknowledged her, and he seemed reasonably happy with his new friend. She'd never prominently figured in either Joan's or Becca's lives, and she had no wish to do so, so there was no wrench there. And soon she would lose Ruby and Jake, her stalwart supports for the past two years. So there was no reason to feel guilty about wanting to be with Russell. The disburdening effect was marvelous.

Ruby couldn't have been more delighted for Tina, and that went far beyond the older woman's concerns over leaving the ranch. For two years she had watched the vitality seep out of Tina's system like water out of a leaking hose. In a very short time, Russell had put it back, and the Tina of now was a far cry from the Tina of six months ago. It was time she had a life of her own, and with Russell she would have a wonderful one.

And Russell was the happiest of them all. When he'd left Red Star he'd envisioned settling down and then finding the woman he wanted to spend the rest of his life with. It had happened in reverse, which made things even nicer. Now he and Tina could settle down together. He rummaged around in his belongings until he found all his travel books about northern California. He gave them to Tina, who pored over them in her spare time, and as in his first days at the ranch, Russell talked about the North Coast all the time. His eyes became bright and alive when he did, and his voice almost quivered with anticipation. He even wanted them to be married there, at a particular chapel he had once seen. Now she realized he'd never really stopped thinking about it. Sooner or later he would have gone, no matter what. Thank God, she was now in a position to go with him.

Plans began in earnest, and it seemed there were fifty things that needed doing. The first was contacting a real-estate agency that specialized in farm and ranch property. An agent came out and spent most of one day with them. Jake gave him a tour of the ranch, and Tina went over the books with him. The agent, Oscar Stilwell, assured them his agency had dozens of prospects who would swoon over the property. He then gave Tina an appraisal, and hammered a For Sale sign into the ground at the entrance gate. Tina never could drive by the sign without experiencing a slight pang of sadness.

The day after the sign went up, Ruby left for a week-long visit with Connie. "I'll be back," she promised. "Jake refuses to leave as long as you're here, so we can't get a whole lot of house hunting done."

"I hope this business with Connie and the kids works out for you, Ruby," Tina said.

"It will. I'll see that it does. You concentrate on your brand-new life."

"Oh, I plan to."

Not that Tina didn't occasionally have misgivings, but they never lasted long. All it took was Russell's lovemaking to convince her she had made the wisest decision of her life. At the next support-group meeting she attended she announced her plans.

Kathryn applauded. "You've lived for your father long enough, Tina. Now it's time to live for yourself. Let others help for a change. Happiness is too elusive to risk it on misguided guilt."

Meanwhile, life went on as usual, only Tina's routine now included visiting Ty twice a week. Sometimes Russell accompanied her, but mostly she went alone. The visits often seemed like a huge waste of time and energy. Her father seldom spoke to her; his focus was solely on Harve. As Edna pointed out to her, Ty shadowed his roommate. If Harve stood up, Ty stood up. If Harve went to the recreation area, it was a sure bet that Ty would be at his elbow. Even when Harve's friends came to visit, Ty stayed by the man's side. Tina wondered if poor Harve got to go to the bathroom alone.

"Is there anything wrong with that, Edna?" she asked the director after observing this behavior during a couple of visits.

"No, not as long as Harve doesn't mind, and he doesn't seem to. Dementia patients often do that—pick out one person to use for a security blanket. So far the two gentlemen seem to be doing fine. Harve has an adoring audience, and Ty has the security of the friendship."

It didn't seem like a healthy relationship to Tina, but she had to remember that her father wasn't a healthy man. Nothing he did could be judged by normal standards. And she had to admit that Ty was doing twice as well as she would have dared hope.

ALL THOSE BUYERS whom Oscar Stilwell had sworn would just be panting to buy the ranch mysteriously vanished. They'd only had two prospects, and nothing had come of either. One had wanted more land, the other not quite so much. Of course, the agent had a rash of excuses. The economy was flat. There was too much property for sale. It was a buyer's market. As the weeks passed, Russell grew impatient.

"Is it absolutely necessary that we wait until the ranch sells, sweetheart? It could take months. Hell, it could take years."

"I'm just afraid the place would get so rundown if it was vacant," Tina said. "And I hate to let the corn and cotton just rot in the field. And pardon me for being crass, but we could use the money."

"I'll bring 'em in," Jake said. "I'll stay here and look after the place, too. I ain't near as crazy about movin' closer to Connie and them kids as Ruby is. I also ain't all that school's-out happy about home ownership. Seems ta me, a fifty-eight-year-old man oughta be simplifyin' his life, not takin' on a mortgage and a lawn and what not."

"Oh, Jake, I can't ask you to do that," Tina protested.

"You ain't askin'. I'm offerin'."

"Well, I can't deny that it would ease my mind considerably. And the Jeep and pickup will stay for you to use. They both have so many miles on them that I'm sure we couldn't get much for either. They won't be a bother for you, will they?"

"Nope. I've been drivin' that Jeep so long it's almost a part of me. Wouldn't know what to do without it. Fact is, I'd 'bout as soon everythin' stayed as is."

Tina smiled. It was strange, but in many ways her thoughts mirrored Jake's. Now that the demands on her time and patience had lessened, now that she had Russell with her, she was quite content on the ranch. She hadn't wanted the place, but it was hers and it had grown on her. During a wakeful period only the night before, she had lain beside a sleeping Russell thinking, *I wish everything could stay just the way it is.* Then she'd reminded herself that such a thought actually was pretty selfish. If everything stayed the way it was, Russell would be robbed of his dream. She didn't want that to happen because she loved him, so she would go to California. Even as she'd thought it, her stomach had given a little lurch. Just to go... maybe never see this place again...

Tina was surprised by these thoughts. She didn't think she'd ever been particularly sentimental about the old homestead. True, the romantic in her loved the tales of her pioneer ancestors, and there had always been something about rural life she had found relaxing. But her real attachment wasn't to a place, it was to a man. So she would go to California.

Now she turned to Russell, who had sat quietly taking in Jake's offer. "When would you like to leave?"

He shrugged. "A week. No more than two."

She nodded distractedly and glanced around. "Lord," she muttered, "this house is full of stuff. Most of it's been around as long as I can remember. What do I do with it?"

Russell, who'd hardly ever owned more than he could carry with him, wasn't sure. "Maybe you should take inventory. List the things you'll want when we get settled and give the list to Jake. When he hears from you, he can call the movers. As for everything else...I don't know.''

"Jus' let me take care of everythin'," Jake said. "What Tina don't want, I'll let Ruby go through. Everythin' else I'll give to charity. Don't worry about it." He grinned at Russell and jerked his thumb in Tina's direction. "That one's a worrywart. Always has been, ever since she was a tyke."

It was a monumental task, going through possessions accumulated over a period of more than fifty years. Furniture was the easy part. She would wait to see what kind of place she and Russell found in California, then send for what she could use. She was sure they wouldn't be able to afford new furniture in the foreseeable future. But there was a small mountain of other items. Every drawer and every closet had to be gone through, and the attic was full of keepsakes that several generations of Websters had found impossible to discard.

After a few hours of sifting through the memorabilia, Tina wasn't sure she had the heart to get rid of them, either. The odds and ends of clothing, furniture and wall hangings were no problem; Jake could haul them to the dump. But there were cartons and boxes and even an old steamer trunk full of letters, diaries, newspapers and magazines, some of them dating back to the late nineteenth century. It dawned on her that those containers held her family's history, to say nothing of a great deal of the history of the South Plains. For her they were just fun to look at and read, but she couldn't shake the notion that they might be very valuable to the right person. A collector, perhaps, or a historian or a museum. Destroying them would be like burning down a library.

Finally she decided she couldn't. They would be shipped to California.

THE DAY FOR Tina's and Russell's departure neared. Ruby, who had been dividing her time equally between the ranch and Connie's house, decided to stay and help Tina get ready. She now had Alejandro eating out of her hand, so much so that when she'd left the last time, the boy had taken her aside and asked if he could come live with her.

"In pretty good English, too," Ruby said. "Oh, the accent was as thick as salsa, but I understood him plain as day. It really... touched me. I've wanted to cuff the kid a time or two, but now...I'm pretty fond of him."

"What did you tell him when he asked if he could live with you?" Tina wanted to know.

"The truth. That the place I'm living in now is for sale, and Jake and I don't have another yet."

"You know you and Jake are welcome to stay here until the place sells, and it looks like that might be some time. Oscar Stilwell now informs me that we've passed the 'good' selling season, that the market will slow until after the first of the year." Tina uttered a little laugh. "It couldn't get much slower than it is now if you ask me. Funny how the market changed the minute I signed those papers. So you and Jake stay, by all means."

"Thanks. We might take you up on that. But Lord, I'm going to miss you, Tina."

"I'll be back, you know. Often. I'll come back to see Dad, and we'll visit then." Tina looked at her watch. "Speaking of which, I'd best be going if I'm going to have lunch with him. Lunchtime is the best time for me to be there. It gives me something to do, since Dad hardly ever says anything to me."

"Then why do you bother?" Ruby asked practically.

"I don't know, Ruby. I just feel...pulled." She grabbed the keys to the pickup. "See you this afternoon."

And what, Ruby wondered, if Tina still felt pulled after she and Russell were in California?

TINA FOUND Ty's room empty, but it was too early for him to have gone to the dining room with Harve, so she went in search of them. Since Harve was a sociable sort who liked having people around, she first checked the recreation room. Not finding them, she went into the TV parlor, finally the courtyard. For good measure, she glanced in the dining room, but the tables were only now being set for lunch. At a loss, she went back to Ty's room, thinking the men might be taking a walk and would soon be back. After five impatient minutes, however, she decided to ask someone. She was on the way to the orderlies' station, when she spotted Ty. He was seated alone on a bench at the far end of the hall, his head down. He looked like a lost child. It seemed so strange to see him without Harve by his side that Tina stopped in her tracks. A fearful premonition swept through her. Collecting herself, she hurried down the hall to her father.

"Dad?"

Ty looked up, squinting. "Who are you?"

"Tina."

"You're...Tina?"

It was the first time he had said her name in months. Sadly she didn't know if that was good or bad. "Yes. Why are you sitting here alone?"

"Someone...put me here." Suddenly he reached for her hand. "Can you take me back...to that other place?"

Tina's free hand went to her chest. "What other place, Dad?"

"Where I was...before."

Oh, Lord, she was naive. Had she really thought things would continue to run as smoothly as they had? "I thought you liked it here, where everyone is."

Ty shook his head. "I want you to get me out of here. They do bad things."

"What sort of things?" she asked gently, wondering if he was hallucinating again.

"They...take people away...like in the war."

Tina frowned. Was he thinking about things like death marches and concentration camps? Maybe he and Harve spent too much time talking about that damned war.

"Get me out of here!"

This time Ty almost had shouted it. A woman walking by stared at him.

The pitiful plea tugged at Tina's heart. Worse, there was real fear in his eyes. What had happened? And where the hell was Harve? Gently she took her father's arm and urged him to his feet. Slipping her arm around his waist, she began propelling him back to his room. Though it had been some time since Ty's walk had been brisk, he'd never shuffled. Now he did. "Let's go back to the room and talk about this," she said softly.

With some difficulty, Tina managed to get him into the room and settled in one of the easy chairs. She took the other one, never letting go of his hand. "You know, that other place doesn't have all the activities and people they have here," she said. "No singalongs, no church service, no Ping-Pong."

"I hate it here. I hate Ping-Pong."

"I see." Hoping she sounded offhanded, she asked, "By the way, where's Harve?"

"Who?"

"Where is the man who sleeps in that other bed?"

Ty frowned. "I . . . don't know."

Tina's breath escaped between her teeth in a little whistle. "Dad, I want to make a phone call. Excuse me just for a minute." She reached for the phone and pushed the number indicated for the director's office. After two rings, a familiar feminine voice answered.

"Edna Lowell."

Tina was careful to keep her voice calm, to mask her rising tide of panic, lest Ty pick up on it. "Edna, this is Tina Webster. I'm in my father's room. Has anything . . . er, unusual happened since my last visit?"

"Oh, Tina, Harve suffered a minor stroke this morning. I took him to the hospital, and they decided to keep him overnight for observation. He's going to be fine, I'm happy to say. I tried to call you when I got back, but you had left the house."

So that was it. Harve had been taken away. "I found Dad sitting all alone at the end of the hall. Under the circumstances, I don't think that was wise."

Edna gasped. "Well, that shouldn't have happened. I left instructions that someone was to be with Ty at all times. I'll do my best to see it doesn't happen again until Harve returns."

"Thank you. I'd appreciate it. By the way, has my sister been to see Dad? Her name is Rebecca Jennings."

There was a pause. "No, Tina, not that I know of, and I stay pretty well informed about visitors. I'm almost sure you and Mr. Cade are the only ones who've been to see him."

I might have known, Tina thought as she hung up. And raising hell wouldn't do a bit of good. She might as well talk to the chair she was sitting in. She couldn't begin to understand her sister, and trying to do so would be a waste of time. Becca could be left out of the equation entirely.

So Tina assessed the situation sensibly. She was very upset that Ty had been left alone on the morning Harve had been taken to the hospital, but perhaps she had overreacted. No home she could put her father in would be absolutely perfect. There were people working at Fairhope, not robots, and Ty wasn't their only patient. Edna certainly couldn't be expected to know what every member of the staff was doing every minute. Tina was thankful that Harve was going to be all right, but her father's dependence on him was alarming. One day without Harve and Ty was lost.

She returned her attention to him. "Now, Dad, about that other place."

Ty looked at her blankly. "What other place?"

Tina's shoulders slumped. He'd already forgotten. Thank God.

At that moment, a very harried-looking young orderly rushed into the room. Seeing Ty, he slumped against the wall. "There you are. I told you to stay put."

Tina eyed him accusingly. She got to her feet and crossed the room to stand in front of him. Lowering her voice, she said, "My father shouldn't be left alone."

"Hey, I'm sorry. I had a phone call. I told him to wait for me."

"He doesn't always remember to do what he's told."

"I was only gone a few minutes."

"A lot could happen in a few minutes. I'll be with him until after lunch, but then, until Mr. Chesterton returns, I want someone else to stay whenever he's awake."

"Sure, ma'am, sure. Sorry," the man said, hurriedly backing out the door.

Lunch was served soon after that, but it was a difficult meal. Ty ate almost nothing, even though the food was wonderful. Tina begged, teased and cajoled to no avail. She even tried feeding him herself, although she hated doing that in front of others. Nothing worked. He was like a cranky child. He hadn't eaten heartily in a long time, but Tina had noticed that he did much better when Harve was around. But what if his roommate was sicker than everyone seemed to think? What if he returned to Fairhope needing some special care of his own? Harve might not be as patient as he'd been in the past. What would happen to her father then?

After lunch, Ty declared he was sleepy, so Tina turned him over to another orderly and left for home, exhausted and heartsick.

RUSSELL WATCHED Tina throughout supper. She seemed remote and lost in thought, but she was often preoccupied when she returned from Fairhope. Those visits took a lot out of her, and since from all reports they did no good, he thought the sooner they got on the road, the better she would feel . . . about everything.

And the more relieved he would feel. As long as they were here, he couldn't shake the nagging fear that something would happen, some emergency—real or imagined—would come along that would shatter the dream. And that fear was with him tonight, much stronger than ever before.

But though Tina was quiet and pensive, almost moody all evening, when they were upstairs in her room, she became sweet and very loving. "I'm wilted," she said. "I think I'll take a bath before I crawl between those clean sheets."

"Mind if I join you?"

She threw him a glance over her shoulder. "You took a shower just before supper."

"Can a body be too clean?"

"I guess not. And you can scrub my back."

As she filled the tub, Russell glanced suspiciously at the small bottle she held in her hand. "What's that?"

"Bath oil."

"Is it going to make me smell like I've been in a bordello?"

"I don't know," Tina said, "because I don't know what a bordello smells like."

They both stripped and stepped into the steamy, fragrant water. Soon cleanliness was the last thing on their minds. Locked in a tight embrace, they entwined their legs and arms. Water sloshed over them, then over the rim of the tub to form little pools on the tiled floor. Their slick bodies slipped and slid until Russell pulled her on top of him and locked his legs around her. He gave her a hot, prolonged kiss while pressing her against his turgid body. For Tina, the ensuing union was unbelievably erotic, intense and tender all at once. It was like making love in slow motion. When they reached their simultaneous climaxes, she was astonished that the bathwater didn't gush toward the ceiling, like the spewing of a geyser.

Later, when the water had cooled to tepid, they lethargically hauled their spent selves out of the tub, toweled each other and went to bed to lie in each other's arms. Minutes passed.

"Tina?" Russell murmured.

"Hmm?"

"Did anything unusual happen at the home today?"

"Why do you ask?"

"Oh . . . you weren't yourself this evening. I thought maybe . . . Is Ty all right?"

There was a pause, such a long one that Russell's insides tensed. He felt her lips against his neck. They moved, and a sound came out, something like a choked-back sob.

"I . . . do have something to tell you," she said in a voice barely above a whisper.

"What's that?"

"Oh, Russell . . . I'm so sorry, but . . . I can't go to California. I just can't."

Whatever she had expected, it wasn't complete silence. Not only silence but the rigidity of his body. He didn't move, not a flicker. He didn't seem to be breathing. She began speaking rapidly, haltingly, disjointedly. "At the home . . . I found Dad all alone at the end of the hall. . . . He even said my name . . . not like he recognized me, but . . . He was so frightened. . . . Harve had . . ."

Somehow the story managed to come out after a fashion. "Oh, Russell, I love you more than anything, but I'm the only one who really cares about Dad. The people at Fairhope are probably the best, but they aren't family. Becca hasn't even been to see him. Isn't that awful? I . . . I'm the only one who really cares, the only one who'll complain if I think he isn't being treated properly."

She tried to pull herself together. "If I were in California, I would worry all the time. There would be too many phone calls, too many trips back. You would grow resentful. I've talked to people who've been through it. Strong, loving, twenty-year marriages falter. It wouldn't be fair to you."

Russell's disappointment was acute. It was something he could taste. For weeks he'd thought of almost nothing but the two of them together in the place he'd dreamed about for so long. All those years of making do and doing without so that someday he could settle down comfortably, without money worries. Then Tina had come along—the icing on the cake. Now this.

Tina waited for some kind of response from him. She wouldn't have believed a human being could remain so motionless for so long. She didn't know if he was stunned . . . or immobilized by anger. She had said everything she knew to say, and she felt drained. "I'm so sorry. I want to go to California. I wish I could go . . . but I can't."

Finally he stirred. The first sound out of his mouth was a lusty sigh. Then the arm around her shoulders tightened, and his chest heaved. His lips brushed her temple. "If you can't go, sweetheart, I won't go, either."

Everything inside Tina seemed to melt. It was what she had wanted to hear more than anything in the world. Now, having heard it, she knew what her next step had to be. She raised on one elbow and looked at him adoringly. She bent and kissed him. Then she traced the outline of his mouth with a fingertip and smiled down at him adoringly. "But you have to," she said, a slight catch in her voice. "Don't you see that? You must go."

Russell wondered if he'd heard right. Had she really said what he thought she'd said? "Tina! You want me to leave?"

"Yes and no. No, I don't want to be away from you, but as much as it pains me to say it . . . yes, you have to go and see it. That's the only way you'll know what you want for sure."

"I know for sure what I want, and it's you."

"Now. I know you do . . . now." Tina sat up and reached for her robe at the foot of the bed. Slipping it on, she got out of bed and began pacing the room restlessly. "The years ahead aren't going to be easy ones. There'll be Dad and the money crunch. There's this ranch. What if it doesn't sell? I'll have to stay here and try to keep it going. I couldn't possibly afford it and a place in town, too. You might start feeling trapped. I have, plenty of times, and it's a horrible feeling."

Russell raised up and propped himself against the headboard, his eyes following her agitated movements. Over the past weeks he had watched the tension gradually leave her face, and he'd fancied himself responsible. But it was back now. "Sweetheart, I've been around. I think I can judge what I do and don't want."

She stopped pacing and turned to look at him. "Please . . . for me as much as for yourself. I've been listening to you for weeks, heard the excitement in your voice whenever you talked about California. Go see it. Go with an open mind. Give it a chance to work its magic on you again. Then if you come back, we'll both know for sure. I won't always feel as though I kept you from your dream.'' She averted her eyes for a minute; when she looked back at him, they were misty. ''Believe me, I know the risk I'm taking.''

Russell didn't think he'd ever seen such earnestness on her face. And he wondered if there wasn't a lot of good sense in what she said. If it would ease her mind, make her feel more secure... He thought he would circle the globe if it would give Tina peace of mind. Lord knows, she'd had precious little of it during the past two years. He patted the space beside him. ''Come back to bed, love. Get some sleep. We'll talk about it later.''

Tina opened her mouth to say something, then closed it. And because she was tired enough to drop, she shrugged out of the robe, crawled back under the covers and into his arms. ''I'm right to insist you go, Russell,'' she murmured. ''You know I'm right.'' She was asleep within minutes.

WHEN TINA AWOKE the next morning, Russell was gone. A note had been pinned to his pillow: ''I didn't want say goodbye. You'll hear from me. I love you very much. Russell.''

She refused to believe it. Bounding out of bed, she put on her robe and ran to his room. Everything was gone. She returned to her room and looked out the window, craning to see the side yard where the vehicles were kept parked. The Thunderbird wasn't there. She backed to the bed, sinking down.

Tina stared across the room in stunned disbelief. She was amazingly dry-eyed, though there was an uncomfortable heaviness in her chest. She tried to give a name to what she felt. It wasn't heartbreak or grief—more of a chilling uncertainty about the outcome. How much better she would have felt if he had left some of his belongings behind.

My God, she thought, *what have I done?*

CHAPTER FIFTEEN

THE BAR of the motel in Gallup, where Russell had gotten a room, was packed to the rafters, and the noise level was indescribable. He wondered if that was the norm for a weekday afternoon. There weren't many solitary drinkers, he noticed. Everyone but him seemed to know everyone else, including the bartender and the two waitresses. The place rang with laughter. Russell sat nursing a Scotch on the rocks and brooding.

What he'd thought was such a good idea at five o'clock this morning now seemed like the silliest thing he had ever done. *Just go,* he'd told himself. *Go before anyone wakes up. No maudlin farewell. No tears from Tina.* He was coming back, after all. He'd treat this California jaunt as a business trip, nothing else.

Still, the hardest thing he had ever done was turn away from Tina's sleeping form, gather up his things and drive away in the predawn darkness. Determinedly he'd driven west from Amarillo, willing his mind to think of nothing at all, not even daring to turn on the radio. He was sure the first sad country song would have melted his resolve.

The first strong misgivings had struck him just as he crossed the New Mexico state line. In Tucumcari, he had come within a whisker of turning around and going back. But that would prove nothing to Tina, and it was for her he was doing this crazy thing. So he'd pushed on relentlessly, not stopping in Albuquerque as he'd planned. Having left the ranch before daybreak, he'd arrived there much too early to call it a day. So now the state of New Mexico was almost behind him, and he was weary to the bone. In fact, he was so tired he probably shouldn't be drinking, but what the hell? He didn't have to do any more driving today, and the booze might help him sleep.

"Ready for another one, pal?" the bartender asked as he moved along the length of the bar, keeping a watchful eye on the customers' glasses.

Russell glanced down at his empty glass, unaware that he had drunk it. "Yeah, I guess so." He watched the man mix the drink. "Is the food in the dining room any good?"

"It is if you like Mexican. Manolo hasn't exactly mastered the art of anything else, but he's new."

"Do you ever eat here?"

"All the time."

"That's as good a recommendation as any." Russell looked out over the crowd, which was getting noisier by the minute. "Do you always do this much business during the week?" he asked.

"Nope," the bartender said, setting Russell's drink in front of him. "A young couple who met in here about eight months ago are getting married tomorrow. Their friends are giving them a wedding-eve party. Sure never thought ol' Clayton would get married. A free spirit if there ever was one... but I guess it happens to the best of us sooner or later."

"It's the predictability of marriage," Russell said. "I think that's the appeal."

"Huh?"

"You know, coming home every night to the wife and kids, always having someone to talk to, someone who's glad to see you when the sun goes down. Good food, comfort, familiarity."

The bartender looked at him curiously. "Hell, pal, who has that kind of marriage in this day and age?" he asked, then moved on as he caught another customer's signal.

Russell smiled wryly and took a hefty swallow of his drink. *Tina and I would,* he thought. He was certain of it. He thought of how he'd felt at the end of every workday when he'd walked through that back door, anxious for the sight of her face. A sharp longing overtook him. The urge to call her was strong, but he fought it. Her voice would be all it took to have him heading back east the next day. Besides, she wouldn't want to just chat any more than he did.

She had told him to keep an open mind, to give things a chance, and that was what he would do. The next time he talked to her, she'd know for sure. Never again would she worry that she had kept him from his dream.

THE FIRST DAY Russell was gone seemed to Tina to last an eternity, and the next day wasn't any better. She had hoped he would call, but he didn't. Maybe it was just as well. What would a call en route accomplish? And if she heard his voice, the yearning would drive her mad. Ruby was at Connie's, Ty was at Fairhope, Russell was on his way to California and Jake was in the fields. There wasn't anything that she absolutely, positively had to do. For the first time she understood why people who lived alone got hooked on television.

On the third day, Tina engaged in a fit of cleaning that the house didn't need, but it proved to be fortuitous activity. That afternoon, Oscar Stilwell brought out another prospective buyer. The house had never looked better than it did then. For the rest of the day she was poised for the telephone's ring, hoping Oscar would call to say he had a contract. He didn't, so Tina went to bed that night hearing neither from the real-estate agent nor from Russell.

On the fourth day she went to visit Ty. Harve had recovered nicely from the stroke and was his normal garrulous self, so her father once again paid little attention to her. Briefly, perhaps pettishly, Tina resented having given up California for a man who treated her as if she wasn't there, but she quickly shook that off. Ty couldn't help it, and he did need her, whether he knew it or not.

Time dragged. Still, she stayed longer than she did normally. She had lunch with Ty and Harve, then stopped in to visit some of the women she had met since Ty had moved in. Her favorite was a spry, eighty-year-old named Bertha McCorkle. Every time Tina had seen Bertha, the woman had been dressed as if she were on her way to church, and this afternoon was no exception. The door to her room was open, and Bertha was standing in front of a mirror, patting her silver hair.

"Am I imposing?" Tina asked from the doorway.

Bertha turned. "Oh, Tina, of course not. It's always so good to see you. Come in and have a seat, dear."

As Tina sat down, Bertha gave herself a quick spraying of perfume, then took the chair next to Tina's.

"You look unusually nice this afternoon, Bertha," Tina said. "Is this a special occasion?"

Bertha leaned toward her conspiratorially, and her eyes twinkled. "Tina, do you know the real reason I live here?"

Tina thought she did. The first time she'd met Bertha, she'd received a full accounting of the circumstances behind the woman's moving to Fairhope. Her daughter baby-sat three of her own grandchildren, all of them preschoolers. In Bertha's words, "Those kids absolutely drive me insane. If I lived in that house, I'd surely have to take tranquilizers...either that or give them to the kids." And her son lived on a farm in North Dakota. According to Bertha, he called once a week, begging her to come live with his family. "But I can't stand that wife of his," Bertha had confided to Tina. "Never could. And she's not any fonder of me."

So Tina had assumed that Bertha was at Fairhope for the same reason a lot of the residents were—she couldn't live alone and had nowhere else to go. Apparently she had been wrong. Judging from the look on the woman's face, she had a confidence she was dying to spill.

"Why, Bertha? Why do you live here?"

"Because it's a good place to meet men."

Tina blinked. "It is?"

"Of course. Just look around at all the men, most of them widowers at that." Bertha brushed at the front of her dress and stood up. "Come with me, Tina. I want to show you something."

Tina stood and followed her out of the room, shaking her head and trying very hard not to giggle. Their destination was the recreation room. At the doorway, Bertha paused and scanned the room. Then she tugged at Tina's arm. "Look over there at the table in front of the window. See those men playing dominoes?"

Tina nodded.

"See the one dressed up so nice and proper in a jacket and tie?"

One of the men had thick gray hair, a gray mustache and was wearing a rather loud plaid jacket. "Yes, I see him."

"He's new. Just checked in yesterday. I haven't had a chance to meet him yet, but I noticed him right off. I think he's nice-looking, don't you?"

It was all Tina could do to keep a straight face. "Yes, I guess so . . . distinguished and dapper."

"Somebody said he's loaded . . . with money, you know. He also looks fairly healthy. I'll never forgive my darling Fred for up and dying on me. It wouldn't have happened if he'd taken better care of himself. But that one over there looks fit. Now all I have to do is figure out a way to meet him."

"Why, Bertha, that's easy. Just step forward, stick out your hand and introduce yourself."

Bertha looked uncertain. "Do you really think that would be all right?"

"Oh, of course. Today women don't wait around to be noticed. They make themselves impossible to ignore. Trust me on this."

"Well . . . if you really think . . . Oh, my goodness!"

The game of dominoes was breaking up. The object of Bertha's interest stood, exchanged a few words with the other men, then turned and headed straight for the door. As he neared, Tina nudged Bertha slightly.

The elderly woman stepped in the man's path and stuck out her hand. "Hello. You're new, aren't you? I'm Bertha McCorkle."

"How do you do, Bertha," the man said, taking her hand. He had a deep resounding voice.

"And this is my friend, Tina Webster."

"It's a pleasure. Lionel Gage at your service, ladies."

Bertha was almost simpering. "Do you like music, Lionel?"

"Not particularly."

"We have some nice dances here."

"I hate dancing."

Bertha's composure slipped a bit. "Well . . . arts and crafts, perhaps. We have . . ."

"Arts and crafts?" Lionel's voice seemed to bounce off the walls. "That's for doddering old ladies."

"You must have some special interest," Bertha insisted.

"Golf! Golf, golf and more golf! It's a gentleman's game, you know. Edna has promised I can practice my putting in the courtyard. Now, if you ladies will excuse me, it's time for my nap." He touched his forehead in a little farewell salute.

Tina and Bertha had no choice but to stand aside and let him pass.

Bertha stared after him; a pinched look crossed her face. "Grumpy old goat, isn't he?"

Tina gave her a rueful smile. "How often do we set our sights on someone, only to find he isn't what we'd hoped he'd be."

"Well," Bertha said with a sigh, "there'll be someone else, you can be sure of that. I wasn't meant to be without a husband. I'll get married again, Tina. You just wait and see."

Hope springs eternal, Tina thought.

After she left Fairhope, she stopped at the mall to do some shopping—more looking than buying. Actually, it was more just to pass the time—anything to keep from going back to that big empty house.

Eventually, of course, she had to return home. As she drove through the entrance gate, she stopped to get the mail out of the box, then continued up to the house. The Jeep was gone, so that meant Jake was gone. With a sigh, Tina opened the back door, tossed the mail on the kitchen table and sat down to go through it. As usual, it was mostly magazines, catalogs and junk. There were several official-looking government envelopes, from the Department of Agriculture, she assumed. Each month they received a slew of such mailings, often containing important information. She set them aside for later reading.

And there was a letter for her... another one from Paul. His chatty little notes had been arriving at frequent intervals. She never answered them. It was difficult to know what to say to him. Tina simply stared at the envelope for a minute. She didn't really want to read it, but she knew she would. Throwing away an unread letter was as unthinkable to her as ignoring a ringing telephone. She got up, poured a glass of tea, then sat down and ripped open the envelope.

Dearest Tina,

I must say I'm underwhelmed by your response to my previous letters. Your reluctance even to correspond with me is puzzling. However, undaunted, I persist.

I've recently been approached by a colleague in Amarillo. He has a rather interesting offer for me.

He has been in practice with his father for fifteen years, but now the old man wants to retire. My colleague has asked me to join his busy, lucrative practice, and I find the idea enormously appealing. There I would be one of two instead of one of many.

I would find living and working in Amarillo especially appealing if I thought there was a chance I could see you. I know I've changed a great deal since the unfortunate dissolution of our marriage, and I wish you would give me a chance to prove that to you. Seeing me wouldn't compromise your honor, or whatever it is that you're so steadfastly protecting. We could have dinner and talk, just the two of us alone somewhere. Without, I would hope, recriminations or accusations.

From all that Becca's told me, I gather these past few years have been difficult ones. Your father's illness must be ghastly for you. I wish I could help you, and I will if you'll let me. One phone call and you would have anything that's in my power to give, which is a great deal. I've done well. You shared the lean years with me. I wish I could share the fat ones with you. I could give you a life of comfort and ease. I could help you with Ty. I could do a lot for you, but I can't do a damned thing if you won't even write to me.

The fact is, Tina, I don't like being alone, and you're the only woman I've ever met whom I've wanted to live with. I still love you, and I know I could make you love me again. How many times must I tell you I'm sorry? Remember the begin ning? It could be like that again. Please, just give me a chance.

And, please, answer this.

Love,
Paul

Tina set the letter on the table and sadly shook her head. Never would she have imagined Paul's pleading like that. It was so uncharacteristic. And he was a charming rascal...but a rascal, nevertheless. She wondered if it was possible for a person to really change inside. He had always been an outrageous flirt, though in the early days of their marriage his lust for his new young wife had tempered the flirting somewhat. But as familiarity had set in, he'd gone back to his old ways. Women just seemed to give a boost to his ego that nothing else could. She'd thought the flirting was harmless. How wrong she had been.

She supposed good manners dictated she acknowledge the letter, but what could she say? *Dear Paul, how are you? I'm fine. The tractor broke down again, and the Jeep needed a tune-up.* She glanced toward the phone. *Russell, please call me. Please.*

God, she was an idiot! There he was, ready and willing to stay with her, but, no, she had to insist he go and see the North Coast. What had she been thinking of? If the place had the ability to enchant him for ten long years, it was entirely possible it would do the same thing all over again.

Absence makes the heart grow fonder, her inner voice reminded her.

Out of sight, out of mind, Tina thought morosely.

She laid Paul's letter aside and reached for the government mail, thumbing through it idly. The same old stuff, she thought. Then her fingers stopped. One of

the envelopes was decidedly not from the Department
of Agriculture. Tina swallowed hard as she looked at
the return address. Internal Revenue Service. And the
envelope was addressed to Ty. There was no way on
earth that could be good news. Nervously she opened
it and read the contents.

It was a form letter with the pertinent information
typed in the blank spaces. It informed her that an error had been made on Ty's tax return of three years
ago. With penalty and interest tacked on, he owed the
government just over eight thousand dollars. The letter instructed him to remit by September 15 or another
penalty would be added to the tax owed. If he had
questions, he was to call so-and-so at such-and-such a
number.

Tina slumped back in the chair and closed her eyes.
Eight thousand dollars! And three years ago would
have been the last time Ty himself had made out his
own tax return, when he'd probably already been sick.
She had done their taxes ever since she'd found his accounts in such a mess.

Again she read the letter, overcome with utter disbelief. How could this be happening? Suddenly all her
other troubles seemed minuscule, indeed. Here was
something major to worry about. How in the hell was
she going to come up with eight thousand dollars by the
fifteenth? It might as well have been twice that much,
three times that much. She would have been hard-
pressed to come up with half that amount. Dear God,
what was she going to do?

Now wait, she cautioned herself. *The IRS makes
mistakes, too.* She remembered the year Ty had been
audited and the government ended up owing him
money. Before she pushed the panic button, she would
go over that year's tax return with a fine-tooth comb.

She might discover that no mistake had been made. But if there actually had been that big an error...well, *then* she would go into full-swivel panic.

THE QUAINT bed-and-breakfast inn where Russell was staying on the North Coast dated from 1870, according to the brief history of the place that was posted in all six of the bedrooms. It had a winding staircase, a library, parlor, dining room and porch. There was plush carpeting on the floors, and the walls were adorned with patterned wallpaper. The Victorian structure held a wealth of antiques, for its proprietor was also an antique dealer. It was exactly the sort of place he had hoped to find.

The breakfast the inn served was not of the continental variety but was huge and filling. After stuffing himself, Russell set out on foot to explore the environs. The little town of Ferndale had been so perfectly refurbished it didn't seem real—more like a Hollywood back lot. The streets were lined with Gothic Revival, Queen Anne and Italianate-style Victorian homes, brightly painted and blooming with pride. The main part of town was filled with antique shops, art galleries and even an old blacksmith shop. It was easy to see that arts and crafts, lumbering and fishing were the area's main industries. Everything was laid-back, delightfully removed from hustle and bustle and perfectly peaceful. It was also great fun to explore.

After several hours of walking, he returned to the inn and considered calling Tina, just to describe the town and the area. Then he thought better of it. Telling her about this picturesque place would be like rubbing salt on a wound. Instead, Russell got into his car and set out to do some sight-seeing on his own, following a back road arc that curved through forest, sheep-grazing lands and gentle pastures, finally ending up at a western cape. From there he had a broad view of the ocean and its menacing shoals.

He tried to envision himself living in this peaceful, beautiful place. Perhaps he would buy a boat and charter it for fishing. Squatting on his haunches, he stared out over the water, mesmerized. He was so pleased that his memories hadn't been blown out of proportion with time. It was as he'd thought it would. It really was paradise.

IT DIDN'T TAKE Tina long to find the mistake. It was there, all right, very real, very forbidding. The arithmetic on the return was sloppy throughout. Her father had been sick a long time.

Throwing her pencil down on the desk, she turned in her swivel chair, stared out the window and considered her options. She had two weeks. She could wait and see if Russell returned. She hated putting "if" in there, but she had to be realistic. He might not come back. But if he did, they would be married, the taxes would be paid and that would be that.

However, it was entirely possible he wouldn't be back in two weeks, so she couldn't count on him for help. She was in a bind, no question about it. There were several sources for borrowing the money—the bank, for one. The Websters' credit was excellent. The trouble was, she couldn't afford a monthly payment, not with what Fairhope cost. She had to live, after all, and she was getting by on the barest minimum as it was.

There was Becca...or rather, there was Derek. Tina visibly shuddered. She liked her brother-in-law, but their relationship had never been close. He'd never really seemed like family, though he'd probably give her the money. However, she knew she would have to accompany the request with something like "I'm not sure when I can pay you back. Maybe when the cotton is harvested." The words would stick in her throat.

Tina asked herself why that was so. Surely Ty's tax troubles were as much Becca's responsibility as they were her own. Why would asking her sister and Derek make her feel like an impoverished relative?

She didn't know, but the sad fact was that it would. After thinking about it a few more minutes, Tina decided that she had taken care of her father for a long time with precious little help from her sister. She could handle this, too... she hoped.

Jake and Ruby? No way. They were helping Connie, which was as it should be. Tina didn't intend for them ever to find out about this.

That left Joan, and she had no idea what her mother's financial circumstances were. Eight thousand dollars was a lot of money. If her mother simply couldn't afford to loan her that much... well, things might get embarrassing. And, again, she would have to tell Joan the pay-back date was uncertain.

Then she remembered her father's long-ago admonition never to borrow money from a good friend or kinfolks. Ty vowed and declared that was the surest way in the world to lose a friend or cause hard feelings in the family. Joan, too, was out.

If only someone would come along who couldn't live without the ranch. Selling it would give her a big chunk of cash. But even if someone came along tomorrow, which was the ultimate in fantasy, it was doubtful the deal could be closed and money change hands in two weeks.

Which brought her back to the bank... and more questions. The last time Ty had borrowed money, the ranch had been much larger and a thriving operation. Now it was merely breaking even. Even though her father had excellent credit, Tina herself had no credit record. Would the bank take a chance on Ty Webster's unemployed daughter? Unlikely. She had no collateral save for the ranch and its well-used vehicles and machinery. She doubted that would impress a loan officer. But she did have the corn and cotton crops. Maybe they would loan her the money on those.

Sighing, Tina turned back to the desk, pulled a note pad toward her and once again figured her monthly expenses. This time she took them down to the bare bones, and still she didn't have enough. She would have to borrow—that was all there was to it. She'd mortgage her crops, do anything to pay the taxes, then worry about how to pay back the money. Debt! How she hated the sound of the word. Being debt-free was the one thing that had made her feel financially secure, no matter how little money she had.

Well, she had to get a job... quickly. She hadn't wanted to until she heard from Russell, but things had changed. She didn't have the luxury of waiting. She'd take anything she could get, just as long as the salary would pay back whoever loaned her the money. If she found work in Leatrice, she would have to limit her visits with Ty to evenings and weekends. If she had to work in Amarillo, it would mean a depressingly long daily commute, and the pickup was a real gas-guzzler. If it wasn't one damned thing, it was twelve others.

Disgustedly Tina ripped the paper off the notepad, crumpled it into a ball and tossed it in a wastebasket. As she did, her eyes spotted Paul's letter. She had brought it into the office thinking she would write him a chatty note that said nothing. She felt her heart skip a beat. *One phone call and you would have anything that's in my power to give, which is a great deal.*

Tina was aghast that she would even think such a thing. That was what came from being desperate. Getting to her feet lest the idea become attractive to her, she hurried out of the office. She wouldn't do anything right away. She still had two weeks. Maybe something would come to her. Did miracles still happen?

At that moment she would have given all she owned to be able to go in search of Russell and pour out her woes to him. She would have settled for just hearing his voice telling her he was on his way back to Texas. But that was ridiculous. He'd been gone less than a week. It only seemed like a month. She needed that sense of having a staunch ally that he always brought her.

Oh, Russell, where are you? What are you doing? Are you thinking about me and, more important, are you coming back?

THE REDWOOD HIGHWAY led north to the Redwood National Park—"the park of parks" the proprietress of the inn had informed Russell. It was the habitat of the coastal redwood, a tree whose ancestors dated to the age of dinosaurs. The guidebook he carried said they lived from five to eight centuries and grew to three hundred fifty feet. *Awesome* did not begin to describe them adequately.

BIG SUMMER READ

Summer Reading At Its Best

In July, Harlequin and Silhouette bring readers the Big Summer Read Program. Heat up your summer with these four exciting new novels by top Harlequin and Silhouette authors.

SOMEWHERE IN TIME by Barbara Bretton
YESTERDAY COMES TOMORROW by Rebecca Flanders
A DAY IN APRIL by Mary Lynn Baxter
LOVE CHILD by Patricia Coughlin

From time travel to fame and fortune, this program offers something for everyone.

Available at your favorite retail outlet.

FREE GIFT OFFER

With Free Gift Promotion proofs-of-purchase from Harlequin or Silhouette, you can receive this beautiful jewelry collection. Each item is perfect by itself, or collect all three for a complete jewelry ensemble.

For a classic look that is always in style, this beautiful gold tone jewelry will complement any outfit. Items include:

Gold tone clip earrings (approx. retail value $9.95), a 7½" gold tone bracelet (approx. retail value $15.95) and a 18" gold tone necklace (approx. retail value $29.95).

FREE GIFT OFFER TERMS

To receive your free gift, complete the certificate according to directions. Be certain to enclose the required number of Free Gift proofs-of-purchase, which are found on the last page of every specially marked Free Gift Harlequin or Silhouette romance novel. Requests must be received no later than July 31, 1992. Items depicted are for illustrative purposes only and may not be exactly as shown. Please allow 6 to 8 weeks for receipt of order. Offer good while quantities of gifts last. In the event an ordered gift is no longer available, you will receive a free, previously unpublished Harlequin or Silhouette book for every proof-of-purchase you have submitted with your request, plus a refund of the postage-and-handling charge you have included. Offer good in the U.S. and Canada only.

MILLIONAIRE! *Sweepstakes*

As an added value every time you send in a completed certificate with the correct number of proofs-of-purchase, your name will automatically be entered in our Million Dollar Sweepstakes. The more completed offer certificates you send in, the more often your name will be entered in our sweepstakes and the better your chances of winning.

PR0I

The park took his breath away. There was a sense of solitude that Russell had never experienced anywhere else, and he had pretty well covered the continent in his day. The giant Sequoias formed a cathedral over his head. Solitary rays of light cut through the roof of the forest, their points dancing across the forest floor. Only ferns and a few small animals lived there. It was almost impossible to believe there was a place in 1990s America that was so ethereally quiet. Yet not far away were a sandy beach and a beautiful lagoon. Everywhere he looked there was something else he wanted to explore.

He located the campground and set up the gear he had purchased in town. The innkeeper had looked him up and down when he'd told her he wanted to do some camping. Obviously she could tell he was anything but an experienced camper, so she had suggested he rent an RV. But that would have been too easy; he wanted to do this right.

He was really roughing it—tent, sleeping bag and kerosene stove—but that seemed only fitting, considering his surroundings. Amenities would have somehow spoiled everything.

In the morning he intended exploring the network of hiking trails that laced through the park. He might spend another day here, who knows? Then he thought he'd drive on up toward the Oregon state line. How far he went depended on how he felt at the moment, what he found farther north. He finally was here, and he wanted to see everything.

After a primitive evening meal out of a can and heated on the stove, he sat on the ground outside his tent, huddling deep in his jacket and drinking strong coffee. He listened to the night sounds and smelled the night scents. It seemed strange to see no stars on a clear night. After months of gazing out over flat, broad prairie and vast, endless sky, this was overwhelming.

In a place like this, he thought, *even I could become a poet.*

CHAPTER SIXTEEN

ON MONDAY MORNING, after a weekend of unceasing worry, Tina was seized by the need to talk to someone about her problem. She couldn't just do nothing and hope for a miracle. There was no guardian angel watching over her. She decided that the poor soul who'd hear her worries was Nate Lomax, the loan officer at the First National Bank. Nate's father had been one of Ty's best friends, and though friendship didn't count for as much in business dealings today as it had in her father's day, she imagined she would get the straight truth from Nate . . . and perhaps some advice, as well. She hated baring her financial woes, but she didn't feel equipped to handle this alone. Besides, Nate had probably heard just about everything through the years. This was farm and ranching country. No doubt ninety percent of First National's depositors had almost gone belly-up at one time or another.

Armed with the ranch's records from the past three years, she went to see the loan officer. After the initial pleasantries and some catching up, she explained her plight to him. He listened sympathetically, with interest. Then he examined her financial statements. Tina began to feel a tingle of hope. At least he hadn't laughed at her.

"I have two crops still to be harvested," she told Nate, "and two vehicles and some farm equipment. I'll put up anything I own except for my house and my land. I'll be going back to work soon, and that will be extra money. You'll get paid back even if I have to work two jobs." Tina hoped he didn't ask her where she was going to be working. That had yet to be established.

Miraculously he didn't. He merely folded his arms on his desk and smiled at her. "Well, it's not the most attractive deal I've heard lately, but it's not the worst, either. Frankly, if it were up to me, I'd approve the loan and take my chances. But it's not up to me."

"Then who..."

"It's up to the bank's directors. I present the deal to them, and they decide. I think I can ramrod it through. They meet again on the twelfth."

Tina's eyes widened in dismay. "The twelfth? Oh, Nate, that's bringing it down to the wire. That money has to be in the mail and postmarked by midnight of the fifteenth."

"I know. I'm sorry, but my hands are tied. Like I say, we can fill out the loan application, and I think I can sell it. If they approve it, we'll cut you a check on the spot. But not until the twelfth."

Tina felt as though she were living under a black cloud. Wasn't anything going to go right for her? "Well," she said helplessly, "all right. I don't know what else I can do. If the loan isn't approved, if I can't pay by the fifteenth, I suppose the worst that can happen is another penalty tacked on to what I already owe."

Nate opened a bottom drawer and pulled out the forms she was to fill out. "Not necessarily," he said casually. "It depends on what kind of person the agent handling your case turns out to be. The IRS actually has the authority to confiscate anything you own that will, in their estimation, satisfy your tax bill."

MINUTES LATER, Tina stood outside the bank building in a daze. The deed was done. She had applied for a First National loan of eight thousand dollars. If it was approved, half would be repaid from the sale of her corn and the remainder of her cattle, the other half when her cotton went to market. She wouldn't be tied to monthly payments, so she could take her time finding a job. If she defaulted on the loan, the bank would be the proud owners of the Jeep, the pickup, the tractor and the plow. And Tina was smart enough to know she was able to strike such a deal only because she was dealing with neighbors. A big bank in the city wouldn't have touched it.

Nate had been kindness personified. He had told her that the Webster name counted for something in the county, and he'd repeatedly expressed his confidence that he could get the loan approved.

But what if he couldn't? The way her luck had been running lately, Tina was turning into the quintessential pessimist. If she came out of this mess without an ulcer, it would be a major miracle.

Every shred of common sense she possessed told her she would be an idiot not to have a backup plan in case the loan didn't go through. It was time for pride to take a holiday. She was going to drag Becca into this. She hated to, but she also hated having the government on her back. Her sister might be thoughtless at times, but she had a heart. *And,* Tina thought, *I'm going to tell her a story that will break it.*

Leaving Leatrice, she drove home and called Becca.

"Oh, hi, Tina. I've been meaning to call you. Have you and that man...er, Russell, done anything rash?"

"No," Tina said without explanation. "Listen, Becca, I'm coming into town. Is it all right if I stop by?"

"Of course. I could use a friend."

That sounded strange coming from Becca. She had legions of friends. "I'll be leaving here in five minutes," Tina said.

After hanging up, she scribbled a note to Jake and in less than five minutes, she was back in the pickup, reversing it and heading for the highway. There was no one in the house to hear the telephone ring and ring and ring.

TINA'S PLAN was simple. She'd tell Becca about the tax bill and explain that she had applied for a loan to cover it. It would have been nice to think that at that point her sister would say something like "Oh, don't do that. Let me give you the money and you can pay me back when you can."

However, there was a good chance she wouldn't, so then Tina planned to say, "If the loan isn't approved, will you give me the money? I'll pay you back the same way I would pay back the bank." And she fervently hoped it wouldn't sound like begging. If her sister came through, Tina thought she just might get the first good night's sleep she had since she opened that damned letter.

Becca was waiting for her with a pout on her face. "Let's have some coffee," she said as she led the way to the sunroom. "Or would you rather have a Bloody Mary?"

Tina looked startled. "At this hour of the day?"

"It was a thought. Probably a bad one. Sit down, Tina."

The sunroom was a cheery place, furnished with white wicker furniture and bold, bright prints. While Tina took a seat, Becca stuck her head through a serving window that opened to the kitchen and asked the maid to bring them coffee. Then she came to sit in a chair near Tina, her mind obviously on something other than having coffee with her sister. She definitely looked annoyed about something, Tina noticed. *My luck is holding,* she thought dispiritedly. *Becca looks in anything but a charitable mood.*

Since she hated for virtually the first words out of her mouth to be about money, she began with the usual banalities. "How're the kids?"

"Fine."

"And Derek?"

Becca's eyes flashed. "He's on my list today."

A marital spat? Great. "I'm sorry. But all couples have tiffs now and then. Becca, I..."

"Tiff? Ha! I am good and steamed at him. He's a big boy. One would think he could stand up to Daddy... but no. Daddy says it's going to be this way, so that's the way it's going to be."

Tina, of course, had no idea what Becca was talking about, but something obviously was going on in the Jennings clan, something that had her sister good and vexed. Becca had a way of dismissing anything that didn't please her, as though it didn't exist, so whatever had her upset now apparently wasn't that easily gotten rid of. And Tina sensed that she was going to hear all about it, like it or not.

She was right. The maid entered the sunroom at that moment, carrying a tray with cups, a coffeepot, creamer and sugar, which she placed on a table that stood between the two women. She poured the coffee, then left the room. As soon as she was out of hearing distance, Becca ignored her cup and plunged right in.

"Milton called his kids on the carpet yesterday afternoon," she announced, as though she was sure Tina would be vastly interested.

"Oh?" Tina said weakly. The "kids" would be Derek, his younger brother and elder sister. Tina knew them by sight only, and she'd exchanged perhaps three sentences with Milton Jennings, the family patriarch.

"Milton says we've all got to tighten our belts. He's 'distressed' over how much money his children and their spouses spend. Would you believe we've all been put on allowances? Allowances! I think that's degrading, and I told Derek as much. He wasn't too happy with me when he left the house this morning, but that's fine. I'm not too happy with him, either. Ten thousand dollars a month per household. That's what we're limited to. Not a penny more."

Tina felt a rock hit the pit of her stomach. She just stared at her sister.

Becca leaned forward and gestured broadly. "Do you have any idea what it costs just to run this house? And, you know, we can't just go to parties. We have to give them, too. If I'm going to bust my buns for this charity and that, we have to donate, too. I can't run around town looking like a frump. I have to have a few nice clothes."

Tina set her cup down and rubbed her temples. Becca continued her raving. Tina then learned what the tuition to the private school the Jennings children attended cost, how much Becca paid her maid and the gardener, how much the kids' tennis lessons were and the exact cost of the country-club membership. She tried to look sympathetic or interested or something, but she was sure her expression was one of utter astonishment. To think there were people who lived that way, and her sister was one of them.

Becca finally wound down. Raising her arms high above her head, she stretched and uttered a bitter little laugh. "Oh, I'm sure we'll adjust, but I do so wish Milton had waited until after Christmas. It just seems to me that the first of the year would be the best time to start austere times." She dropped her arms and smiled at Tina. "Sorry. I was so upset. It's nice to have someone to rant to. I feel better. I'll be supersweet to Derek tonight. Now, Tina . . . was there any particular reason for this visit?"

"No, I . . . I just had to come into town for a few things, and I . . . thought I'd stop by. No reason in particular. I can't even stay but a minute."

USUALLY, ONCE TINA was in Amarillo, she would make a point of visiting Ty. But today she felt so wretched she didn't dare call on him lest she upset him, too. And she didn't want to see her mother, either. She simply left Becca's house, got in the truck and drove straight home.

Ten thousand dollars a month! A king's ransom to her, but apparently her sister was accustomed to more. She shook her head wearily. So much for the backup plan. She was at the bank's mercy, and there was nothing to do but wait anxiously.

Jake was finishing a late lunch when Tina entered the kitchen. She sighed ruefully. "Poor Jake. Are you existing on sandwiches these days?"

"Don't mind. Danged good, if you ask me."

"Well, I'll fix us a really nice supper. I'll bet you miss Ruby's cooking more than anyone. Have you heard from her?" She reached in the cabinet for a glass just as Jake stood and carried his plate to the sink.

"Not since Thursday. I thought I heard the phone ringin' as I was headin' for the house 'while ago, but they'd hung up 'fore I could get to it." Jake looked at her with concern. "Is somethin' buggin' you, Tina?" he asked solicitously.

"No, I . . . I mean no more than the usual. Dad and all. Why do you ask?"

He reached out and with his thumb rubbed the space between her eyes. "Can't imagine. If you ain't careful, that's gonna be permanently puckered."

"Well, you've always told me I worry too much."

When Jake had left the house to go back to work, Tina rummaged around in the refrigerator, looking for something to eat. The larder was becoming bare. A trip to the supermarket obviously was in order and that meant spending money. She had always been frugal, but she was turning into a penny-pincher. She finally opened a can of soup and made do with that for lunch.

She finished her uninspired meal, put a load of clothes in the washing machine and had just settled on the living-room sofa, when the front doorbell rang. It was such an unusual sound that it startled her. Almost everybody used the back door. Then it dawned on her—Oscar Stilwell. He always came to the front door. That was probably who had called earlier.

Oh, please, please, please, she prayed, swinging her legs off the sofa and standing up. *Let him have someone with him who falls in love with this place.* Hurrying across the foyer, she swung open the front door. Her expectant expression faded.

Paul stood framed in the doorway, hands on hips, his sunglasses dangling from one corner of his mouth. He looked devilishly handsome. Everything about him said that here was an enormously successful young executive or professional with plenty of disposable income. Over his shoulder Tina caught a glimpse of his automobile. She knew very little about makes of cars, but it was sleek and sporty and looked brand-new. How she wished he hadn't come. She just didn't feel up to sparring this afternoon.

"Obviously," Paul said, "I can't take a hint."

"What are you doing here?"

"Why is that always the first thing you ask me? The polite thing to do would be to ask me in first."

Tina stepped back. "Please, come in."

"Thanks." He brushed past her, stopping to drop a kiss on her forehead before proceeding on. Tina closed the door and followed him into the living room.

"Can I get you something to drink?" she asked.

"No, thanks."

"Have a seat."

"After you."

Tina crossed the room and sat in Ty's old chair. It was so butt-sprung she sank into it. Paul sat down on the sofa and favored her with his most charming smile.

"Now you may ask me what I'm doing here."

"What are you doing here?"

"I came to Amarillo to discuss that job offer with my colleague. Or do you even read my letters?"

"Of course I read them. I was going to answer it, but . . . I've had a lot on my mind lately, and . . . I was going to answer it."

Paul sat back. "I understand you finally had to put Ty in a home."

Becca's hot line to Paul was no doubt the source of that piece of information. What else had she told him? About Russell? Probably not. Becca wouldn't want Paul to hear anything that might discourage him. Paul was persistent, but not so much so that he would risk being rejected in favor of someone else. "Yes, I did. It's a very nice place, better than I'd hoped to find."

"Then it must be expensive."

"It is, relatively so."

"Tina, please let me help you." His voice was impassioned. "You wouldn't take a damned thing from me when we split up, and that always made me feel like a rat . . . which, love, is exactly what I suspect you were trying to do. Well, take something from me now. Any amount. All you have to do is name it. And don't tell me you don't need it. I'm betting you do."

Tina studied him. "Why, Paul? Would giving me money salve your conscience?"

"Maybe. Maybe it would."

Tina stilled. She didn't want to think what she was thinking, that all she had to do was open her mouth and the worst of her worries would be behind her. Just say the word and the money would be hers. An amount that doubtless meant nothing to Paul and would mean the world to her. Damned small payment for the heartache and anguish he once had caused her. *Ask for it, ask for it. Swallow your stupid pride for once and buy yourself a good night's sleep.*

"Are you worried that you'd be obligating yourself to me?" Paul asked.

"I would be. I'd have a debt that had to be repaid."

"Oh, God! Ten years from now. Twenty. Never. I don't care. Just let me help out. Let me do my good deed for the decade."

It would have been so easy. Too easy. And Tina wasn't an idiot. Of course it would obligate her to him. Furthermore, it would keep him in her life. There wasn't much of her life she was sure about anymore, but she was sure she and Paul were a thing of the past. "Thanks, Paul, that's very nice, but..." She swallowed hard. "I really don't need anything."

His shoulders slumped and he uttered a little laugh. "You and that damned conscience. I don't believe a word of it, but there's no way I can force money on you. You're a hard woman to deal with." Shrugging, he got to his feet. "I tried. Now I've got to get back to the city. I have an appointment in an hour."

Tina stood and walked with him to the door. They stood there, facing each other. "I won't bother you anymore," Paul said.

"You're not bothering me. By the way, are you going to join the practice in Amarillo?"

"I'm not sure, Tina. I'm really not."

"Well, good luck with whatever you decide to do."

"Thanks. Take care of yourself."

"I will. Goodbye, Paul."

"Goodbye."

For several minutes after he left, Tina stood with her back pressed against the door, her chest heaving. Then she pushed herself away and headed down the hall for the office. She couldn't complain about her luck anymore. The solution to her financial problems had been handed to her, and she'd turned her back on it. Yet she felt strangely good about her decision. If she had taken that money, she would have regretted it, she was sure of it.

The office was cool and quiet. Plopping down in her swivel chair, she sifted through the mail. Nothing seemed to require her immediate attention, so she picked up the Amarillo paper, scanned the front page, checked the weather, then turned to local news. The first item she encountered sent her hand to her mouth. She read it, then read it again. Her heart started knocking against her ribs. "Oh, my God!" she whispered. "Oh, my God!" Grabbing the phone, she punched its buttons with shaking fingers.

THE FOLLOWING MORNING at a quarter after ten, the front doorbell rang. Tina had been waiting... pacing, actually. Over and over she had cautioned herself not to get her hopes up, but they were up. She couldn't help it. Taking a deep breath, she opened the door.

Two men stood on the porch. One was tall and slender with graying black hair and chiseled features. Tina recognized him from having seen him on television talk shows. Next to him stood a much shorter, more portly man with rust-colored hair and a sprinkle of freckles across his nose. Both men were dressed neatly but casually in slacks and knit shirts.

"Miss Webster?" the taller of the men inquired.

"Yes."

He stuck out his hand. "I'm Bennett Cole."

She took his hand, and he shook it firmly. "How do you do. It's such a pleasure meeting you." Her voice sounded gushy to her own ears; she hoped she wouldn't come across as star-struck.

"And this is Edgar Burdick," Bennett Cole said, indicating the man on his right. "He's my research assistant and my expert on just about everything."

"I'm so happy to meet both of you," Tina said. "Please come in."

"If you have even half of what you say you do," Cole said, "I'm alive with excitement."

"I described the things to you as accurately as I could, but...well, I guess you'll just have to look at them yourself. This way, please." Tina gestured to the stairs. The men stood aside to allow her to precede them upstairs.

On the outside she was calm and collected, but her insides churned with expectation. She couldn't believe someone as famous as Bennett Cole was actually in her house, just as she hadn't been able to believe the item in yesterday's newspaper.

Cole, the author of a dozen bestselling mammoth family sagas might possibly have been the world's best-known author. Certainly he was in the top ten. Tina herself had read everything he'd ever written, and she thought they were wonderful. Cole's novels were renowned not only for their incredible length—a thousand pages weren't uncommon—but for the exhaustive research that went into them. Tina had read somewhere that his work-in-progress was to be set in the Panhandle-Plains area, a fact she had quickly forgotten until yesterday. The newspaper item had stated that Cole was using Amarillo as his base while he researched the book, and the author would like to buy or borrow any family memorabilia that would be useful to him. A phone number had been included in the article. Tina had immediately thought of her attic.

"Forgive the attic," she said as she ushered her visitors to the third floor. "There was just too much for me to tote downstairs."

"This is fine," Cole assured her.

Tina had assembled the cartons and steamer trunk into an isolated cluster in the middle of the attic floor and had rustled up two chairs. "Please have a seat. These are the things I thought you might be interested in."

Like archaeologists homing in on an important excavation, Cole and Burdick sat down in the chairs, and each opened a carton.

Burdick withdrew a letter, scanned it for a moment, then turned to his companion. "My, God, Ben, look at this date!"

"May I get either of you something to drink?" Tina asked.

"No, no thanks," Cole said. "Miss Webster, this might take some time."

"That's all right. Take all the time you need."

"You did say, I believe, that you would be willing to sell any or all of these things? I prefer to buy rather than borrow. I'm a bit of a collector myself."

"Yes. I have my own family's memorabilia, and if any of this would be of help to you ... well, I'd enjoy it if some of my ancestors' stories found their way into your book. I'll be downstairs in the kitchen if you need me." She hurried out of the room.

Actually, Tina was having mixed feelings about selling her family's history, but those letters and newspapers and magazines had been languishing in the attic for who knows how long, doing nobody any good, least of all her. If they were valuable... Again she cautioned herself against too much hope. They might be worthless.

She sat at the kitchen table, drinking coffee and reading yesterday's newspaper from cover to cover. An interminable hour passed. Then she heard the men coming down the stairs. Taking a deep breath, she went to meet them.

Bennett Cole's eyes were alight with excitement. "Miss Webster, it was a lucky moment for me when you saw that article in the paper. What you have up in that attic is priceless ... at least it is to me. Your possessions can shave months and months off my research. I'll be honest with you—there probably are knowledgeable people who would pay a small fortune for them. Ed and I've been discussing this and...would somewhere in the neighborhood of ten thousand dollars be agreeable to you?"

Unbelievably, Tina's knees did not buckle beneath her, though her spirits went soaring off on some wild, uncharted course. She even managed to keep a straight face and pretend to be considering the offer. "I think...I think that's a fair price, Mr. Cole," she managed to say.

Cole rubbed his hands together with satisfaction. "Good, good. Write her a check, Ed. Now, Miss Webster, I'll have to ask you to sign a paper, a legal formality. It states that you are willingly selling your possessions for that price and that you agree that I can use them in any way I see fit."

She nodded numbly. She signed the document Edgar Burdick produced, then accepted the check and her copy of the agreement. The writer and his assistant then made several trips from the attic to the van they were driving, relieving Tina of the boxes and the trunk. At last the van drove away, stirring up a cloud of dust as it headed toward the highway.

Then and only then did Tina let out a war whoop. Clutching the check to her chest, she danced around the foyer. She'd done it! Call it luck or whatever. She had done it, and she hadn't had to go into debt or go begging. Never again would she think there was no

such thing as a guardian angel. She had one, and the
angel loved her!

She allowed herself another minute or two of rejoic-
ing. Then she marched to the phone to call Nate Lomax. She profusely thanked him for his help but asked
him to tear up her loan application. She no longer
needed it.

"WHAT'S PUT that sparkle in your eye, Tina?" Jake
asked suspiciously as they were finishing supper.

"Oh . . . I had a little problem, but I worked it out.
That's always a good feeling."

"Damned if that ain't right. Well, I'm headin' into
Leatrice for a spell. I won't be gone long. I'll be back
'fore bedtime. You ain't scared, are you?"

"No, I'm not scared."

"Lock up after me. Need anythin'?"

"Not a thing, Jake. I'll be fine."

"See ya in a bit."

Tina dawdled over cleaning up the kitchen, then
went into the living room and checked the night's of-
ferings on television. Nothing. She settled on the sofa
and leafed through a magazine, then another. The
house seemed cavernous when she was the only one in
it, and it was eerily quiet. An edgy restlessness overtook her. She should have been the most relaxed person on earth; her problem had been solved. But she was
about to jump out of her skin.

Finally she reached for the telephone on the end table and dialed Ty's room at Fairhope. It was useless to
try to talk to her father over the phone, a study in
frustration, so she always called Harve and asked him
whatever she wanted to know. Tonight, however, there
was no answer, so she dialed Fairhope's office.

The night manager answered. "Fairhope Manor."

"This is Tina Webster. My father, Ty Webster, is in 104 with Mr. Chesterton. I'm calling to inquire about him. Is he all right?"

"Why, he's fine, Miss Webster. I believe he and Harve are in the television room right now."

"Thank you. I...I didn't get over there to see him today, and I...I worry."

"I understand. Perhaps you can come tomorrow."

Well, that was most unsatisfying, Tina thought as she hung up the phone. But, then, so were most of her visits to the home. Sighing, she returned to the kitchen and made a cup of instant coffee. Though the days were getting shorter, there still was plenty of daylight left. Carrying her cup, she went out the back door and sat on the stoop to enjoy her drink and the sunset.

And sitting there alone, sipping coffee and watching the setting sun's glorious display, she knew the source of her uneasiness. Russell. She'd been so distraught by her financial plight that she had put her anxiety over Russell on the back burner while she untangled the other mess. Now he was in the forefront again, very real and sorely missed.

Tina reminded herself that he really hadn't been gone so long. After all he was visiting the place he'd thought about for so many years, finally fulfilling his dream. There was a surprise around every bend in the road, he'd once told her. Well, discovering all those surprises would take time. She was still sure she had done the right thing in insisting he go.

Suddenly she recalled something she had read many, many years ago when she was much younger. It had gone something like—If you love something, set it free. If it comes back, it was meant to be. And that's what she had done with Russell and it had been the right thing to do. But knowing she'd been right didn't ease the aching loneliness, especially when she crawled into that big empty bed at night.

She no longer asked herself what she would do if he didn't come back. She would cope because she would have to. But she would miss him every single day of her life. No one would ever take his place in her heart.

Tina didn't know how long she sat on the stoop, letting her coffee get cold and staring across the broad expanse of pasture, before she heard wheels rumbling along the road toward the house. She glanced at her watch. Jake hadn't stayed in town as long as he usually did. She poured the remainder of the coffee onto the ground, then set the cup on the stoop beside her and hugged her knees, waiting for him.

But the figure rounding the corner of the house wasn't Jake. Tina shot to her feet. "Russell!" she cried.

He hurried toward her, his face full of concern. She flew into his arms, felt them tighten around her, and she melted against him. He was back! She lifted her face to receive a deep, thorough kiss.

Raising his head, he frowned. "Are you all right?"

She cocked her head quizzically. "Yes, I'm fine. Now I'm great."

His shoulders slumped with relief. "Thank God!"

"Russell, what on earth?"

He uttered a little laugh. "You're going to think I'm nuts, but . . . three days ago, I woke up with the worst feeling in the pit of my stomach. I just knew you were in some kind of trouble. I couldn't even think straight.

I tried calling and got no answer. Eventually I threw everything into a bag and hit the road.''

Tina frowned. Three days ago would have been Sunday. Jake had gone to see Ruby and Connie and hadn't returned until after supper. She had spent some time in Leatrice trying to take her mind off her problems.

"I've been driving like a madman ever since," Russell went on. "The feeling was so strong. Once yesterday during a pit stop, I tried calling again, and again there was no answer. A couple of hours later, I called again. I thought maybe you were sick or had had an accident or that something had happened to Ty..." He rubbed her back, as if reassuring himself that she was really all right. "Then everything's really fine? No trouble?"

Tina smiled up at him adoringly. She'd probably tell him about her tax woes in a day or two, but not now, not when there were so many happy things to talk about. "Everything's just dandy. Even dandier now that you're back. You're really back. You really are."

"You didn't doubt I would be, I hope."

"You saw the North Coast?"

"Yeah, I saw it. It's beautiful, just as I remembered. But as much as I loved seeing it, I never gave a minute's thought to not coming back. I just weighed giant redwoods, rugged coastline and quaint Victorian towns against you, and they didn't stand a chance. I'm going to take you there someday, Tina, but for now... For now we'll stay here, where we're needed."

Tina took him by the hand. "Are you hungry?"

"Starved...and for more than food. I need a big helping of you."

"Then you've come to the right place. Right this way."

Russell kicked the West Texas dust off his boots and followed her into the house.

CHAPTER SEVENTEEN

TINA, RUSSELL AND JAKE were having breakfast the next morning when the back door opened and Ruby stepped into the kitchen.

"Ruby!" Tina cried with delight.

"Hi ya, babe," Jake said, surprised. "What brings ya here so early in the mornin'?"

"The adoption went through, thanks to yours truly," Ruby said. "Now I'm back until this place is sold out from under me."

There were murmurs around the table. "But I thought... I mean, Connie..." Tina began.

Ruby dropped her handbag on a chair and reached for the apron hanging on a peg at the back door. Tying it around her ample waist, she said, "I've learned one thing, folks. Raising kids is something you should do when you're young. Those three just about wore me out. Connie wanted them. Connie's got them. I'll be here to help when she really needs me, but not on a full-time basis, no, sir."

Jake slapped the table and cackled gleefully. "Good for ya, babe."

Ruby didn't seem especially surprised to see Russell. "Are you back for good?" she asked him.

"Wild horses couldn't drag me away," he said with a grin.

Tina's eyes shone with delight. "Oh, Ruby, I'm so glad. Sit down and have coffee with us. There's something I've been thinking about, and I want to run it by all of you. This is as good a time as any."

When everyone was seated and all eyes were fastened on her, Tina folded her arms on the table. "As we all know, buyers aren't exactly knocking down the door wanting this place. Harvest is almost upon us, and the market looks good. Well, it looks pretty good. We aren't in debt, so we ought to be left with some operating capital for... next year." She quickly glanced around the table to see if anybody blanched. No one did, so she was sufficiently encouraged to continue. "I've been giving some thought to there being a next year for the Webster Hereford Ranch."

Russell, Jake and Ruby exchanged glances, but no one said anything. They simply fastened their rapt attention on her once more. Tina cleared her throat and went on. "But if we do keep the ranch in operation, I don't want any more of the just getting by and breaking even. I'd like to see us expand, to make this place more like it was when Dad was in charge. I'm talking about maybe planting more cotton, more wheat, maybe doing away with the corn altogether. Maybe slowly upgrading the livestock. Very slowly, I'm afraid. Good breeding stock doesn't come cheap. And if we do plant more crops, we might want to figure if contracting out the harvests costs more than making payments on our own combine would."

Tina wasn't sure when she had begun to think about this seriously. Seeds of the idea had been planted weeks ago, but at the time it had seemed impractical if not impossible. Her life had been so full of uncertainties. But the seeds had begun germinating last night when, lying warm and sated in the circle of Russell's arms, she had thought and thought, then asked herself some questions. Did she really want to get a job in Amarillo, a nine-to-five, paycheck-every-other-Friday sort of thing? And Russell had been a fiercely independent trucker for years. Would he want to punch a time clock? Or did they want to build something to hand down to the next generation? If hopes were realized, there would be a next generation. Ruby's return seemed to be the sign she'd needed to know it might indeed be possible.

"I know the downside," she said. "The caprices of nature, the uncertainty of the market from year to year, the shortage of reliable help, Jake's back..."

That brought an outburst from Jake. "Hey, hey. It acts up every now and again, but I ain't no cripple. I can still put in a day's work. When it's bad, we'll jus' have to let ol' Russell take over."

Jake's vote, Tina knew, would be to keep the ranch. She looked at Russell, quizzing him with her eyes. He was the one she was most worried about. One didn't have to be exceptionally bright to know how he'd felt about ranch work in the beginning. Maybe it was no more attractive to him now than it had been then. "What do you think? This has to be a mutual decision."

It was strange. Only weeks ago he'd thought ranching to be two notches above working on a chain gang on any desirability scale, but in California he'd missed it. He'd missed Tina acutely, of course, but he'd also missed Jake and Ruby, the house and the land. Maybe his dream had just changed course.

Russell rubbed his chin thoughtfully. He knew that if they kept the ranch and worked it, he and Tina would never go to California. Oh, they might visit someday, maybe even retire there, but this would always be home. Oddly, he didn't mind. "I'm for keeping it," he said.

Tina sat back, a satisfied smile on her face. "I've had to devote the past few years to Dad, but I'm young, strong and healthy. There's a lot I can do that I simply didn't have time for before. But we do need to get serious about hiring some more help. What I have in mind can't be done by four people. I'll run ads in papers for miles around. We might get lucky. Then again, we might not."

"I'll tell ya what ya oughta do," Jake said. "Ya oughta marry Russell here and start havin' some kids. Ain't never been a mom-and-pop farm or ranch that didn't depend on young'uns to help out with the chores."

Tina looked at Ruby. "What about Alejandro?"

Ruby pursed her lips. "Might be a good idea. Weekends and summers. That might do that kid a world of good. Working with the men probably would appeal to all that macho garbage he dotes on. I'll talk to Connie about it."

Tina glanced around the table. "Is that it then? Do I take this place off the market?"

Three heads nodded their approval. "Well, now that I know I still got me a job," Jake said, looking at Russell, "ya ready to head for the mine? Time's a'wastin' and daylight's burnin'."

"As ready as I'll ever be."

Chair legs scraped across the floor as they stood and carried their plates to the sink. Tina and Ruby got to their feet and began clearing the table. Jake gave Ruby a playful smack on her rump as he went to the back door.

Russell paused long enough to give Tina a quick kiss. "See you ladies at lunch," he said.

The back door swung open. Russell stepped out on the stoop, and from force of habit, he shaded his eyes and glanced out at the horizon . . . a practically unbroken 180-degree horizon. It never ceased to amaze him, the sense of limitless space. This was a land of baked red earth, endless blue sky and blazing yellow sun. He hadn't been able to wait to see it again. He guessed he had known more happiness here than he ever had anywhere else. The ranch and the land it stood on had grown on him. After all those rootless years on the road, it was good to feel he belonged somewhere. It was just good to be home.

My lovely green Eden, he thought with a smile, then went down the steps and followed Jake to the Jeep.

TWO WEEKS LATER, Tina and Russell were married in Fairhope Manor's chapel . . . unusual, perhaps, but she couldn't bear the thought of getting married without her father present, even if Ty was unaware of the significance of the event. Before the ceremony, Russell managed to get Ty into a suit and tie. The suit, Tina noticed sadly, all but hung on his thin frame. Still, she thought he looked grand.

It was a simple wedding that turned into a festive occasion. Tina wore a coral silk dress with flutter sleeves, and she made a point of wearing the pearl earrings Russell had given her. She cast an admiring glance at her groom. He was dressed in a dark business suit that made him look like the chairman of some prestigious board.

Ruby was Tina's attendant, and Jake was Russell's. Tina did a double take when she saw Jake. She had never seen the man in a coat and tie. "You look like a banker!" she screeched.

"This goddanged thing," he said, indicating his tie, "comes off the minute you two say 'I do.'"

All the residents who were able to attended the ceremony and the reception afterward, most of them dressed to the nines. And being allowed punch and cake in the middle of the afternoon was a real treat. Even Becca and Joan showed up. Tina had not been at all sure they would. Her sister wore something of a pinched expression, but Joan's was stricken. In the recreation room where the reception was being held, Tina approached her mother.

"I can't believe that's Ty," Joan confided with tears in her eyes.

"It takes some getting used to, Mom. Have you spoken to Dad? You're part of the distant past, so he just might remember you."

"I . . . haven't yet, but I will, I promise."

"Let's do it now," Tina insisted, and without giving Joan a chance to protest, led her cross the room to where Ty was seated next to Harve.

"You're the prettiest damn bride I ever saw," Harve boomed.

"Why, thank you, Harve." She gently nudged her mother.

Joan reached down and took one of Ty's hands in hers. "Hello, Ty. It's . . . wonderful to see you again."

"Hello," Ty said. "How's the family?"

Joan hesitated. "They're . . . fine, thanks."

Ty squinted up at her. "Don't I know you from somewhere?"

Joan slid into a chair on the other side of him. "Yes, we met many years ago."

"I thought so. During the war."

"Well, no, actually—" She caught Tina's quick shake of the head and stopped.

"Did I ever tell you about the time my outfit put a refrigeration..."

Tina smiled and walked away, going in search of Russell. She found him in the center of a gaggle of women, the youngest of whom was probably seventy-five. When he saw her, he graciously extricated himself from his admirers.

"You ready to leave?" he asked under his breath.

"Yes."

"Ruby and Jake suddenly have a burning desire to spend the night with Connie."

"How nice," Tina cooed. "So the newlyweds can have some time alone."

"How about stopping at a deli for our wedding feast?"

"Suits me."

"Is there anybody we have to say goodbye to?" Russell asked.

Tina glanced across. Ty was still talking, and Joan was still feigning rapt interest. Becca had joined the group and was engaged in conversation with Harve. "No. Let's go."

But as they were leaving the recreation room, Tina spied someone. Stopping for just a second, she dropped her bridal bouquet into the lap of the beautifully clad Bertha McCorkle.

Harlequin Superromance®

This May, Harlequin celebrates the
publication of its 500th Superromance with
a very special book . . .

THE SILENCE OF MIDNIGHT
by Karen Young

"A story you'll treasure forever."

Jake and Rachel McAdam have been married for
eighteen years when suddenly their whole world
comes crashing down around them. As sheriff of
Kinard County, Florida, Jake is sworn to serve and
protect its citizens, yet his small son Scotty had been
snatched from under his nose. And just when Rachel's
faith in Jake is at its lowest ebb, fourteen-year-old
Michael arrives on their doorstep, claiming to be her
husband's illegitimate son.

"A novel of love, betrayal and
triumph, The Silence of Midnight will
touch you deeply."

Look for . . .
Harlequin Superromance #500
THE SILENCE OF MIDNIGHT
by Karen Young

Available wherever Harlequin novels are sold

FREE GIFT OFFER

To receive your free gift, send us the specified number of proofs-of-purchase from any specially marked Free Gift Offer Harlequin or Silhouette book with the Free Gift Certificate properly completed, plus a check or money order (do not send cash) to cover postage and handling payable to Harlequin/Silhouette Free Gift Promotion Offer. We will send you the specified gift.

FREE GIFT CERTIFICATE

ITEM	A. GOLD TONE EARRINGS	B. GOLD TONE BRACELET	C. GOLD TONE NECKLACE
# of proofs-of-purchase required	3	6	9
Postage and Handling	$1.75	$2.25	$2.75
Check one	☐	☐	☐

Name: _____

Address: _____

City: _____ State: _____ Zip Code: _____

Mail this certificate, specified number of proofs-of-purchase and a check or money order for postage and handling to: HARLEQUIN/SILHOUETTE FREE GIFT OFFER 1992, P.O. Box 9057, Buffalo, NY 14269-9057. Requests must be received by July 31, 1992.

PLUS—Every time you submit a completed certificate with the correct number of proofs-of-purchase, you are automatically entered in our MILLION DOLLAR SWEEPSTAKES! No purchase or obligation necessary to enter. See below for alternate means of entry and how to obtain complete sweepstakes rules.

MILLION DOLLAR SWEEPSTAKES
NO PURCHASE OR OBLIGATION NECESSARY TO ENTER

To enter, hand-print (mechanical reproductions are not acceptable) your name and address on a 3"×5" card and mail to Million Dollar Sweepstakes 6097, c/o either P.O. Box 9056, Buffalo, NY 14269-9056 or P.O. Box 621, Fort Erie, Ontario L2A 5X3. Limit: one entry per envelope. Entries must be sent via 1st-class mail. For eligibility, entries must be received no later than March 31, 1994. No liability is assumed for printing errors, lost, late or misdirected entries.

Sweepstakes is open to persons 18 years of age or older. All applicable laws and regulations apply. Sweepstakes offer void wherever prohibited by law. Prizewinners will be determined no later than May 1994. Chances of winning are determined by the number of entries distributed and received. For a copy of the Official Rules governing this sweepstakes offer, send a self-addressed, stamped envelope (WA residents need not affix return postage) to: Million Dollar Sweepstakes Rules, P.O. Box 4733, Blair, NE 68009.

✂

HS1U

ONE PROOF-OF-PURCHASE
To collect your fabulous FREE GIFT you must include the necessary FREE GIFT proofs-of-purchase with a properly completed offer certificate.

(See center insert for details)